TRIAGE

JACK KETCHUM

RICHARD LAYMON

EDWARD LEE

Edited by Matt Johnson

LEISURE BOOKS   NEW YORK CITY

A LEISURE BOOK®

January 2008

Published by

Dorchester Publishing Co., Inc.
200 Madison Avenue
New York, NY 10016

If you purchased this book without a cover you should be aware that this book is stolen property. It was reported as "unsold and destroyed" to the publisher and neither the author nor the publisher has received any payment for this "stripped book."

Copyright © 2001 by Matt Johnson

"Triage" copyright © 2001 by Richard Laymon
"In the Year of Our Lord: 2202" copyright © 2001 by Edward Lee
"Sheep Meadow Story" copyright © 2001 by Dallas Mayr

All rights reserved. No part of this book may be reproduced or transmitted in any form or by any electronic or mechanical means, including photocopying, recording or by any information storage and retrieval system, without the written permission of the publisher, except where permitted by law.

ISBN 10: 0-8439-5823-5
ISBN 13: 978-0-8439-5823-2

The name "Leisure Books" and the stylized "L" with design are trademarks of Dorchester Publishing Co., Inc.

Printed in the United States of America.

10 9 8 7 6 5 4 3 2

Visit us on the web at www.dorchesterpub.com.

CONTENTS

Either a Very Long Note or a Very Short Introduction, From the Editor

This book was supposed to be a two way collaboration, but it got all twisted around, like a great many collaborative (and non-collaborative) efforts. The original idea was for Jack Ketchum and Richard Laymon to collaborate on a novel, to be published by my specialty press in a real purty signed, limited edition with bells, whistles and super-crunchy extras. But Jack got busy with pressing matters, as did Richard. So Edward Lee, a close friend/drinking buddy/gifted author, said to me "I've collaborated with Jack, and I'd love to collaborate with Dick if Jack can't do it. Dick's cool." I said "Okay" or possibly "Neat," and made a phone call.*

The idea for the Laymon/Lee collaboration was based on Richard's concept that a mystery person came to a workplace bent on destroying someone who had no idea why they were being targeted, or even who the

---

*The phone call was actually to the Thai restaurant down the block to set up some delivery, but the "And made a phone call" was pretty dramatic, right?

psycho was. But as they collaborated, Laymon and Lee had separate ideas about where the story should go. They both dug each other's ideas so much, they wanted to write their own stories based on the original concept instead of direct collaborations. Lee told me this, and I said "Okay, go ahead. And we'll get that handsome devil* Jack Ketchum back on board for his own story." Three stories by three big boys in the horror field, all known for their cutting edge styles. Again, neat.

So, that happened. And each of them took that same concept in very original directions, and were just all around damn good. The project was at that golden-brown stage where it looks fantastic and smells like a winner. Except . . .

Richard Laymon, a giant in the horror field (and no small tater in other fields) passed away on February 14, 2001. He was a kind, funny man, graceful and absolutely generous in his treatment of those he dealt with, and a truly good friend. After his passing, Ann Laymon, his wife, and Kelly Laymon, his daughter, expressed their wishes for this project to go forward. So here it is, all done up real nice, with three novellas that will knock you out of your shoes or pants or underpants or whatever it is you wear when you read.

As if it needs to be said, this book is dedicated to the memory of our friend Richard Laymon, whose Cartmann-esque authority we shall always respect.

Matt Johnson
Seattle
June, 2001

*Note to editors: Compliment the talent whenever possible.

TRIAGE

Richard Laymon

CHAPTER ONE

Almost quitting time. The last hour always dragged on and on, especially on Fridays.

Sharon looked at the clock above the office door.

Ten minutes to go. Ten long, long minutes. Then freedom, the weekend.

If Mr. Hammond had been away as he often was, the others would've left by now. But you don't take off early when the boss is in.

Not that Sharon would've left early, anyway. She got paid for a full day of work, so she worked a full day. Unlike Susie and Kim and Leslie, who would've been long gone by now if Mr. Hammond hadn't been here.

Sharon liked the office better when she had it to herself.

Susie, Kim and Leslie weren't exactly horrible. Sharon supposed they were fairly typical office work-ers: capable but not very ambitious, friendly enough when not being petty, full of complaints about every aspect of the job, mostly interested in their hair and nails.

Shut away in his office with a client, Mr. Hammond couldn't see that Susie was applying lavender nail polish as the final minutes of the workday drifted away. Nor that Leslie was checking her lipstick in a compact mirror. Nor that Kim was speaking on the phone, probably to one of her several boyfriends.

They've been at this job a lot longer than me, Sharon thought. Before you know it, maybe *I'll* start growing two-inch nails and . . .

No way.

Christ, she thought, I'd kill myself if I had to spend my whole life in a job like this.

No I wouldn't.

Anyway, it's not going to happen.

She looked at the clock again. Eight minutes till five.

As she grimaced about the slow passage of time, the burning returned. Acid indigestion. The result of today's lunch at Simon's Deli. Great Reuben sandwiches: pastrami and sauerkraut piled high, drenched in melted Swiss cheese between two slices of grilled rye bread. The best. Simon's meant a long drive through lunch hour traffic and acid indigestion later in the afternoon, but she had a hard time staying away. At least twice a week, she made the drive. And paid the price.

She glanced again at the clock. Six till five.

Time sure flies. . . .

She opened a side drawer of her desk and took out a roll of Tums. After peeling away a strip of the wrapper, she used her thumb nail to pry a tablet loose. She popped the pink disk into her mouth and chewed.

Her telephone rang. In the quiet of the late afternoon office, the sudden noise made her flinch. Swallowing the Tums, she reached across her desk and picked up the handset. "Law Offices of J.P. Hammond and Sons, Sharon speaking. May I help you?"

"I'm gonna get you."

The voice of the man on the phone sounded sly and mean. Underneath her blouse, goosebumps scurried up the skin of Sharon's back. Inside the cups of her bra, her breasts went crawly and her nipples hardened.

"Excuse me?" she asked.

"*I'm gonna get you, Sharon.*"

"Who is this?"

"*I'm gonna get you NOW.*"

Dead air. He was gone.

Sharon slammed the phone down and jerked her hand away.

Kim, phone still to her ear, swiveled on her desk chair and frowned at Sharon. "What's your problem?"

"That call . . ."

"I've got a call of my own, honey. You wanta hold it down?"

"Sorry."

The front door of the office swung open and a man stepped in.

Him?

He must've made the call from the hallway, probably with a cell phone.

He wasn't holding a cell phone, though.

Both his hands were busy with a shotgun. A short, black thing with a pistol grip.

Susie, at the desk nearest the door, normally greeted visitors with "May I help you?" Usually followed by "Please take a seat." Today, not speaking a word, she dropped her nail polish. The bottle thunked on her desktop and rolled.

"I'm here to see Sharon," the man said.

The same voice she'd heard on the phone.

Susie nodded, swiveled, pointed a finger toward the rear of the office. Straight at Sharon. "That's her."

"Thanks," the man said and shot Suzy in the side of the head. As the shotgun bucked, the noise of its blast crashed in Sharon's ears. Susie looked as if she'd been swatted by a baseball bat except that some of her head seemed to blow apart, spraying red.

Susie was still falling out of her chair when the man pumped a fresh shell into the chamber of his shotgun and swung the muzzle toward Leslie—and Sharon threw herself down behind her desk.

Her knees pounded the hardwood floor. Another detonation rocked the office. Then she couldn't hear anything except the ringing in her ears.

Her reactions weren't what she would've expected. She didn't go numb with terror. She didn't ask herself who this man might be or why he had barged into the office to kill people. He was a fact. A horrible fact like a truck suddenly bearing down on her for a head-on.

She flinched as another blast crashed through the office.

Then came two more very quick shots.

Shit!

Hunkered down behind the leghole of her desk, she realized she was staring at her purse. She grabbed it, pulled it closer, peered down into it: wallet, lipstick, tampons, Marlboros, hair brush, Kleenex, note pad, Bufferin, more rolls of Tums, ballpoint pens, a matchbook from Simon's Deli.

KRAWBOOM!

She snatched out what she needed.

Hands strangely steady, she flipped open the Simon's Deli matchbook and plucked out a match. It flared to life on the first try. She applied the flame to the note pad and flames curled over the pages.

She dropped the burning pad into her wastebasket. Half full of paper wads.

As fire bloomed from its top, Sharon grabbed the wastebasket with both hands. Though she had no idea where the man might be, she sprang up.

He stood a few feet away, just to the left of her desk, head down, both hands occupied with feeding bright red shells into his shotgun. He looked up.

Sharon hurled the flaming wastebasket at his face and broke to the right.

Lurching backward, the man flung up both arms.

As Sharon ran around the side of her desk, he bashed the wastebasket out of his way and fiery papers flew out at him.

Sharon dashed for the office door.

Saw bodies on the floor. Susie. Kim. Leslie. Head-shot. Sprawled in puddles of blood.

Far to the right, Mr. Hammond's door remained shut. *Hiding in there with his client?*

Sharon leaped over Susie, but her shoe came down on blood as slick as ice. Her leg flew up. Crying out and flapping her arms, she dropped backward and sat down hard, her right buttock pounding the side of Susie's head. Nothing under her left buttock, she tumbled sideways.

Rolled through blood.

Belly down, she raised her head. The killer wasn't after her. Not yet. He stood near the front of her desk, surrounded by small fires, trying to rip his flaming shirt off his body.

Sharon shoved at the slippery floor, stood up, whirled around and staggered to the door. She jerked it open. Glancing back, she saw the killer fling his shirt away.

That's it. Now he'll come.

The last thing she saw before she broke into a run was the killer crouching to pick up his shotgun.

CHAPTER TWO

Alone in the corridor, Sharon ducked her head and pumped her arms and ran with long, quick strides for the EXIT door at the end of the hallway.

The elevators were in the other direction, but she knew better than to try for them. They were too far away. Besides, there was little chance of an elevator arriving in time.

She had to get out of the corridor fast.

I'll never make it.

In her jarring vision, she saw the EXIT door growing larger, watched her legs reaching out for it, one after the other, thighs encased in trousers that had been white only seconds ago. White and dry, now crimson and sodden and clinging.

In her mind, she saw the shirtless killer stagger out behind her from the Law Offices of J.P. Hammond and Sons, swing the shotgun in her direction and pull the trigger. She imagined the noise of its blast. Saw her own back open up, pieces of blouse and skin and blood flying off in tatters and splashes. Saw the force of the impact throw her forward, knock her off her feet, smash her to the floor.

Why is he doing this? I don't even know him!

Running full speed, Sharon turned sideways at the last moment, struck the low metal crossbar with her hip to free the latch and pounded the door open with her shoulder. On the other side, a quick grab of the railing saved her from a plunge down the stairwell.

She glanced over her shoulder. The door had already swung too far shut to allow her a peek down the corridor.

Is he coming? she wondered.

Better believe it.

She raced down the stairs, taking them one at a time but very fast, keeping a hand close to the railing in case of a stumble. The wooden stairs thudded and creaked with her footfalls.

She wished she didn't need to make so much noise, but figured it didn't really matter.

He knows where I went.

Fleeing down the stairs, she felt a sense of repetition. She'd seen a woman doing this in a movie or TV show. Or in dozens. Read this sort of thing in novels, too.

The clever gals often tried to trick the bad guy by running *up* the stairs instead of down them.

A little late for that.

I wouldn't have done it anyway, she thought.

Don't fuck around with cute tricks when your life's at stake.

Sharon realized she heard no one coming down the stairs above her. Were her own noises masking his?

She didn't dare stop to find out.

Maybe he took the elevator and he'll meet me at the bottom.

Maybe I *should* try a trick—the one where you don't take the stairwell all the way down.

She'd started at the fifth floor, already descended past the fourth and third floors and was hurrying across the landing above the second.

She stopped.

No sounds of anyone pounding down the stairs.

He *isn't* coming. Not this way.

Not unless he's being very stealthy.

Stealth, however, made no sense for him; he needed to close in on Sharon and gun her down, the quicker the better.

He's not in the stairwell, she thought. So he probably *does* plan to intercept me on the ground floor.

She turned around and chugged upstairs to the door with 3 on it.

She pulled it open.

The third floor corridor looked exactly the same as the fifth.

Except that the fifth probably now had bloody shoeprints on its floor, red smears on its EXIT door. . . .

Blood.

She let go of the door. As it drifted shut, she looked down. Her right hand had put a smear of blood on the handle. She also must've brushed against the door with her knee because there was a smear of blood lower down.

A few drops were sprinkled about on the floor around her feet.

I'm leaving him a trail!

Her throat tightened. On the verge of weeping, she realized how *much* she'd counted on hiding. Find herself an empty office, a closet, a restroom . . . *disap-*

pear and wait for the killer to give up looking, wait for the police or firemen to come.

He'll just follow the blood.

If it weren't for the blood . . .

Trembling, she unbuttoned her blouse, pulled it off and tossed it aside. She kicked off her shoes. Not bothering to unfasten her belt or waist button or zipper, she jerked her trousers down her legs. She stepped out of them, then peeled off her socks.

In just her bra and panties, she crouched and found a clean section of trouser leg below the right knee. She rubbed her hands on the white fabric, staining it.

Then she stood up and backed away from the pile of bloody clothes.

She turned around. Moving quickly but quietly, she climbed the stairs to the fourth floor. She stopped in front of the door and checked her hands. They were trembling badly, sweaty and still slightly bloody. Her sweat must've moistened whatever blood had remained on her hands after the quick wipe on her trouser leg. She swung her arms behind her back and rubbed both hands on the seat of her panties. The slick nylon was moist and clinging.

She looked at her hands again. Much better.

She eased the door open, leaned sideways and peered through the gap.

Another long, empty corridor.

She opened the door wide, stepped out of the stairwell and held the bar while the door swung slowly shut. Still facing the door, she took a few backward steps. She saw no traces of blood on the door or on the hardwood floor, so she turned around and walked down the corridor.

Except for her own breathing and the thumping of her heartbeat, she heard no sounds at all.

Will anybody hear me if I scream?

Maybe *him*.

She hurried to the first door. Plastic lettering on the door read DENNIS K. EDGEWOOD, DDS.

A dentist. Probably with a small staff: a receptionist, a hygenist . . .

Sharon reached out, grabbed the doorknob and tried to turn it.

It didn't budge.

Locked?

She tried the knob again, let go of it and rapped gently on the door. The solid wood muffled the sound of her knuckles. She pounded harder.

Come on! Where are you?

Nobody answered her. Nobody opened the door.

Of course not, Sharon thought. Five o'clock on a Friday afternoon. Half the offices in the building had probably closed down by now.

She hurried toward the next door.

Better luck with this one, she thought.

But she wasn't even halfway there when the *ding* of an arriving elevator, soft and musical, pierced the silence like a shriek.

CHAPTER THREE

The nearest door was a few yards away on the other side of the corridor. Sharon dashed for it.

MEN

What if it's locked?

I'm screwed.

But it was the only door she had a chance of reaching before someone—maybe the killer—stepped out of the elevator.

She hit it with her shoulder. It swung open and she lurched in. Whirling around, she grabbed the door. She threw her weight against it and forced it shut against the power of the automatic door closer.

Can *he* hear that? she wondered.

Probably not. The elevators were pretty far away and they made noises of their own.

At last, the restroom door silently stopped, snug in its frame.

Sharon stepped away from it. Her upper arm had put a moist smear on the wood, but it was hardly noticeable and it would probably dry quickly.

She turned around.

Like the men's restroom on the fifth floor, this one had two paper towel dispensers on the wall near the door. There were two sinks with mirrors above them, four urinals, and three toilet stalls.

Two regular stalls and one extra-large stall equipped for the handicapped.

None of the doors was completely shut. They were only partway open, though. Sharon gave each a gentle push as she walked by. They swung wide enough for her to see the toilets.

The stalls were empty.

The last toilet hadn't been flushed.

She hurried over to the first stall and stepped into it. Standing sideways, her back almost touching the metal partition, she swung the door shut.

Shut it, but didn't latch it.

Like the others, it needed to be ajar.

The door slowly drifted open while Sharon climbed onto the toilet seat.

She stood facing the front of the stall, her feet apart, her knees slightly bent, her hands resting on her thighs, and wondered why in hell you almost never found public toilets *enclosed*.

Don't you *want* privacy when you use them? So how come they have wide open spaces at the top and bottom?

They don't want you having *too much* privacy, she thought. People'd be using them all the time for quickies.

Makes it mighty damn inconvenient if you're trying to hide from a killer.

Instead of smiling at the thought, Sharon grimaced.

The awkward stance was getting quickly tougher. She'd been exhausted *before* climbing onto the toilet seat. Now, the muscles in her legs and buttocks ached and shook. Her back felt sore. Sweat seemed to be running out of every pore, hundreds of dribbles sliding down her skin. Even the bottoms of her feet felt sweaty, making the toilet seat slick.

How long do I want to keep this up? she wondered.

Long as it takes.

He'll never find me here.

Never?

What if I left a trail? I couldn't get *all* the blood off. And I probably dripped sweat.

No, I'm all right here.

Maybe.

Besides, it's not like he's going to *devote his life* to searching the building for me. He's probably gone already. Nobody in his right mind sticks around after blasting three people with a shotgun.

Plus, he's burnt.

Maybe just minor burns, but they'd have to hurt.

I wonder if the building's burning down.

Probably not, Sharon thought.

No fire alarms had gone off. No sprinklers, either, so far as she knew. The fires hadn't really amounted to much. A dozen or so paper wads and the bastard's shirt on a hardwood floor.

Besides, maybe he stuck around long enough to stomp out the flames. That'd explain why he wasn't hot on my tail two seconds after I ran out of the office.

But the smoke detectors and sprinklers *should've* gone off. There must have been enough fire for that.

For all I know, the damn things don't even work.

What if nothing happened? No alarms went off. No sprinklers. What if nobody reported the shots?

Maybe no one *heard* them.

Who knows how far the noises carried? Who knows how many offices were empty by the time the guy attacked?

J.P. Hammond must've heard the shots. His client, too. Mrs. Hayes. They were right there in the next room.

Maybe they didn't last long enough to phone the cops.

If no alarms went off . . .

If nobody called the cops . . .

If the killer has the guts to stick it out . . .

He can take his sweet time searching for me.

Sharon wiped her face with both hands, but her hands only seemed to smear the sweat around.

This really sucks, she thought.

Better than being dead.

The aches and tremors grew worse. After a while, she thought, Why am I doing this to myself? Nobody's here. I don't have to wear myself out *ducking.*

So she stood up straight and swiveled her body to the left. With both feet on the same side of the toilet seat, she reached out and hooked her hands over the edge of the stall. Then she stretched and sighed.

Standing upright seemed to take only a fraction of the effort involved in hunching down.

Though sweat still poured down her body, her aches faded and her trembling subsided.

Should've stood like this from the start, she thought.

Course, I'll be screwed if someone barges in.

From her new position, she had a fine view down from the top of the stall's partition . . . a fine view of the restroom door.

Just duck fast if it opens.

If it does open, she thought, chances are it *won't* be the killer.

Who would I like it to be?

A cop.

Yeah, that'd be nice. Not just any cop, but one of those SWAT guys looking like he's all set for combat.

That'd be nice.

Suppose I can't have a cop? Who'd be second choice?

Matt Scudder?

Can't have him, he's a cop.

I can, too—he only *used* to be a cop.

Do fictional characters count?

Hell, if fiction counts, I want Bond. James Bond, but none of those movie guys. Not even Connery. Good as he was, he wasn't *Bond*. There's only one *real* Bond, the guy in the books.

Yes!

That'd be something!

The bathroom door swept open.

CHAPTER FOUR

Sharon flinched and ducked, jerked her hands down from the edge of the stall, then braced herself steady with her knuckles just below the top.

The quiet, shuffling sounds of footsteps traveled closer.

I'm in the first stall! If he needs to take a dump . . .

Some distance away, the footsteps went silent. A man cleared his throat. A zipper hissed. A strong, steady stream began drilling the enamel of a urinal. A man began to hum a quiet tune.

The tune sounded familiar.

I am a lineman for the counteeee. . . .

Anyone who'll hum Glen Campbell while he takes a leak has to be a good guy, doesn't he?

Sharon straightened up, raised herself on tiptoes, turned her head and saw the man at the urinal.

Definitely not the killer.

From behind, at least, he looked like a regular guy: maybe six feet tall, only slightly overweight, maybe forty to fifty years old, light brown hair neatly trimmed and a little thin on top. He wore the outfit of a businessman—sport shirt, gray slacks and black wingtips, but his shirt was half untucked in back. Long day.

Apparently a long day without a recent restroom break.

Not waiting for him to finish, Sharon bent her knees and the stall seemed to rise around her. She looked down at herself.

Guy's gonna get an eyeful.

Though both cups of her bra were blotchy from blood that must've seeped through her blouse, the wet, clinging material was nearly transparent. She could see a *freckle* on her left breast.

Good grief.

She liked to wear skimpy undergarments, but she hadn't counted on *this*.

Let's hope the guy's a gentleman, she thought.

She heard him zip up.

Pivoting, Sharon returned her right foot to the other side of the toilet seat. As she reached out and pushed the stall door completely shut, the urinal flushed with a rush of surging water. The flush ended quickly.

Footsteps.

"Excuse me, sir," she said.

The footsteps stopped.

Keeping the door shut with one hand, Sharon hopped down to the floor.

"I'm in this stall over here," she explained.

"Uh-huh."

"Could you help me?"

"Out of toilet paper?"

Surprised by the question, she checked. "No, there's plenty."

"What seems to be the problem?" He sounded friendly but perhaps a little wary.

"I'll come out."

"Okay."

She drew the door inward. Though she tried to step out of its way, the guy got to see the edge of the door rub across her left breast.

Blushing, she muttered, "Damn doors."

The man fixed his eyes on her face. "Whoever makes these stalls obviously has a nasty streak."

She smiled.

The man, more like fifty now that she could see his face, had a rough and weathered look. Frowning, he started to unbutton his shirt.

Sharon felt a flutter of alarm. "What're you doing?"

"Taking off my shirt."

"Hey, no. . . ."

"It's all right," he said. Underneath it, he wore a T-shirt with Homer Simpson blurting *"Dohhh!"* When his sport shirt was off, he held it out to her. "You can use it more than me."

"Oh." She started to reach for his shirt, then stopped. "No, but thanks. I'll get it all messed up."

He looked her over. Sharon blushed some more. "Go ahead and wear it."

"I'm a little bloody." Hadn't he noticed? "I don't want to ruin it."

"Doesn't matter."

"Well . . ." She accepted the shirt from him. "Thank you. That's very nice of you."

"No problem."

27

"I'm Sharon," she said, slipping her arms into the short sleeves. "I work upstairs. On the fifth floor. At J.P. Hammond and Sons."

"I'm Hal Clark."

Holding the shirt closed with her left hand, she put out her right. "Nice to meet you, Mr. Clark."

They shook hands. His felt big and solid and warm.

"Hal," he said. "Just Hal."

Keeping her hold on his hand, Sharon said, "Hal, somebody came into the office a while ago and shot everybody."

His grip tightened slightly. Though his expression didn't change at all, Sharon thought she could see color draining from his face.

"He had a shotgun," she explained. She let go of Hal's hand and started to button the shirt. "He *phoned* me. He said, 'I'm gonna get you, Sharon.' I don't even know who he is, but he called me and said that. He knew my name. And I no sooner hung up the phone than he came in the door and started shooting everyone. Susie, Kim, Leslie. From what I saw, looked like he shot all of them in the head. I think he shot some of them more than once. To finish them off. I only got away because he had to reload."

"This happened when?" Hal asked.

"Just a little before five."

"Guess I missed it."

"It happened."

"I don't doubt it. What I mean, I'd gone down to the street to put some money in the meter."

"And just came back up in the elevator?"

He nodded. "Maybe ten minutes ago."

"I was afraid he might be in it. That's why I hid in here."

Hal glanced at his wristwatch. "It's a quarter after, now." He frowned at Sharon. "You pretty sure your co-workers were dead?"

"They almost had to be. Headshots with a big shotgun like that. I don't know about Mr. Hammond, though. He was in his office with a client. I have no idea what happened to them. Didn't stick around to find out. When I made it into the corridor, I just ran like hell. I figured the guy would be right on my tail." She shrugged.

"What we'd better do right now," Hal said, "is get you tucked away safe in my office. It's just down the hall. Follow me."

At the restroom door, he stopped. "Hang back a second. I'll make sure the coast is clear." He pulled the door open, walked out into the corridor and looked both ways. "Okay."

With her fingertips, Sharon caught the slowly shutting door. She pulled it toward her and stepped out. Except for Hal, the corridor looked deserted.

"This way," he whispered.

Hurrying toward the far end of the corridor a few paces behind Hal, Sharon walked past the LADIES restroom, a couple of unlabeled doors, several office doors, and the elevator bank.

Hal glanced at the elevator doors, then looked back at Sharon.

She shook her head. "No thanks. He might be waiting at the bottom."

Beyond the elevators, Hal stopped at a door on the right side of the corridor. He used a key on it, stepped in, and held it open for Sharon.

She read the lettering on the door: CLARK CONSULTING SERVICES.

Consulting services? Consulting about what?

She entered the office.

Hal shut the door, then hurried through a reception room. It reminded Sharon of her dentist's waiting room, but no one was waiting.

"Come on back," Hal said.

She followed him across the waiting room, through another doorway and into a pleasant, comfortable-looking office. Hal gestured toward an easy chair in front of the desk.

She sat in it.

He hurried around his desk. "I want you to wait here. I'll lock the door on my way out. Don't open it for anyone."

"What'll you be doing?"

"I'm going upstairs for a look." He opened a drawer and reached in. His hand came out with a large, dark pistol. Though Sharon was no expert on such things, she'd read a lot of crime novels. She guessed it was probably a .45 caliber model 1911 semi-automatic. The sort of pistol Mike Hammer liked to use.

Holding the pistol in one hand, Hal reached into the drawer again. His hand came out with two fully-loaded magazines. He dropped them into a front pocket of his trousers.

"Are you some kind of a cop?" Sharon asked.

He shook his head.

"P.I.?"

"I do odd jobs. The odder the job, the more I like it." He flashed a boyish smile at her.

"Gimme a break."

He grabbed the top of the pistol and jacked a round into the chamber.

"Don't you think we'd better call 911?" Sharon asked.

"I never call 911."

"Oh, wonderful."

"We had a little trouble in the building last month, should've taken two minutes to handle, some lame-ass attorney phoned the cops. They cleared out the building and we couldn't get back in for four hours. Fucked up my whole day." Again, he flashed the smile. Then he hurried around the desk. "You sit tight. I'll take care of this."

"No way."

Hal stopped in the doorway and frowned over his shoulder.

Sharon stood up. "I'm not staying here by myself."

"You'll be perfectly safe."

"Oh, sure. Unless the bastard blows your head off. Then he gets your wallet and keys and even if you don't make it easy for him with a business card, your name's on the office door . . . probably on a directory downstairs, too. Before I know it, he comes waltzing in here looking for me."

"I suppose that's a possibility. A *remote* possibility. But if you really want to come along . . ." He shrugged. "Who am I to stop you?"

"Thanks."

CHAPTER FIVE

Hal pulled the office door shut. Looking Sharon in the eyes, he said, "You don't really want to go back up there, do you?"

"I'd rather do that than stay by myself."

"I'll take you down in the elevator, make sure you get out of the building okay."

"And then *you'll* go up by yourself?"

"Yep."

"If you're going up, I'm going up."

"Why?"

"You're only doing it because of me."

"Doing it because I want to."

"You wouldn't know anything about it if I hadn't told you."

"I suppose that's the truth. But that's not much of a reason for risking your life."

She supposed he was right about that. Still, she wanted to go with him.

Maybe I just want to *be* with him?

She'd only known Hal for a few minutes, but she liked him. He seemed friendly and decent and brave. Old enough to be her father, she supposed, but she wondered how much that really mattered.

I'm going upstairs with the guy, not marrying him.

"Anyway," she said, "the killer's probably long gone."

"More than likely," Hal agreed. "But you never know about these things. Just stay behind me and keep your eyes open."

Sharon followed him. He walked quickly, holding the pistol close to the side of his right thigh.

The corridor was silent except for the sounds of Hal's shoes and Sharon's bare feet. Still, she worried that someone might be sneaking up behind them. Every few strides, she twisted halfway around and looked back.

The corridor behind them was empty.

"It's like nobody's here but us," she said, her voice little more than a whisper.

"Just about everyone probably *has* cleared out by now. Friday afternoon. Add that to the fact that there's only a fifty percent occupancy rate in this building."

"What?"

"About half the office spaces are vacant. You didn't know that?"

"I knew the place seemed awfully *quiet*."

They passed the door of the men's restroom.

"Well, now you know why it's quiet."

"Why's it so empty?"

"Old. No decent parking. Legionnaires' disease."

"*What?*"

"Legionnaires' disease. Killed twelve, fifteen people."

"Here?"

"They caught it here. I don't know all that much about it. Happened a long time ago, but I understand it came from the air-conditioning."

"Jeez."

"I suppose it's the main reason the rent's so cheap."

"Is it *safe*?"

Hal turned his head and gave her a funny smile.

"You know what I mean," she said.

"I've been in my office eight years. Nobody's dropped from Legionnaires' disease while I've been here."

"I never heard anything about it."

"They like to keep it quiet. Not because there's any real danger at this point, but it has a way of scaring people off." At the end of the corridor, Hal said, "Hang back a second."

Sharon waited a few feet behind him while he opened the stairwell door.

Propping it wide with his shoulder, he stood motionless and listened. He looked up and down. Then he gave her a nod and she stepped through the doorway.

The air inside the stairwell felt warmer than the air in the corridor.

Hal eased the door shut. Looking at her, he pressed a forefinger against his lips.

She nodded.

They began climbing slowly, silently up the stairs. As Sharon's fear began to grow, she realized she'd been feeling pretty much okay for the past few minutes. Now, she was breathing harder. Her heart was pounding. Her muscles trembled and sweat poured down her body. She had a heavy, sick feeling in her stomach, a cold tightness in her bowels.

I must be out of my mind.

No, she told herself. It's all right. Nobody would stick around this long after blasting an office full of people. The cops are probably already here.

Even if they're not—and even if the killer hasn't run off yet—Hal's got the .45 and we'll have the element of surprise on our side.

I hope.

I must be out of my mind.

As she stepped across the landing halfway between the fourth and fifth floors, she imagined herself whispering, "Gotta go." In her mind, she swiveled around and trotted down the stairs, moving fast, rushing down and down and down, feeling guilty. *Sorry, Hal, I'm just a coward at heart.* Rushing down and down the twisting staircase, then making a turn, maybe on the first floor landing, only to find *him* grinning up at her—shirtless and charred, giving her a big white-toothed grin, pointing the shotgun up at her face and saying, "*Told* you I'd get you, Sharon."

Looking down at her, Hal raised his eyebrows.

She realized that she had halted on the landing. She forced a smile, then resumed climbing.

Hal, a few stairs from the top, waited for her. When she stopped on the stair below him, he whispered, "Do you want to go down?"

"I'm sticking with you."

"You don't have to."

"I know."

"Want to wait here? I'll take a quick look around and come back."

She shook her head.

"More guts than sense," he said.

"Look who's talking."

A corner of his mouth tilted upward. Reaching out with his left hand, he gave her shoulder a gentle squeeze. Then he turned around and climbed to the top of the stairs.

For a few moments, he listened at the door. He met Sharon's eyes and shook his head.

What's that supposed to mean?

He opened the door a couple of inches, peered out, then opened it wider. With Hal blocking her view, Sharon couldn't see much. Not until he opened the door all the way.

The corridor was empty.

No cops. No firemen. Nobody.

The corridor looked the same as usual: windowless, illuminated only by recessed lights in the ceiling, all the doors shut.

Sharon did notice a slight tang of smoke in the air.

"Nobody *called*," she whispered.

"Apparently not. Which office is it?"

"First door on the right."

Hal nodded. "Tell you what, you stay here. He's probably *still* gone, but I'll take a look in the office. Be ready to run if anything goes wrong."

"Okay."

CHAPTER SIX

Sharon waited with her back to the EXIT door. She could feel the push-bar's coolness through the tail of Hal's shirt and the seat of her panties.

A quick backward lurch would depress the bar and throw open the door for her escape.

Nothing's going to happen, she told herself as Hal walked toward the door of J.P. Hammond and Sons.

Still, she felt tight and trembly.

Why does he have to do this? Why can't he just call the cops and let them take care of it?

Some sort of macho thing, she supposed.

Holding her breath, she watched Hal stop beside the office door. He raised his pistol toward the side of his face as if ready to bring it down and fire. With his left hand, he reached out and turned the knob.

Still standing off to the side, he shoved the door wide open.

Nothing happened.

He crouched, turned, and peered into the office. For a long while, he didn't move. Just watched and listened. Then he stepped through the doorway and out of sight.

Sharon expected the silence to erupt with gunshots. The silence remained.

She stepped away from the EXIT door and walked toward the open door of the office, her bare feet squeaking on the hardwood. Along the way, she noticed scattered dots and specks of blood on the floor. Nearer the office, faint traces of her shoeprints began to appear. She walked beside them.

Are they all from me? she wondered.

She saw no second set of shoeprints.

Does that mean he never left?

Maybe it just means he didn't step in blood. . . .

She came to the doorway and looked in and couldn't figure out what she was seeing. The office furniture wasn't where it belonged. Looked as if it had all been shoved aside to make a big clear space in the middle of the floor.

Straight in front of her, toward the middle of the cleared area, everyone seemed to be *piled up*.

A heap of bloody bodies?

Bloody, *naked* bodies?

That's what it looked like, but Sharon could hardly believe such a thing was on the floor in front of her.

"Hal?" she asked, her voice so soft she could barely hear it herself. She tried again. "Hal?" Better.

"Yeah." His voice came from somewhere inside the office, but she couldn't see him. "You might not want to come in," he warned.

"Did you find him?"

"No. Looks like he cleared out." Hal walked into view from the left, the pistol swaying by his side as if his arm had grown weary of holding it up. He turned his head toward her. "You were supposed to wait, you know."

"Yeah."

"You didn't need to see this."

"It's okay," she said.

It wasn't okay. It was very far from okay.

What did he do to these people?

Walking into the office, she stared at them. The sight sickened her but intrigued her. So many bare legs, buttocks, hands, breasts . . . bloody skin, clean pale skin, hair, gaping wounds. A face here. A vagina there. And there a flaccid penis.

He got Mr. Hammond.

She'd *thought* there must be more in the pile than just Susie and Kim and Leslie. Mr. Hammond was obviously in there, too. And probably his client, that woman, Mrs. Hayes.

One little mistake, Sharon thought, and I would've been in the pile with the rest of them.

How did I luck out?

She looked at Hal. He met her eyes, shook his head. "Now we know why he didn't come after you," he said.

"Too busy playing with the bodies," Sharon muttered. "Why would he do something like that?"

"Sick fuck."

"But he came here to get *me*."

"That's what it sounded like."

"He could've *gotten* me if he'd tried."

"Guess you weren't his highest priority at that point."

She groaned.

Then someone else groaned, too. Someone in the pile of bodies.

41

"My God!" Sharon blurted.

Rushing toward the pile, Hal stuffed the pistol down the back of his waistband. He crouched and took hold of a bloody wrist and pulled, saying, "You'll be all right."

Clearly the woman whose wrist he was pulling *wouldn't* be all right. Half her face was gone. She was probably Leslie. Her large, bloody breasts wobbled as Hal dragged her off the heap.

The survivor whimpered quietly.

"I'm almost to you," Hal said.

He began to remove another body. A short-haired, blonde woman, facedown. The client, Mrs. Hayes?

With one hand, Hal grabbed her upper arm. With the other, he grabbed her hip. He pulled at her, rolled her over. As she flopped toward him, the bloody naked man underneath her raised his shotgun and fired point-blank into Hal's face.

CHAPTER SEVEN

The sight of it staggered Sharon, knocked her breath out, felt like a blow to her mind. She seemed to split up instantly into several Sharons: one thought *This didn't just happen*; one wanted to scream in horror; one felt heartbroken over the sudden loss of Hal; one thought *Knew this'd happen*; one thought *Get outa here!*

All the Sharons watched the blood-drenched naked man sit up among the dead and smile. His teeth and eyes were white in a crimson face.

"Hop on in," he said. "The water's fine."

She whirled around and fled.

Maybe he'll miss. Oh, sure.

From behind her came the *snak-clak* of the shotgun's action as the killer chambered a fresh round.

Here it comes!

She dived for the floor.

BOOM!

She crashed down, her ribcage pounding the threshold, her bare thighs squeaking on the hardwood floor as she skidded.

43

Thinking she'd been missed by the gunshot—but not really sure—she scurried for the corridor.

I'm functioning.

Expecting another shot, she didn't even wait for her legs to clear the doorway. Flung herself to the side. The frame scraped her right buttock. She kicked her legs out into the corridor, belly-crawled in a frenzy, glanced back, saw she was out of the doorway, scampered to her feet and ran.

Ran hard and fast, arms pumping, feet slapping the floor.

Running in the wrong direction.

She realized she should've gone to the left like before, but she hadn't been *planning*, just reacting, just trying to get the hell *out*, and now she was racing down the corridor *away* from the stairwell.

Away from her nearest way out and toward the stairwell that was three times as far away.

With a bank of elevators much closer.

She glanced back.

He wasn't out of the office yet.

Try!

Veering across the corridor, she raced for the elevators. Both sets of doors were shut. The plastic call buttons on the panel between them were dark.

Arm out, forefinger extended, she lunged for the call buttons and hit the down. It lit up. Then she jabbed the up button.

Up, down, who cares? OUTA here, that's all.

Staggering backward, she turned and looked down the corridor.

Maybe he won't come after me this time, either. Maybe he wants to stay and play. . . .

He sprang out of the doorway, landed sideways on both feet and slid.

With flare.

Tom Cruise. Risky Business.

But instead of white briefs, this guy wore nothing but blood. He carried his shotgun like a guitar.

Mind reeling, Sharon looked away from him. Both call buttons were still lighted.

Both sets of elevator doors remained shut.

The killer, still smiling, danced toward her. In no hurry at all.

Knows he's got me.

She glanced at the EXIT door. Too far away. It had probably been too far away from the start, but she might've made it. No chance of that now. Her only chance was an elevator.

She watched the killer. He wasn't much closer than before, bopping from side to side, swinging, strumming the side of his shotgun as if performing a rock 'n roll tune that only existed in his head.

"Leave me alone!" she yelled.

"Gonna get you, Sharon." Then he sang out, " 'cause I'm stuck in the middle with you."

"Who *are* you?"

"Don't you remember me?"

"No."

"Bet you will from now on."

"Do I know you?"

"Do you?"

She shook her head.

Where's the fucking elevator?

"Think hard," he said.

"What's your name?"

45

"That'd be telling."

Ding!

Sharon looked. The down button was dark.

The killer broke into a run.

Sharon lurched for the opening doors. And slid to a stop.

Inside the elevator stood a young woman and a girl. The woman in a neat white blouse and jeans. The cute blonde girl in a jumper. Ten years old? Eleven?

Mother and daughter?

They both gazed out at Sharon.

The girl's eyes got big and her jaw dropped.

The woman said, "Oh, my Lord."

"Hold the elevator please!" the killer called.

Sharon blurted, "*No!* Get outa here! Quick!"

The elevator doors were wide open.

"You'd better get in," the woman told her.

"Go. Go." In the corner of her eye, she saw the killer bearing down.

The doors stayed open.

They won't close in time!

"Go!" she yelled again, then swung away from the woman and girl and ran.

Ran, but not away from the killer.

Straight toward him.

CHAPTER EIGHT

She meant to block him, knock him down if she could, slow him down at the very least and give the elevator doors a chance to shut.

As she hurled herself at him, his shotgun swept up and over her shoulder and the barrel clubbed the side of her head. Through the quick burst of pain, she thought she could still take him down. But he was no longer in front of her.

In front of her was a corridor wall. She twisted, trying to save herself from striking it headfirst.

Her shoulder crashed against the wall and she bounced off and fell. She hit the floor rolling. On her back, she elbowed the floor to halt herself.

The girl cried out, *"Mom!"*

The woman shouted, *"No! Get out!"*

Sharon yelled, *"Not them!"* She sat up just in time to watch the elevator doors slide shut.

Alone in the corridor, she heard faint, fading screams.

CHAPTER NINE

Sick with rage and despair, Sharon struggled to her feet. She hobbled toward the elevator bank. The down button was dark, the up still lighted. She jabbed a finger against the down button, then staggered over to the right-side elevator and put her ear to the door crack.

She heard no more outcries, no sounds of a moving elevator.

It's stopped somewhere?

It'll be back on its way up any moment, she thought. He probably just stopped it long enough to deal with the passengers.

Deal with them. Kill them? The mother. The little girl.

Suddenly in tears, Sharon pounded on the doors. She shouted, *"Leave them alone! You want MEEE! Don't hurt THEMMM! Please!"*

Another Sharon seemed to be watching her cry and pound the doors and plead. This one was shaking her head. Smirking, she said, *You're missing your chance to get away.*

The crying Sharon thought, *I don't care.*

Another Sharon seemed to be shrugging, saying *What's the use anyway?*

The determined Sharon said, *Run and hide! Now!*

What, in a toilet stall? Give me a break.

And a scene began playing in her head. A scene like a clip from a movie.

She saw Hal get shot in the face, saw his head jerk back as his face exploded into a red shower, saw him flop to the floor dead . . . with his .45 semi-auto in his hand.

It's in his hand NOW.

Sharon shoved at the elevator doors, stumbled away from them and ran for the office of J.P. Hammond and Sons.

She was nearly there when she heard the *ding!*

He's back!

She cut toward the office doorway and slowed down. Just as she leaped over the threshold, she heard the quiet sound of the elevator doors sliding open.

Made it!

She rushed toward the bodies, but slowed down when she felt blood under her feet.

Though most of the bodies had no faces, only Hal was wearing clothes. She knelt beside him and wrenched the pistol out of his hand.

On his T-shirt, Homer Simpson blurted *"Dohhh!"*

Sharon stood up with the pistol. It felt big and heavy. Its hammer was back.

Cocked and ready to fire.

She turned toward the door and saw it standing open.

Shit!

During a heatwave more than a month ago, the air-conditioning system had gone down (the same system that had spread the Legionnaires' disease?), and Susie had stood on a chair with a screwdriver and disabled the arm that made the door shut automatically.

That's why it's still open, Sharon thought. And because *I* forgot to shut it.

Shut it now!

She moved toward it, skating her feet over the slick floor.

Lock it! He sure as hell hasn't got a key on him.

When her feet found friction, she ran for the door.

How close is he? she wondered.

She wanted to look.

Don't!

Instead of slamming the door, she leaned forward and peeked around the edge of the doorframe.

"Hi, honey," he said.

He was ambling up the corridor, still a fair distance away and in no hurry at all. The shotgun, held by its pistol grip, swung by the side of his right leg as he walked. His left arm was clamped across the backs of the girl's thighs.

She was draped over his shoulder.

Behind them, in front of the elevator, lay a motionless body in jeans and a white blouse.

"Do you like children?" the man asked.

Sharon didn't even try to answer.

She saw how his penis, bouncing slightly with the motions of his stride, seemed to be pointing mostly at her face.

"This one's Taffy," he said. "You ask me, sounds like a cat's name. Taffy."

Sharon scurried backward and slammed the door. With her trembling left hand, she pinched the button in the middle of the knob and twisted it.

CHAPTER TEN

"Open up!"

Sharon knew he didn't have a key. He had the shotgun, though. Could he shoot through the door with it? Maybe, but the door was heavy and solid. Putting a hole all the way through it might take several shots. . . .

Maybe depends on what sort of loads he's using.

She glanced down at Hal's .45 in her hand.

This'll sure as hell go through.

But I might hit the girl.

Backing away from the door, she wondered if the man would try to shoot it open.

Hope you do. Use up your ammo on the door, you won't have any left for me.

Naked, he obviously wasn't carrying extra shells around with him. As soon as he used up those already in the shotgun, that would be it.

How many?

He'd had no time to reload after shooting Hal, so he was at least one shell short of full capacity. Maybe more. Sharon didn't think he had used the shotgun on Taffy or her mother. But he'd obviously shot Mr. Hammond and Mrs. Hayes; she hadn't heard the blasts, but she must've been in the stairwell by then.

That's a couple more shells gone, if he didn't reload afterward.

With Hal, Hammond and Hayes, he might be down *three* rounds or even more.

How many does the damn thing hold?

Taking more steps away from the door, Sharon thought about how he'd been busy reloading in front of her desk just when she'd jumped up to throw the wastebasket at him.

So how many times had he fired before that?

One each for Susie, Leslie and Kim. That's three. But she'd heard more than three shots. Four? Five? Maybe *that* was when he killed Hammond and Hayes.

No. He did that after I left. Those early shots were all used on the office girls.

So say the shotgun holds five.

After the last reloading, he might've already fired three times.

"Open the door, Sharon."

"Eat shit and die!"

"Taffy says please."

"I've already called the police," she yelled. "They're on the way."

"Is that so?"

"We called from Hal's office."

If only.

Shit!

She whirled around. The office's desks and chairs had been shoved toward the walls to clear the area for the body pile. In the rush, a lot had fallen off the desks: books, papers, case files, monitors, keyboards, phones.

She spotted a phone on the floor between a desk and a wall. It would be hard to reach.

Her own office phone was still on top of her desk, but at the far end of the office. The bodies were in her way.

Must be a closer one.

Susie kept a cell phone in her purse.

Where's her purse? Where're *any* of the purses? Where're all the clothes?

She didn't see them anywhere.

Had the killer thrown them into Hammond's office?

She couldn't see inside it; the connecting door was shut.

"I'll have to blow off Taffy's head if the cops show up," he announced from the corridor. "So it's a pity if you've already called them. If you *haven't* called yet, you might want to think twice. First sign of cops, Taffy gets it in her sweet little face."

"Yeah, sure. She's already dead."

"Think so?"

There came a shocked, high squeal. It sent waves of chills up Sharon's skin.

"Ask the nice lady not to call the cops," he said.

A girl's sobbing voice choked out, "Eat shit and die." Then came a gasp. Then a thud and a sharp grunt.

"That was her head hitting the door, Sharon."

Sharon heard the girl gasping for breath, crying softly.

"Not dead yet," the man said. "You want her?"

"Leave her alone."

"Open the door and you can have her."

"You'll kill us both."

"I'll let Taffy go."

"No, you won't. You won't let *any*body go."

"Sure I will. What do you think, I'm some sort of *monster?*"

Sharon felt a sneer twist her lips.

"I'm not a monster, am I, Taffy?"

After a moment of silence, the girl screeched.

The man laughed softly, then said, "Sharon?"

"What?"

"I understand your reluctance to open the door."

"That so?"

"You're right in suspecting that I'll kill you both. Aside from my other reasons for being here, I can hardly leave witnesses behind. Any reasonable man would eliminate both of you."

"That's right."

"Do I *look* like a reasonable man?" He laughed again, then said, "I'll make you a deal."

"Oh, sure."

"I'll go away if you tell me who I am."

"Sure you will."

"I will. Trust me." He laughed again. "Anyway, what've you got to lose? If you figure out who I am, I'll go away. I'll leave you and Taffy alive."

"What if I don't know who you are?"

"Oh, that'll be very bad. For both of you. Very, very bad. Bad for you, fun for me. Your only hope of saving yourself and Taffy from death—and a fate *worse* than death, as they say—is for you to tell me my name."

Sharon groaned. Then she muttered, "Okay."

"What?"

"I'll *do* it!"

"Okay! Very good! Let's get started. Who am I?"

"Rumple-fucking-stiltskin."

"Wrong."

Taffy let out a squeal of pain.

"Damn it!" Sharon cried out.

"Oh, I forgot to mention . . . each wrong guess, Taffy gets pulled."

CHAPTER ELEVEN

Through the door, she could hear Taffy crying. "Leave her alone!"

"She's in your hands, Sharon."

"She's in yours!"

"But you have the power to set her free. The *truth* shall set her free. Who am I, Sharon?"

Just keep him talking, she thought. That's the thing. Doesn't matter who he is. Better that I *don't* know. Telling him who he is would end the game. When it's over, no telling what he'll do.

Keep it going.

But try to avoid wrong answers.

"Can you give me a clue?" she asked. He didn't answer right away. Afraid to wait, she said, "You do look awfully familiar."

"Do I?" He sounded pleased.

"Very."

Not an outright lie. He looked familiar in the way that most strangers looked familiar to Sharon. Nearly everyone, it seemed, resembled somebody she knew one way or another. . . . from real life or movies or TV.

"I'm sure we never went *out* together," she said. "We didn't, did we? Go out together?"

"You don't *remember* who you go out with?"

"Sure I do. I mean, mostly. Maybe not if it was like a *really* long time ago. But I'm sure I would've remembered *you*."

"Think so, huh?"

"Yeah."

"Why's that?"

"A handsome guy like you."

Taffy let out another squeal. It made Sharon flinch. "Hey!" she yelled.

"Better watch what you say."

"I'm sorry!"

She heard the girl sobbing through the door.

"Just don't hurt her, okay?" Sharon blinked sweat out of her eyes.

I'm drenched.

Flop sweat?

Hal's shirt was clinging to her back. Her bra and panties felt sodden. Though she wasn't standing in blood, the floor was wet and slippery under her feet.

Flop sweat *plus* the building's damn western exposure. The air-conditioning could never quite cope with all that heat. When it's not killing people with Legionnaires' disease, she thought, it's cooking us to death.

"What're you doing?" the man asked.

"Trying to figure out who you are. I think I've almost got it."

"You better hope so."

"We never went out together, right?"

"What do you think?"

"I'm pretty sure we didn't."

"Like you *would*."

"Would what?"

"Go out with me."

Now we're getting somewhere!

"Did you ever ask?"

"What do you think?"

"I don't know," she said. "You tell me."

"Of course not. You would've *laughed* in my face. You never even knew I existed."

This sounds like some kind of high school shit, she thought. In those days—not so very long ago, though it sometimes seemed like eons—she'd been a varsity cheerleader, president of the senior class, prom queen. She'd gone steady with Bud Wayne, the most popular guy in school. No telling *how* many losers must've been roaming the hallways, dying for so much as a smile from her.

Is this one of them? Thinks maybe it's his turn now?

But that was in Seattle, for Godsake! Did he *track* me to L.A.?

Would've been easy enough, she thought. Not like I've been trying to *hide* from anyone.

"Give up?" he asked.

"No! I'm thinking. I've almost got it."

With the back of her left hand, she wiped her sweaty face. It didn't help. Clamping the pistol between her knees, she took off Hal's shirt. She mopped her face, then her arms and sides and chest and belly.

A lot better.

She tossed the shirt to the floor and took hold of the pistol again. She leveled it at the door.

Why not just pop one through?

She pictured the other side of the door, the killer holding Taffy up in front of him, Sharon's slug blasting through the back of the girl's head.

If I just knew where she was!

I don't even know for sure where *he* is, she reminded herself. He's very close to the door, but maybe off to one side or the other. Maybe sitting. Who knows?

Afraid she'd been silent too long, she said, "You're from high school, aren't you?"

"Ha! Very good! Maybe you *do* remember."

"Well, it's kind of vague."

"I'll bet it is. Hard to remember someone when all you ever did was look through him as if he wasn't even there."

"Did I do that to you?"

"What do you think?" He sounded like a disappointed kid.

"I'm sorry," she said. "I never *meant* to ignore you. It wasn't anything *personal*."

"Know what, Sharon? *Everything's* personal. And everything has consequences."

"I didn't *mean* to ignore you. If you'd ever come up to me, *talked* to me, let me know how you felt. . . ."

"Oh, sure."

"Did you want to take me out?"

Bad choice of words, she thought.

"I wanted you to notice me. To *like* me."

"Maybe I *would've*, if you'd ever approached me. What was I supposed to do, walk up to every boy I saw and ask him if he wants to *date* me?"

Taffy cried, *"OWWWW!"*

Sharon winced. "Hey!"

"Taffy notices me. Don't you, Taffy?"

Sobbing, the girl blurted, "Yes!"

"Leave her alone," Sharon begged. "Please. Stop hurting her. Let her go. This is between you and me. She never did anything to you. Come on, she's just a kid. Let her go."

"Who am I?"

The words of an old poem whispered through her mind. *I'm nobody, who are you? Are you a nobody, too?*

"How am I supposed to know who you are if you never introduced yourself?"

"That's your problem."

"It isn't fair!"

He laughed.

"I'm *sorry* I ignored you. I really am."

"I bet you are. Now. Everyone's *always* sorry afterward—when it comes to payback time. But they're never sorry when they're *ignoring* you."

"But you must've . . . *liked* me, or it wouldn't have been a problem. You must've liked me *a lot*. Right?"

"Of course."

"And you wanted us to be friends. You wanted me to be your girlfriend. You wanted to *go* with me."

"Yeah."

"Well, you've got my attention now. I'll go with you now. Right now. We can go out to dinner and . . . anything you want. Okay?"

"Too late. It's way too late."

"No, it's not."

"Tell me who I am or I'm starting on the girl."

"But that's crazy! How can I possibly . . . ?"

A cry of pain from Taffy silenced her.

CHAPTER TWELVE

"Let me think for a minute," Sharon said. "I remember you now. It's just a matter of coming up with your name."

Being careful not to fall on the slippery floor, she hurried over to the inner office—Mr. Hammond's private domain—and eased open its door.

On the floor in front of the attorney's desk was a pile of clothes, just as she'd expected.

Naked bodies piled in one office, their effects piled in the other.

Sick, Sharon thought.

Sick and weird and somehow familiar.

I know your name, you fucker. It's Adolph. Or maybe Heinrich.

She was tempted to call the names out, but knew they would only buy pain for Taffy. Also, he would hear the difference in her voice, know she was on the move.

Stick with the plan.

She hurried over to the pile and studied it.

What was he wearing?

Jeans? Camouflage pants?

She tried to picture the way he'd looked when he was still wearing clothes.

Jeans?

Maybe. Seems like.

She saw blouses, socks, a brown purse, shoes, panties, slacks, a skirt, a black purse, a blue necktie. . . . A *lot* of stuff. Even a pair of glasses. Mr. Hammond's bifocals.

Every stitch worn by six people, five of them piled dead in the other office, one standing out in the hall with Taffy and a shotgun.

Just gotta dig *his* pants out of the heap.

Would he bring a wallet with him for a thing like this?

Maybe. From all she'd read, most criminals weren't exactly beacons of intelligence.

"Sharon?" the man asked.

Don't answer.

Not just yet.

Not seeing any jeans (wearing them was against Mr. Hammond's rules, even on Fridays) she dropped to her knees, set down the pistol, then grabbed clothes by the handsful and flung them out of her way.

"Sharon!" This time Taffy's voice, pitched high and trembling.

She found a blue denim leg, grabbed it and pulled. Out from under a pair of thong panties, a black wingtip shoe, a pale blue camisole and Kim's shiny green blouse—the camisole and blouse now torn and splashed with blood—came the rest of the blue jeans.

His?

Must be.

"Tell him!" Taffy cried out. *"He's hurting me!"*

66

"Just a minute!" she yelled.

Now I've done it!

But she felt something the size and shape of a wallet in the left rear pocket of the jeans.

"Sharon!" the man called. "What're you doing? Where are you?"

Though her body shook with tremors, she managed to shove her left hand into the pocket and drag out the wallet. She flipped it open.

"*Stop it!*" Taffy cried out. "*Let go! Don't you do that! No! That hurts!*"

Wallet in one hand, pistol in the other, Sharon sprang up and ran into the outer office.

"*No!*" Taffy squealed. "*Please please please! You shouldn't! Owwww!*"

Sharon's feet slid on the bloody floor. Skating to a halt, she turned toward the door and flipped open the wallet.

Taffy was sobbing, whimpering.

"I remember your name!"

"You do, do you?" His voice sounded strange. Tight and breathless.

She squinted at the driver's license. "Andy!" she called out. "Andy Carvell!"

"Ha! You're right!"

"Let Taffy go!"

"Well, I don't know."

"You promised!"

"I know, but . . . we're having such a good time out here."

"*Are not!*" Taffy blurted, sobbing. "*It hurts!*"

"Damn it, let her go! We had a deal!"

"You didn't cheat, did you?"

"I *remembered!*"

"Deal's off if you cheated."

"I didn't cheat!"

"I think what you did was run into the other office where I piled up everyone's stuff and you found my billfold. I think *that's* how you 'remembered' my name."

"Did not!"

"Yeah, that's it. Too bad. Cheaters never prosper. Say bye to Taffy."

"Don't!"

The blast crashed in Sharon's ears. She jumped and cried out, then lurched forward and jerked open the door.

Ready to shoot Andy, but he wasn't there.

Taffy was. Wearing only her white socks, she lay crumpled on the corridor floor, a pool of blood spreading out around her.

Shot in the head.

Sharon felt her mind suddenly split again into several Sharons. One thought, *Oh my God, he did it!* Another, *He wouldn't do that to a little girl. It's some kind of trick. Special effects.* Another Sharon thought, *All my fault!* Another, *I'm gonna kill him if it's the last thing I ever do!*

And another seemed to sneer. *Shouldn't have opened the door, idiot.*

Andy leaped from somewhere to the right of the doorway. Facing Sharon, he skidded past the threshold with the shotgun down low by his side.

As he slid by, she got off one shot.

So did he.

An instant after the .45 roared and leaped in Sharon's hand, a red furrow appeared on Andy's left upper arm.

At almost the same moment, a shotgun blast took her in the left knee with a hard sharp coldness like getting clobbered by an iceball. She felt her leg go out from under her. Trying to stay up, she hopped forward on her right leg but her balance was gone to hell.

Out in the corridor, she tried to swing her pistol over toward Andy for another shot.

Taffy got in the way of her right foot, knocked it out from under her, and Sharon crashed to the floor.

CHAPTER THIRTEEN

Sharon wondered why she hadn't passed out. Aren't you *supposed* to pass out when someone demolishes your knee with a shotgun?

She *wished* she would.

I don't want to be here!

He'd already wrenched the .45 out of her hand. Now he was pulling her by the wrists, dragging her through the doorway.

Is everybody in this building deaf? she wondered.

Gone for the weekend.

Thank God it's Friday.

Somebody should've heard the shots!

When Sharon was all the way back inside the office, he let her arms fall. Then he stepped around her and shut the door.

"Our first date," he said. "We'd better start by patching you up, though. Wouldn't want you to pass out and miss some of the fun."

He left her and hurried into Hammond's office.

Gotta get outa here, Sharon thought. She pushed herself up to her elbows. Feeling her weakness, seeing what was left of her knee, she knew she would be going nowhere.

I'm not getting out of here till someone takes me out.

"You'll be fine," Andy said, coming back. He had some clothes in his hands. A pair of trousers and a skirt. "Just a little scratch." He laughed. "Maybe *not* so little." He knelt down beside her. "Just lie back and relax," he said. "We'll have you all fixed up in no time flat."

She stayed on her elbows.

"Lie *down*."

She settled onto her back. And flinched and cried out when Andy pulled at her knee.

"Foreplay," he said.

When he began to wrap her knee, Sharon tried to lie still but the pain made her shudder and writhe.

"Not hurting you, am I?"

She whimpered and didn't try to answer.

"Well," Andy said, "turnabout is fair play. You've certainly hurt *me* a lot. It's about time you got some back."

"I . . . never meant . . . to hurt you."

"Acted like you didn't even see me. Like I didn't exist."

"No reason to . . . do all *this*. All these people. That . . . that poor girl."

"Collateral damage," he said. "But fun."

"You sick fuck."

"That's me." He gave her knee a hard swat.

That's when she passed out.

CHAPTER FOURTEEN

When Sharon came to, she kept her eyes shut. The blazing pain in her left leg reminded her immediately of what had happened to her.

And to the others.

To Taffy.

Why hasn't he killed me yet? she wondered.

Oh yeah, it's our first date. Doesn't want me to miss the fun.

From the feel of her body, she knew that she had already missed *some* of the fun. Missed the part where Andy removed her bra and panties. Except for the garment (someone's skirt or trousers?) binding her knee, she was naked.

At least he's not *doing* anything to me.

Not at the moment.

Where is he, anyway?

Where am *I*?

The hardwood floor wasn't underneath Sharon anymore. She was sprawled on an uneven, lumpy surface, soft in some places, hard in others. She moved slightly.

Whatever was underneath her wobbled, tickled her just below the small of her back. A tuft of hair? She furtively flexed her buttocks and recognized the feel of what was nestled between them.

He's under me!

She opened her eyes.

Andy, standing just beyond her feet, smiled down at her.

Who's under me?

Oh, my God.

"Welcome back," Andy said.

In a sudden frenzy, she tried to get herself off Mr. Hammond's body. Her wound erupted with pain. Crying out in agony and revulsion, she bucked and thrashed and twisted, then saw what *else* was happening and screamed in horror.

Two women, one on each side of her—Susie and Kim, she thought—were lurching, trying to sit up, shaking their ruined heads at Sharon as if angry at being disturbed.

The necks of both women were *bound by belts* to her outstretched arms.

Still dead, after all.

Andy watched, his mouth slightly open, excitement in his eyes.

Not letting the pain stop her, Sharon struggled even more fiercely, lifting Susie and Kim off their backs, shaking them. Their breasts leaped. Their heads bobbed and swayed. Blood flew off their demolished faces, speckling Sharon's arms. Kim had no jaw. Susie did, but it was loose and flapping up and down, teeth clashing together.

Breathless, drenched in sweat, slipping and sliding on Hammond's body but still *on* it, Sharon made a final try, a *big* try to get off him. She relaxed her left arm, letting Kim sink to the floor, then thrust herself toward Kim while she used all the strength in her right arm on Susie.

Pulled by the belt around her neck, Susie sat up.

Yes!

Sharon rolled, towing Susie after her.

Rolled to the left, onto her side, feeling the push of Hammond's hipbone against her own hip, wanting to go on rolling until she was *off* him—never mind she would be dragging Susie down on top of her, never mind she would land facedown on Kim's body— better that than Hammond's penis under her crack . . . but she couldn't roll any further.

Not the way her left arm was sticking straight out, belted to Kim's neck.

Not without dislocating her shoulder.

She whimpered in pain and despair.

Out of strength, she could no longer hold off Susie.

Her right arm fell and Susie slumped over her, torso coming to rest slick and heavy on top of Sharon's side, her face inches from Sharon's face, one eye gone, the other eye open and staring straight at Sharon with that flat, blank look that nobody has but the dead.

Andy began to clap his hands.

Then he stopped clapping and said, "*Another* fine mess you've gotten us into, Olly."

Sharon closed her eyes.

"I sure hope you aren't too tuckered out to enjoy our date. As the poets say, 'The best is yet to be.'"

CHAPTER FIFTEEN

When she could find enough breath to speak, she gasped, "Get her off me. Please."

Andy stepped around Susie's side, bent over and pulled her by the shoulder. She flopped off, jerking at Sharon's arm, tugging Sharon flat onto her back again.

"What do you say?" Andy asked.

"Thanks."

He looked down at her. "You could sure use a good hosing off."

"No. Please."

He chuckled. "Oh, don't get your shorts in a knot. I didn't mean *that*. What kind of guy do you think I am?"

She didn't try to answer.

Andy walked away.

She lay there, still breathing hard, sweat pouring from her body.

All that, she thought, and I'm back where I started. *You wish.*

Though still flat on her back with Hammond underneath her, she wasn't *quite* where she'd been. Before starting, her legs had been resting on top of his legs, straight out and close together. Now her legs were wide apart, her heels on the floor. And her buttocks were spread more than they'd been before and she could feel him between them.

Deeper in.

And bigger?

Almost against her will, she flexed her buttocks. They tightened, squeezed him.

Long, slippery, slightly stiff.

He *isn't* getting a hard-on, she told herself. He's dead. Nothing's going on down there. Unless maybe rigor mortis.

"Here we go," said Andy, striding up to her with a five-gallon plastic bottle of Sparkletts water cradled in his arms.

He stopped near her feet. "Give us a minute, we'll have you squeaky clean." He wrestled with the bottle and upended it.

Water *blubbed* out, splashing Sharon, the tepid gush making its way up her right leg from foot to thigh, crossing her pelvis then moving down her left leg. When the water pounded her bandaged knee, she cried out and bucked.

The pouring stopped.

A moment later, she felt her legs being shoved farther apart. By Hammond's legs.

What's he *doing?*

It's not him, she realized. It's Andy shoving Hammond's legs apart. Andy now standing between them, dumping water straight down onto Sharon's vagina.

The throbbing gush of water buffeted her, slid its way downward, cooling her, sluicing in between her buttocks, drenching Hammond's penis.

Then the water moved slowly up her body, splashed a trail from one hip to the other, flooded her navel, continued upward, drummed against her ribcage, cascaded onto her left breast, then her right, then her left again, then her right, *blubbing* from the bottle, dropping like soft bombs onto her breasts. He seemed to be using her nipples as bull's-eyes. She felt them tingling, growing stiff.

Now the bottle must've been light enough for Andy to handle with ease, because he raised it overhead and reached it forward, sending the water up Sharon's neck to her face. As it struck her chin, she squeezed her lips together and shut her eyes. The water splashed her lips, her nose, her eyelids, and ran down the sides of her face.

It cooled her forehead. It drenched her hair.

Suddenly, the water stopped.

Sharon opened her eyes, blinked, and saw Andy standing above her, holding the bottle high, pouring the last of it onto his own face. It spilled down his body.

The late afternoon sunlight, slanting in through the windows, turned his skin golden and made the streaming water gleam like liquid fire.

Sharon stared at his erection.

This is it, she thought. This is when he does it.

She groaned.

Andy tossed the bottle. It made a hollow *whomp* when it struck the floor. Then it rolled. He smiled down at Sharon. "Are you ready for some action?"

She didn't answer.

He glanced at himself. "A beaut, huh? Think it'll fit?"

"Fit it up your ass," she said.

Dumb fucking thing to say, she thought. But it was already out and she couldn't call it back.

CHAPTER SIXTEEN

In the beginning, he kept her on top of Hammond, her outstretched arms still belted to the necks of Susie and Kim, her legs far apart, her heels on the floor.

He spent a long time crawling on the others, kneeling on them while he looked closely at Sharon. He circled her a couple of times, just staring. Then he began to touch her. He ran his open hands down her body as if to memorize her curves and textures. He explored her with his fingertips. Caressed her, pinched her, delved.

Every so often, he sighed with pleasure.

Sometimes, he whispered to her. "I've wanted to have you like this for so long. I've *dreamed* of it."

And, "Do you like that? Does that feel good? It does, doesn't it."

And, "See what you've been missing?"

Then he began on her with his mouth. He kissed her gently on the eyes, then on the lips. She wanted to turn her face away. He wasn't hurting her, though, and that might stop if she made him angry. So she lay motionless and made no protests. When he pushed his tongue between her lips, she opened her mouth and allowed it in.

She thought about biting it.

Whatever she might do to him, however, he could do so much worse to her.

Soon, he removed his tongue from her mouth. He made his way lower and hovered over her breasts, licking them, kissing them. He kissed each of her nipples. He swirled his tongue around them, flicked them, sucked on them. Then he drew each breast deep into his mouth, pulling at them until they popped out of his mouth with a loud *slurp*.

He made his way lower, kissing, licking.

Soon, his mouth was between her legs. His tongue slid over her, eased into her, probed and wiggled.

She squirmed.

His mouth went away. "Like it, don't you? *Love* it, don't you?"

"No."

"Sure you do. But wait'll you feel *this*."

He slid his penis into her. It felt solid and huge. He eased it in all the way, then slowly retreated until it was almost out, then clutched her shoulders and *shoved!* Her body jerked with the power of the thrust. She cried out.

He did it again and again.

Each time, the impact jostled Sharon's entire body and she felt her buttocks slide back and forth on Hammond.

He *is* getting bigger, she thought. Bigger, harder.

He isn't dead?

His body had been at the bottom of the pile, then hidden under Sharon; she'd never actually seen his wounds.

But she'd been on top of him for a long, long time and she'd never felt any movement.

Except for *that.*

If he's alive, she thought, how come he isn't breathing?

Maybe he is and I just can't feel it.

Andy pounded deep—all the way in—and stayed there, grunting, twitching, shuddering, throbbing and spurting.

So much for that, she thought.

Now he can kill me and get it over with.

CHAPTER SEVENTEEN

He didn't.

As the office darkened, he straddled Sharon's body. He rubbed himself on her breasts and pushed them together and slid between them. His motions rocked her body gently from side to side. Hammond, slippery between her buttocks, felt larger, harder.

He's alive, all right. Must be.

If he's alive enough to get a boner, maybe he's alive enough to help.

Maybe he'll save me!

Later, in deep darkness, Andy lifted her head in his hands and went into her mouth.

Later still, he climbed off her. A lamp came on, its brightness hurting her eyes. Kneeling on Susie, then Kim, he freed Sharon's arms from the belts.

He rolled her off Hammond. . . .

Pain exploded from her knee.

* * *

She came to, facedown on Kim, her face buried in the pulped remains of the woman's face. Andy was on top of her, clutching her shoulders as he thrust. . . .

Trying to breathe, she sucked blood and bits of flesh into her mouth. She choked.

Andy kept on plunging.

CHAPTER EIGHTEEN

Darkness.

Silence.

Not quite silence, really. Sharon heard ringing in her ears. The ringing seemed to come from inside her, from every hurt part of her body.

Somebody was underneath her. Kim, she supposed.

Somebody was on top of her, too. No longer thrusting, but big and stiff inside her.

She opened her eyes, glimpsed the blur of Kim's face in the darkness, and shut her eyes again.

What happened to the lamp? she wondered.

It had been on, but now it was off.

Maybe it burnt out.

No.

Andy had turned off the lamp. Her memory of it was so vague it seemed almost like a dream . . . she must've been barely conscious at the time. . . .

Andy pulling out of her. Climbing off of her. The lamp remaining on, remaining on, and finally going off. Then the sound of the office door quietly bumping shut.

It *must've* been a dream, she thought.

Because he hadn't really left. He was still up there, the same as before.

It's not over.

She'd thought it was over. He'd gone away, leaving her alive. It was obviously just a dream, though. He couldn't let her live. Not after what she'd seen, not after what he'd done to her. He *had* to kill her.

The door crashed open.

She gasped and flinched.

The body on top of her wobbled.

Men yelled, *"POLICE! . . . POLICE! . . . DON'T MOVE! . . . NOBODY MOVE! . . . POLICE!"*

The room filled with light.

Someone said, "Holy fucking shit."

She heard boots thumping around. Hard breathing. White noise from radios. Creaks and rattles and shaking sounds, metallic clicks. A few seconds later, someone called out, "Clear!"

Looking away from Kim's pulped face, Sharon blurted, "Help! Help me! It's him! Get him off me! He's who did it!"

Boots rushed toward her.

The length of hardness slid out of her. The weight tumbled off her back.

Someone crouched beside her. A hand touched her back. "I'm a police officer, ma'am. You'll be all right. Everything's fine. An ambulance is on the way. Tell me your name. Can you tell me your name?"

"Sharon."

"Sharon, you'll be fine. We'll take good care of you. Okay?"

"Okay."

"Nobody'll hurt you now."

She started to cry again.

CHAPTER NINETEEN

When the policeman hurried out of the way to make room for the EMS crew, Sharon saw Hammond on the floor beside her. He had a face. It was gray and his eyes were wide open.

Dead eyes.

He looked as if he'd been shotgunned in the throat.

Some time ago.

She glimpsed his penis.

Then her view was blocked by men who'd come to help.

She shut her eyes and thought, *No way.*

CHAPTER TWENTY

While Sharon remained in the hospital, a pleasant, gruff-voiced homicide investigator named Phillip Dawson visited her a few times, asking questions and keeping her informed on the progress of the investigation.

Andy's driver's license had been found on the office floor.

The real Andrew Carvell had been found murdered weeks ago, the presumed victim of a car-jacking.

Fingerprints had been discovered in and around the crime scenes, but so far the police hadn't been able to come up with a suspect to match them.

They'd collected hair and fiber samples, too. And semen galore. They had no inkling, however, as to the identity of the man who'd left them behind.

"I know how to find out who he is," Sharon had said. "You need to go to my apartment."

A few hours later, Lt. Dawson returned with Sharon's high school yearbooks.

"He'll be in these," she said.

She leafed through the four yearbooks, searching for the face of the man who had called himself Andy Carvell.

Not there.

She searched the books again and again.

"But he *said* he knew me from high school! He *said* so. He had a crush on me but I ignored him and that's why he *did* all this."

"Well," said Lt. Dawson, "maybe he was absent on picture day."

EIGHT MONTHS LATER

Sharon tossed her crutches into her car, then climbed in and shut the door.

The interview had gone pretty well, she thought.

I'll probably get this one.

Not that she really wanted another office job . . . especially not in a building *this* near to the other one.

It'll only be for a while. Finish my degree at night school, and I'll be on my way.

She started her car and pulled out of the parking lot, turning left before realizing she should've made a right.

Oh, well. It won't kill me to drive past the place. Not as if *he's* there.

He's nowhere.

I hope.

As she neared the old building, she lost her nerve. Too much had happened there. Too many people had died. She'd gone through too much agony and terror and humiliation there.

Though it seemed like a gutless thing to do, she

hung a right onto a sidestreet, drove for a block, made a left and kept going for several blocks before cutting to the left again and returning to the main road.

Neatly avoiding the place.

Avoided *seeing* it, she corrected herself. Didn't miss *thinking* about it, though.

I'll be thinking about it the rest of my life.

She flexed her buttocks.

Felt nothing but the car seat through her panties and skirt.

That Hammond thing never happened, she reminded herself for the umpteenth time. *The Andy thing sure happened, though.*

Andy or whatever his name was.

Still out there someplace.

Or maybe not. Maybe he got arrested for some other crime, or died or something.

Feeling hungry and seeing the familiar sights, Sharon suddenly realized she was on a direct course for Simon's Deli.

Her mouth suddenly watered for one of their famous Reuben sandwiches.

If I get the job, she thought, I'll start eating there again.

Have to lay in a fresh supply of Tums. . . .

She smiled and kept driving.

Soon, a chain link fence appeared on her right. She took her foot off the gas pedal, slowing as she passed a sign that read:

SCHOOL ZONE
25 MPH
WHEN CHILDREN ARE PRESENT

This was a Friday, a school day, lunch hour.

Children were present.

Dozens of them. Not exactly children, though. More like teenagers.

Half a block ahead, a crossing guard in a pith helmet, orange reflective vest and jeans stepped off the curb holding a miniature STOP sign and started to lead half a dozen students across the road.

Sharon eased down on the brake pedal, slowed, stopped.

The crossing guard nodded at her, smiled and stepped in front of her car. He looked forward. Then his head jerked sideways again.

Their eyes locked.

You're from high school, aren't you?

Ha! Very good. You do *remember!*

She muttered, "Fucking shit."

The man who'd called himself Andy threw down the STOP sign and ran.

The kids yelled and laughed at him.

"Lookit the fag run!" one guy shouted.

They laughed all the harder when the crossing guard's pith helmet flew off his head.

But the laughter stopped when the gunshot rang out.

The crossing guard, halfway across the street, flopped on the pavement and skidded.

The kids all turned their heads and looked at Sharon.

"Get out of here," she shouted.

They took off running.

No other traffic was nearby.

The crossing guard, left calf bleeding, pushed himself up to his hands and knees and looked around at Sharon. "Leave me alone!" he cried out.

She stepped on the gas and swerved toward him.

He wasn't quick enough to get out of the way.

Her left front tire crunched both his feet.

She stopped on top of his right foot, shifted to Park, set the emergency brake, and lowered her 1911 model Colt .45 (just like Mike Hammer's, just like Hal's) onto her lap.

Leaning out the window, she said, "Tell me who I am and I'll let you go."

The crossing guard kept on screaming.

"What do you say?" she called. "Is it a deal?"

"Sharon!"

"Sharon what?"

"Sharon Wade!"

"That's right!"

"Get off me! Get off my foot!"

"A deal's a deal," Sharon said. She pulled forward and felt her front tire roll down onto the pavement. With the tire a few inches in front of his foot, she stopped her car again.

"Oh! Thank you! Thank you!"

"One more thing," Sharon said, looking down at him from her window. "How'd you find out my name?"

"The news! The news! It was all over the news!"

"But how'd you know it *then?*"

"I . . . followed you . . . back from lunch. Got it . . . off your registration."

"But I keep that in my glove compartment. You broke into my car?"

"It was . . . yeah. Had to."

"But that's cheating." Sharon shifted to reverse. "And cheaters never prosper."

When her tire crushed his foot again, his screams

ripped through the noon air. They nearly concealed the sounds of approaching sirens.

"Wanta make things more interesting for the emergency room doctors?" Sharon shouted.

"*NO!!!*"

"I do."

"*PLEASE!!!*"

She reached out the window with her .45, aimed down at him and emptied the pistol—five hollow points—being careful to keep the slugs below his waist and away from major blood vessels.

IN THE YEAR OF
OUR LORD: 2202

Edward Lee

For Ann & Kelly Laymon

ACKNOWLEDGEMENTS

As always, my career is in debt to far too many to name here, but for this, I need to thank the late, great Richard Laymon—one, for inviting me into this project, and, two, for his innumerable gestures of friendship.

PART ONE

"I make peace and create evil: I the Lord God do all these things."

—*Isaiah 45:7*

(I)

Almost off-shift. The last hour always dragged on and on.

Sharon looked at the CF Standard Time chronometer above the cove transom. Ten minutes to go. A passive vid-port occupied the entire exterior sidewall of the cove: a giant moving mural blooming with stars and space. Every data center on board had one . . . to induce the crew to muse upon the immensity of God. But Sharon knew that the vision would make the last minutes of her shift seem like an hour. If Captain-Reverend Peter had been away as he usually was, the other techs would've left by now. But you don't take off early when the boss is in.

105

Not that Sharon would've left early, anyway. She owed the Christian Federate a full shift, so that's what it would get. Unlike Susanna and Kim and Leslie. They were usually long gone on mid-shifts when Peter had business elsewhere on the ship. Sharon liked the cove better when she had it to herself. Susanna, Kim and Leslie weren't exactly horrible; Sharon supposed they were fairly typical data integrators: capable but not very ambitious, friendly enough when not obsessing over their hair and nails. And they only attended Mass once a week, the minimum mission requisite.

Shut away in his master cove with one of his diagnostic assistants, Captain-Reverend Peter couldn't see that Susanna was covertly applying lavender nail polish as the final minutes of the work day ticked down. Nor that Leslie was checking her lipstick in a holomirror. Nor that Kim was speaking quietly on the comm, probably to one of her several male acquaintances.

They've been at this job a lot longer than me, Sharon thought. *Before you know it, maybe I'll be growing two-inch nails and . . .*

No way.

It all seemed vain to her. Most makeup had been banned years ago, when the Exploratory Corp had changed the hair regs (bald for males, one-inch cuts for females). Lipstick and nail polish were still allowed provided that the colors met code. Sharon thought it looked whorish, though. She wished they'd change the regs again and just get rid of it all. *We're Christian servants, not models from the old days.*

She looked at the clock again.

Five minutes till 1700.

It's never going to end.

Over the intercom, the familiar, sedate voice flowed: the thrice-daily off-shift blessing.

" 'In them—in the heavens and the stars—hath He set a tabernacle for the faithful. His going forth is from the end of heaven, where there is nothing hid and none shall travail.' "

Psalms, Sharon guessed. *With a few edits!*

"Precious servants, go in peace," the voice bid.

"To love and serve the Lord," she finished, not surprised that her cove mates hadn't joined her in the reply.

Sharon's comm buzzed. In the quiet of the late-shift cove, the sudden noise made her flinch. She reached across her desk and picked up the comm. "Data Regiment, Spec 4 Sharon speaking. May I help you?"

"I'm gonna get you."

The voice of the man on the comm sounded malicious. Underneath Sharon's shift utilities, goosebumps scurried up the skin of her back. Her breasts went crawly and her nipples hardened.

"Excuse me?" she asked.

"I'm gonna get you, Sharon."

Sharon was irate. "This is an illegal communication! Identify yourself immediately!"

"I'm gonna get you NOW."

Dead air. He was gone.

Sharon slammed the comm down and jerked her hand away.

Kim, her own comm still to her ear, swivelled on her grav chair and frowned at Sharon. "Got a problem?" Kim always said that—when she was annoyed, which was most of the time. She and Sharon had been dom-mates for the last four sub-light missions; Sharon knew her *habits* fairly well.

"That call," Sharon murmured.

"I've got a call of my own, honey. You wanta hold it down?"

"Sorry."

The cove entry swung open and a man stepped in. *Him.*

Sharon knew it had to be him. He was bald, like all male regulars, and he wore yellow Class I utilities, a subordinate loader or r-dock worker. He must've made the call from the central accessmain, probably with an illegal comm unit.

He wasn't holding a comm unit, though.

He was holding a high-amp milliwave pistol.

Susanna, whose desk was nearest the manway, normally greeted visitors with, "May I help you?" Today, however, she dropped her nail polish. The bottle thunked on her desktop and rolled.

"I'm here to see Sharon," the man said.

The same voice she'd heard on the comm.

Susanna nodded, swivelled, pointed a trembling finger toward the rear of the data cove. Straight at Sharon. "Th-that's her."

"Thanks," the man said and shot Susanna in the side of the head. As the gun bucked, the noise of its half-second discharge crackled in Sharon's ears. Meanwhile, her colleague's head seemed to erupt from one temple, ejecting cooked brain matter and steaming blood.

Just as the man was pressing the recharge switch, Sharon threw herself to the floor behind her desk.

Her knees pounded the floor. Another discharge crackled through the cove. But Sharon's reactions weren't what she would've expected. She didn't go numb with terror. She didn't ask herself who this man might be or why he had barged into the cove to kill people. He was a fact. A horrible fact like a fifty-ton mag-lev pallet suddenly bearing down on her head-on.

Deal with it or die.

She flinched as another blast crackled through the office. But—

The security signal button. I've got to hit the security signal.

Then two more very quick shots.

God on High, save me. . . .

Sharon popped up from behind the desk, jerked forward, and hit the glowing security tab on her holo-screen, just as—

KRIIIIIIIIIISH

—another milliwave discharge burned a half inch from her cheek.

At least she'd done it, but she didn't consider the unreality of expecting a response team to arrive before this madman killed everyone in the cove. Hunkered down in the leghole of her desk, she realized she was staring at her shift-tote. She grabbed it, pulled it closer, peered down into it: ID-fold, creditbook, file-flat, hairbrush, tampons.

KRIIIIIIIIIISH

Another discharge sizzled through the air. Leslie and Kim both screamed from their own work stations but their screams were brief. Other screams rang out, more subdued: Captain-Reverend Peters and his assistant. Soon a smell like barbequed meat filled the cove.

And Sharon quickly realized that there was nothing in her shift-tote she could use as a weapon.

But what of the shift-tote itself?

God, I beg of thee. Please let this work.

Sharon knew that the feed cables on her desk-link were filled with potassium ethanolamine, a systems coolant. When exposed to air, it would freeze within several seconds—as well as freeze any material it came in contact with.

She glanced aside, closed her eyes for a moment after glimpsing the bodies of first Kim, her roommate, and then Leslie. Both had taken full milliwave bursts to the chest, their hearts broiled mid-beat, smoke rising from opened mouths. Now footsteps could be heard coming around the other side of the cove.

And then the man's voice:

"Sharon. Hiding is pointless. Come out. I'll be merciful and quick."

She put her fingers on the cable's drain plug. DANGER, it read. DO NOT RELEASE WITHOUT WORK ORDER AND HAZMAT AUTHORIZATION. Her fingers lingered on the plug.

The man's boot-tips could be seen coming around the work station. His voice seemed to echo: "Under heaven lay umbra. . . ."

Sharon grit her teeth, released the drain plug, and let the bitter-scented coolant empty into the shift-tote. Would the fluid dissolve the tote's polysynth fabric? Would it freeze immediately?

Was she about to die?

Believe in Him, she thought of the scripture, *and He will help thee.*

Sharon sprang up from behind the desk and flung the tote at the intruder. The milliwave gun was aimed right at her chest, but before the man had time to fire, he threw both arms up to block the tote.

He was a second too late.

The tote plowed into his face, prolapsing, and its blue-green contents bloomed. An agonized yell bubbled from his mouth.

Sharon ran around the side of her desk and dashed for the cove exit. When the door rose, guns were in her face. Now Sharon herself screamed.

"Duck."

Two securitechs in full emergency response gear stood like golems in the entranceway. Sharon ducked just as their stout Colt-Heckler flechette rifles fired over her head. She turned at their armored feet, saw the mile-per-second rounds dot the intruder's chest. The impact slammed him to the wall where his face, already crystalized from the splash of coolant, shattered like glass.

The bare skull seemed to peer at her, then he fell dead.

The first tech helped Sharon up, inhuman-looking in his ballistic visor and body armor. "Are you all right, sister?"

Sharon felt winded yet energized. "Yes, yes, I think so."

His eyes could barely be seen behind the face shield. "Praise be to God," he said. "We sing praise and thanks to God for saving thee."

God. Yes! she thought. *Please, God, accept my thanks!*

The other securitech prodded the dead assailant with his rifle muzzle. He raised his visor, looked back at Sharon and his colleague, and grinned. "This crazy fucker is fuckin' fucked. Think we fucked his fuckin' day up enough?" He winked at Sharon. "Yeah, he's one dead motherfucker, the chump fuck."

(II)

The C.F.S. Edessa was the latest in the Christian Federate's fleet of long-range Exodus-Class exploratory platforms. Named for the raped St. Mary, of Ephraem's parable, the ship fully utilized the newest innovations of elemental hybridization and NHC (non-heat-conducting) materials. A thousand feet long and but seventy wide, the vessel could sustain the lives of its 150-man-and-woman crew for a decade if necessary and could propel itself at slightly less than one-half the speed of light for, theoretically, an indefinite time span. Cold fusion breeder reactors provided equally indefinite power for all of the vessel's systems; fuel cells and nitrogen-recharge inductors provided all water and air.

The spirit of God provided just about everything else.

The time: 1800 hrs. The date: 2202. The mission: routine resupply of free-drift Utility Station Solon, located approximately forty billion miles beyond Pluto's farthest ecliptic orbit.

JESUS IS WATCHING YOU

Sharon peered at the familiar sign behind Major-Rector Matthew's desk. The signs and posters were everywhere, with other signs like it, all care of the Morale Department—she'd seen them a million times. But why should the message and her Savior's graceful face so immediately catch her eye now? Christ's gaze, though benevolent, revealed no answer.

"Ah, Specialist Grade-4 Sharon Beatrice Lydwine," spoke the Major, entering the front cove from one of the security station's anterooms. Descendent surnames were only used for admin purposes.

Sharon began to rise to the position of attention.

"No need, no need," Matthew caught her. "Here in my station, we can dispense with the formalities. Sharon . . . a pretty name. Is it after the rose?"

"No, sir. The plain. The open tract between ancient Jaffa and Caesarea."

"A holy place, yes—" Suddenly, though, his comm buzzed. "Excuse me a moment. . . ."

"Yes, sir."

As the officer quietly conversed with a tech somewhere else in the Edessa, Sharon caught herself looking at the sign again.

JESUS IS WATCHING YOU

Often, at odd moments such as this, she wondered if it were true, if God really could be everywhere at once, omnipotent, all-powerful. *Jesus is watching me,* she thought. *I hope so.*

"He is, isn't He?" Major-Rector Matthew said, having finished his communication.

"Pardon me, sir?"

"Jesus *is* watching you." The gaunt man smiled selflessly as Christ Himself. "And I'd say He was watching you very precisely earlier in the data regiment. He was watching your *back.*"

"Thanks be to God," Sharon said, her hands clasped in her lap. *Jesus saved my life today.* It took a while for the reality to set in.

Matthew adjusted the height of his grav chair. The lumeplates overhead, plus the light from his intranet screen, made the sixty-year-old security chief appear a hundred, bald head glowing dully. "Yes, thanks be to God. But the Edessa and its entire crew owe *you* some thanks too."

"I don't understand." She didn't, and now she felt a subtle discomfiture. During her attack, she'd felt cool and objective, not afraid. Now, though, some psychological backlash was gripping her. Nervous. Jittery. A profuse perspiration suddenly slicked her underarms and between her breasts.

What was he saying? The crew owes me thanks? For what?

"We've seen the digichip recordings, Sharon. You behaved quite bravely. You fearlessly exposed yourself to milliwave fire in order to engage the security signal. Under a clear threat of death, you summoned some very impressive initiative and creativity. You fought back, defeated your foe. Even if my securitechs had been late, the attacker would've died from the wound you inflicted. Loose on the ship, God only knows how many more he would've killed. You saved lives today, Sharon."

That idea hadn't occurred to her. All she could think of just now were the bodies she'd seen.

"Therefore," the Major-Rector continued, "I'm promoting you to Specialist Grade E-5, effective at once."

"Thank you, sir," she replied, not really hearing his words.

"And once we return to the moon, I'm putting in orders to New Vatican, for a Distinguished Service Crucifix."

Now she heard the words, and objected. "Please don't, sir. I'm unworthy. I was just doing my job, for the mission, for God."

Matthew sat upright, dismayed. "But . . . it's one of the highest valor medals a woman can be awarded. It's made of genuine gold."

"Then I'll melt it down and give it to the poor," Sharon insisted. "I don't want medals, sir. I'd feel . . . uncomfortable."

Matthew nodded. "Ah, I see. You're distressed by what you were forced to witness today. Five fine servants of God brutally murdered." He crossed himself. "I've known Captain-Reverend Peter for years; we served together in the Indochine Airlift in '189, and twice in Yemen before the 60th Amendment." His aged eyes scanned an open file on his holoscreen. "Oh, and I see here that one of the victims was your dom-mate. . . ."

Sharon closed her eyes. "Spec 2 Kim Katherine. She was the regiment's transfer and reallocation tech."

"I'm very sorry." Matthew exhaled, about to broach an unpleasantry. "As humans, of course, we despair when our friends and fellow Christians die. But God so loved the world that He gave us eternal life. We're really being selfish, aren't we, when we mourn those who die? Your dom-mate, Captain-Reverend Peter, the others? They're in God's mansion now, everlasting in perfection. But you and I must go on, with our duties, our lives." The Major-Rector leaned closer to Sharon. "The man who attacked you today—I need to know if you've ever seen him before—before we launched, that is. Do you know his name? Have you ever been personally acquainted with him?"

Now the official business was at hand. Sharon had to remind herself that this wasn't just a supervisory chat. It was a *debriefing*. "No, sir. I've never seen him before in my life, not even since we launched."

"What are your impressions of him, I mean, now that it's all over?"

She didn't have to reflect. "He must be part of the Red Sect. I've read a lot about them in the newsflats since I received my Dinar clearance, data not released to the general public." Then the eerie remembrance floated back across her mind. "It was what he said, just before I threw the coolant at him. He said 'Under heaven lay umbra.' Those words are part of their credo or something."

" 'Under heaven lay umbra, hiding the chosen,' " the elder recited the intercession in its entirety. "A convoluted way to suggest that somewhere between God and the earth are an *ungodly* chosen people—the Red Sect themselves, no doubt—who are hidden from the rest of the world by something—some abstraction, perhaps. Hence, the 'umbra,' a shadow of some sort, a shading. Federate Intelligence has always believed this to be a planetary reference, such as the shadow projected during an eclipse."

With all the havoc that the so-called Red Sect had inflicted over the last hundred years, they affronted any logic that existed in the fundamentals of terrorism. Christians and Jews, Buddhists and Moslems and Atheists alike were all open targets to this secret terrorist regime, but in doing so they never made any demands, never made any political statements, never insisted on prisoner exchanges. They just demolitioned churches and mosques and murdered people, all without saying why. No one knew who their leader was, no one knew anything about their organizational base—indeed, no one even knew what they believed in. They weren't Druze nor Haddinites, they weren't Red China Underground nor Fourth Commitern, nor were they Luciferics. All of these terrorist organizations, in the death and destruction they wrought, made their ideals, beliefs, and demands perfectly clear.

But not the Red Sect.

They killed and hid. They destroyed and kept silent. They perpetuated the most appalling acts of sexual atrocity, religious blasphemy, and cultural taboo . . . all without ever saying why.

They'd unleashed a gengineered virus in Africa and killed 100,000,000. From suicidal air-skiffs, they'd dropped phosphorous bombs on Westminster Abbey and the Washington Cathedral on Christmas Eve. In '192, they'd commandeered several thousand tons of Agent Blue and defoliated 50 percent of the protected sectors of the Rain Forest. And in '179, they'd gassed the Sacred College of Cardinals.

A year later they'd nuked Vatican City with hand-made plutonium devices and killed the Holy Father.

"They've never made their agenda known," Matthew continued. "It's possible that they don't even have one. But be that as it may, we've got a serious problem here."

Sharon understood at once. "If one Red Sect member got onboard, there could just as easily be others."

"Precisely."

"I presumed he used a counterfeit ID pass, switched identities with a genuine crewmember?"

"No," the officer answered. "The entire crew is accounted for. Our intruder somehow stowed away and found some effective means to—"

"Hide," Sharon finished, "as if in shadow. As if within an umbra."

Matthew seemed dolorous now. As chief of the Edessa's security, the responsibility was ultimately his to protect the crew from terrorist infiltration. Yet now he seemed deceptively shaken, even afraid. "Anyway, you know that your Federate Restricted Information Clearance forbids you from telling anyone about what happened."

"Understood, sir."

"We can't have an outbreak of panic twenty billion miles from Earth." His gaze narrowed at her. "The reason I asked if you'd ever seen your assailant before is based on what we saw and heard on the digitape. When he entered the cove, he specifically asked for you."

"Yes, sir. And during his comm-call, he named me specifically too. He said 'I'm going to get you, *Sharon*.'"

Matthew contemplated this, resting his chin atop two outstretched fingers. "And your Federate Occupational Specialty is—"

"Thirty Delta 50, sir. I'm mainly just a nav-processor and redundancy-systems monitor. At all times, the coordinates in the back-up navigational drives are constantly matched with those programmed into the central Macro-Analysis Computer. I monitor the data matches. If there's a discrepancy, I send it to operations."

Matthew's old face perked up at a thought. "So you have access to the mission's coordinates?"

"Yes, sir."

"Potentially, then, could you alter the ship's course?"

"No, sir. It's an operational impossibility. No one on board can do that. It's all pre-programmed. Even if an emergency situation occurred—say, a comet spur, or we found ourselves approaching an uncharted asteroid belt—the MAC would change our course automatically. The only thing special about my job is that it sometimes makes me privy to navigational information about course trajectories and debark descriptions. That's it."

"Then, even if the assailant had killed you, the ship's course wouldn't be affected," he said more than asked.

"That's correct, sir."

"It doesn't make sense, but then, the Red Sect, since their formation, have *never* made sense, at least not in any way that seems logical to the Christian Federate. If he truly wanted to sabotage the mission, there are dozens of other stations on the ship that would prove far more vulnerable." Matthew's gaze narrowed again, more darkly this time. "Hmm. The mission. I suppose we have to ask ourselves why the Red Sect would go to such trouble to sabotage a routine resupply mission in the first place."

"Maybe it's—" but Sharon cut herself off. It was not her privilege to offer hypotheses to a senior officer unless directly asked.

But Major-Rector Matthew looked right back into her eyes, his own eyes clearly troubled. "Maybe that's it. Maybe it's not a *routine* mission at all."

(III)

Sharon believed what Major-Rector Matthew had said earlier—that it's actually selfish to mourn those who die. *They're in God's mansion now, everlasting in perfection,* he'd affirmed. "So I guess that means I'm selfish," she muttered to herself. She walked down the central manway, heading back to her dom-room, knowing how oddly empty it would feel without Kim there. True, she and Kim had never really been friends, but at least they got along. Sharon kept close-mouthed about her objections to some of Kim's habits. For one, Kim sometimes lied on her time-file at the cove, and for another, Sharon knew that Kim was seeing several men on the ship—a severe violation of the Christian Federate Military Code. But Sharon never said anything— only God could judge.

God. Not me.

She hadn't really been close to Susanna or Leslie, either; nevertheless, she liked them. And Captain-Reverend Peter had been one of the nicest tech commanders she'd ever worked for. Sharon knew she'd miss them all very much. No, she shouldn't mourn, but, now that she thought of it, even Christ mourned, didn't He? *My soul is exceedingly sorrowful,* He said on the Mount of Olives at Gethsemane the night before He died, *even unto death.*

She couldn't shake the lingering despair; she seemed to be dragging it along behind her like a cape in tatters. By now, the bodies of Kim, the Captain-Reverend, and the others would have been summarily cremated in the central fuel cell, their ashes jettisoned into space, and since the dead were no longer mourned, no funeral services were held, just the ship's lone chaplain reading the Final Rites. Though she'd been born well after the passing of Public Law 482 (the Eugenics Act of the Christian Congress), her biological parents—both missionaries for the Defense Corp—had been killed during a revolt in the state formerly known as California. She'd been four at the time, too young to even remember them—and too young to mourn.

Until today, in fact, she'd never personally witnessed death.

Perhaps that explained the despair, even after all of her conditioning in the technical convents.

Death was new to her.

"Hey, sister! There she is!"

The voice startled her; her contemplations had left her walking down the manway in a daze. A handsome face smiled at her—though the smile seemed a bit sly—and at once she found herself looking at a tall handsome man, blue-eyed, thirtyish, dressed in security fatigues. He stood at parade rest, beneath the transom which read: PROPERTY STATION: RESTRICTED, and he was holstering a Webley Model 2000 automatic caseless revolver—the standard sidearm for Security Corp. His name tag read: THOMAS, PVT-I.

Then it dawned on her. . . .

"You're the securitech . . . from the data cove," she said.

"That's a fact. Call me Tom." He shook his head, smiling as if impressed. "I'll tell ya, that was some fast action you pulled back at the cove."

Sharon could think of nothing to say in response.

"You feeling all right? Sometimes it's easy to get shook up."

"I'm . . . fine. Thank you for inquiring."

"Ooo, yeah, you really put the drop on that dude. Did you see the way his whole face kind'a *busted* off his head when he fell over?"

Sharon gulped at the mental replay of the image. "Really, it's not something I feel very good about."

Tom cocked a brow. "Aw, come on. That freak had it coming and then some. And you gave it to him in spades. All I did was a little clean-up."

Sharon was unnerved. "We killed a man today. We're not supposed to *kill*. 'Thou shalt not kill.' Ever hear of that?"

Tom winced funkily. "Gimme a break. Ever hear of this, sister? 'Whoso sheddeth blood, his blood shall be shed'? Sounds to me like the Book of Genesis says it's okay to kill killers. That guy deserved airing out. You should get a medal for the job you did."

I just turned one down, came the ironic thought. Still, this discourse bothered her and she didn't want any more of the same. "I have to go, Private. God be with you."

"Aw, sister—so heartless. I gotta stand this guard-post for the next twelve hours. You're the first pretty face to come along all shift, and now you're leaving. Just my luck."

She intended to keep on walking—she didn't like the innuendo. But she also knew that standard sentinel shifts were only eight hours maximum. "Twelve hours?" she questioned. "Isn't that unduly long?"

He chuckled. "Sister, I don't know what unduly means but if you ask me, it's *too* long."

Next she found herself appraising him. She noticed five 3-year service strips marking his blue fatigue sleeve. "It's none of my business, Private—"

"Call me Tom—"

"—but how is it that you've been in the Christian Federate Army for fifteen years but you're only a private E-1?"

Another chuckle. "I made it to buck sergeant once—for about two days. Let's just say I've got a language problem."

Did he mean a learning deficiency? "Your English sounds fine to me."

"Not *that* kind of language problem. And I quote the Christian Code of Military Justice: 'All men and women in service, regardless of branch, will refrain at all times from offensive language, gestures deemed to be obscene, and any and all mannerisms, locutions, and behavior that can be defined as profane.'"

Then Sharon remembered his absolutely atrocious language after he'd shot the Red Sect man back at her cove.

"Ain't that a fuckin' kick in the dick? I got two Silver Bishop Stars, two Médaille de Laterans, and a fuckin' Vatican Medal of Honor, and I can't make E-2 because I cuss on occasion. One day I'm gonna tell the

CO to kiss the back of my fuckin' balls. What's he gonna do? Bust me down to fuckin' E-0?"

Sharon winced. "Please!"

He leaned over closer to her, as if to reveal a secret. "That's why I'm standing this damn twelve-motherfuckin'-hour guard shift. Punishment, you know? My sergeant reported me—for cussing after I shot that guy."

"Well, you deserve it," she retorted. "It's *ungodly* to talk like that."

A quick facial expression sluffed her objection off. "God doesn't give a shit if I cuss. Just as long as I get the job done. Think Christ fuckin' cares if I say shit, fuck, cocksucker, and motherfucker? I believe in Him. I accept Him as my lord and savior. He doesn't give a flying tenpound *fuck* how I talk."

"Really, I've got to go—"

"Hey, wait." Tom lightly grabbed her arm, tugged her back and winked at her. "Don't you even want to know what I'm guarding?"

She was about to respond with an emphatic *no*, but simply his tone of voice got a hook in her.

"All right, *Private*. What are you guarding?"

Now he leaned so close, she could feel his breath on her ear. "Him."

"Who?"

"Him. You know. That Red Sect piece of shit we aired out today."

The information astonished her. "You mean he's still alive?"

"Fuck no. He's deader than dog-shit, fuckin' cold meat on the slab. I'm guarding his motherfuckin' corpse—"

"Please stop talking like that!" she implored.

"Sorry. Can't help it."

"Anyway, you must be lying," she felt sure. "I know the disposal regs. He would've been cremated right along with the others. Immediately. Deceased bodies aren't allowed to remain on board during any sub-light mission."

"Hey, to you and me he's a deceased body. But to CID and Security Corp . . . he's fuckin' *evidence*."

This information piqued her curiosity even more, to the extent that she ignored his profanity.

Evidence, she thought.

Tom elbowed her lightly in the side, that sly grin of his ever-present. "Wanna see him?"

(IV)

No she didn't want to see him, not objectively at least. But something deeper in her being needed to. She needed a last look at the man who'd murdered her colleagues and had tried to kill her.

"Don't worry, there aren't any digicams here; it's considered a security vault." Tom took her past the bulkhead, quickly resealed the door behind them. Ahead of her stretched a single narrow corridor lined with pressure doors. A dark crimson light glowed overhead.

"What *is* this place?" Sharon asked.

"Security Corp's property unit," Tom answered, leading her on. "All restricted equipment—mainly weapons and comm gear—are kept here. Also, all classified logs, system specs, and data banks. And one more thing."

The last pressure door was marked: PATHOLOGY. Tom used a chip-pin and took her in.

Distress made Sharon feel as though eels were swimming rabid circles in her stomach. An acrid, antiseptic scent tinged the air. Tom switched on a lumeplate and suddenly the small unit shimmered in harsh white light. Initially, Sharon had to squint.

A simple morgue platform occupied the center of the unit, and what occupied the morgue platform was a human form sealed in a silver steribag.

"Don't worry, he's clean. First thing they did was rad the hell out of the son of a bitch. He can lay here at standard vessel temp and won't start to stink for a year."

"Charming," Sharon said. A small holochart hovered above the platform; it read:

DO NOT DISPLAY IN UNRESTRICTED AREAS

NAME OF DECEDENT: Unknown
DISPOSITION: Unknown
T.O.D.: 1659 hrs C.F.S.T.

COMMENTS (PHYSIOLOGICAL):

C.O.D.: General organ-system failure due to multiple flechette [2mm] discharge into upper- and midchest region.

OTHER: All facial tissues and musculature destroyed by **profuse contact with data-line coolant potassium ethanolamine**

(GENETIC):

1) 11-probe DNA scan affirms 2 positive tests:
   a) Decedent tested positive for ABZ
      Genotype Syndrome (artificially induced
      cytoplastic aspect exclusive to terrorist
      group known as "Red Sect.")

   b) Decedent tested positive for congenital
      cutaneous *nevus* consistent with exclusive
      pigmental skin condition known as the
      "Red Sect Mark."

M.D. on Duty: W.O. Simon
Clinical Recommendations:
HOLD FOR EVIDENCE SECTION; CLASSIFY
IMMEDIATELY

"Oh no!" Sharon objected. "I might not be cleared
high enough to see this!"

"Relax," Tom assured. "I won't tell, and I already
told you this cove isn't 'live.' No digitapes and no aural sensors. That stuff's not allowed in any restricted
depository. That's why they have dumb-ass grunts like
me to guard the place."

This provided little relief; she was still technically
breaking Federate Military Law. *Not much I can do
about it now,* she figured. *I'm already here.* "ABZ
Genotype Syndrome. I had plenty of training blocks
on genetics but I've never heard of that."

"That's because 'that' is classified. New Vatican
wants the general public to know as little as possible
about the Red Sect . . . not that we know much anyway. Average Joe and Jane on the street would panic
and jump to conclusions; they'd think the Red Sect
are mutants, which they aren't."

"So what's this ABZ genotype?"

"All we know about the Red Sect is that they're a secret organization formed at least a couple hundred years ago. They wanted themselves to be exclusive so when genetic-engineering technologies grew advanced enough, they cultivated their own gene-marker—ABZ—and from there on, ectogenically produced a first generation. Similar to the Christian Federate's Public Reproduction Law which called for all pregnancies to be *in vitro*, to screen out all disease genes. Only the Red Sect took it a step further."

Sharon wasn't sure she understood. "Then how does this genotype make them exclusive?"

"They can only reproduce with themselves."

"So it's a reproductive marker," Sharon got it.

"Right. Something about split nucleotides, introns, RNA implants, egg-head shit like that."

Sharon frowned, but now she understood. "There'd be no susceptibilities for disease—just like the Christian populace—and there'd be no dangers of biological defects from inbreeding, because those genes would've been screened out as well."

"And because they can't reproduce outside of the Sect, they don't have to fertilize their eggs in vitro anymore." Tom winked at her again. "They do it the good old fashioned way. The old tube-steak injection."

Sharon recoiled at the words, just as her years of sexual desensitivity training had taught her to. "You're *awful*," she told him.

"Hey, it's what nature intended, so don't jibe me with all that nunnery crap. And if you tell me you don't think about it yourself—then you're a liar."

Sharon rejected the comment. Yes, she did think about it on very rare occasions—just simple unformed curiosities—and went immediately to Confession when she did. By doing so, she was absolved, and even the priests would tell her that this was normal, since all men and women were born in original sin. She was happy that she'd worked so hard to quell these sinful musings. She knew that many did not. And the few times when her dreams turned sexual, she didn't worry about it. In the last ecumenical council, the Pope had declared that dreams did not equate to sin.

"Shit, I'll bet you're even a virgin, aren't you?" Tom, rude as ever, asked next.

"Of course!" she retaliated. "And it's none of your business anyway, so stop talking about things like that. I only came in here to see—"

"To see the dead meat, that's right. Let me find the right chip-pin and I'll open the bag."

Sharon's gut sunk again. Simply the way he'd said that—*I'll open the bag*—sounded utterly grotesque. But then again, she knew she shouldn't be here, and she could easily walk out right now.

But she didn't.

As Tom perused a ring of chip-pins, Sharon looked back up at the holochart, noticed the name of the medical officer who'd signed off on the autopsical scans.

W.O. Simon.

"Who's Simon? I thought the ship's physician was Commander-Deaconness Esther."

"She is. Dr. Cold Hands we guys call her. She doesn't have proper clearance, so she couldn't do the post, doesn't even know what happened. You've been debriefed, right? You know that you can't mention what happened to anyone."

"I'm fully aware of that, *Private*," she couldn't resist.

She'd worked hard for her rank, didn't like to be talked down to. "Major-Rector Matthew already had me in."

Tom laughed. "We call him Major-Rectal Mattie. The guy's a dork and a half."

"He seemed like a capable and patriotic officer. As usual I don't know what you're talking about."

"Fine, but to answer your question, Simon is a medical warrant officer who used to be with Security Corp. So the mission signed him on as Dr. Esther's assistant. But if you ask me, Simon's daddy must be one of the Christian Joint Chiefs 'cos I can't see any other way for a guy that dumb to make warrant officer. He's so dumb he couldn't find his asshole with both thumbs and a bucket of servolube."

"Well I didn't ask you!" she exclaimed over more profanity.

"Say it a little louder, sister. I don't think they heard you back on the Epsilon Eridani Outpost."

Sharon continued to frown objection, but he was right. This wasn't the place to be raising her voice. Her eyes drifted back to the holochart. "So it's true about the mark, I see."

"The Red Sect mark? Oh, yeah. Every member of the Sect has it."

"I've only read about it, never seen one. It's like a tattoo or something, right?"

"No, not a tattoo. It's a birthmark, another thing they genetically bred into themselves. It's blood-red, covers the entire chest, and it's the same pattern on each and every one of them. Creepiest thing you've ever seen. And now if I could only find the right fuckin' chip-pin, I'd be able to show it to you."

As profane, egotistical, and rude as Tom clearly was,

he did seem to know a lot about this most mysterious terrorist sect. Sharon's curiosity wouldn't let go. "The newsflats are always talking about how no one knows anything about the Red Sect. But it seems to me all you have to do is capture a member and interrogate him."

"Never happen, sister." Tom still bumbled with the chip-pins. "Red Secters are hardcore motherfuckers—er, sorry. These fuckin' people—even the chicks—make the Christian Army Rangers and the fuckin' Marine Corp 2nd Spaceborne Division look like a bunch of hundred-and-fifty-year-olds sucking slop through straws at a priest hospice. We've captured dozens of Red Secters."

"Don't you interrogate them?"

"To my knowledge only one of them ever lived to make it to an interrogation cove. I was there on TDY. They bring this guy in after he smoked an entire day nursery full of little kids. Used napalm sticks. Anyway, the interrogation techs put hydro-clamps on him, crushed his ankles, knees, and elbows lickety-split. The guy didn't give up *any* intelligence info, not a peep, and he didn't even scream. Just laid there on the table and smiled. So then they cut a hole in his skull with a gammadrill and start sticking hot-probes into the pain centers of his brain. The fucker just laughed till he croaked."

"But you just said that dozens have been captured."

"Right, but before we can slap on the magcuffs, they kill themselves."

"What, poison lancets or something? Sub-lingual Trichlorex tabs?"

"Fuck, no. They commit suicide with their bare hands. Serious. Finger in the eyeball to the brain, self-strangulation, stuff like that. I caught one myself once. Remember when the Washington Military District was on Alert State Orange? I was on rover patrol when a Red Secter set off a mag-pulse bomb at a Navy convent. It made all the sisters spontaneously hemorrhage. I caught the sick piece of shit over at the rectory; he slit the abbess's throat and was raping her right on the altar while she bled to death—"

Sharon quailed.

"—and I catch him, see? I'd like nothing more than to put a full-beam milliwave burst right into his fuckin' head but I got orders from the F.O.D. to bring him in alive. Before I could run halfway across the chancel, the fucker grabbed his own head and twisted it around till his neck broke."

Sharon tried to shove the image away. *Ask another question,* she told herself, if only to escape the graphic discourse. "It just seems strange that this cult can exist for all these years, killing millions of people, but nobody knows anything about them."

"*You* don't know anything about them, general pop doesn't know anything about them, and even Security Corp doesn't know much. But I know plenty."

Enthused, Sharon's eyes widened. She waited. "And?"

"Oh, well, I can't tell you. Your clearance isn't high enough."

Sharon fumed. "You really are a—"

"Asshole?"

"If I used language like that, yes, I'd say that would be the word I was looking for."

Tom was clearly enjoying this. "Damn straight. Asshole is my middle name, sweetcakes."

"That's *Spec 5* sweetcakes to you," Sharon came right back. "And addressing any female personnel, regardless of rank, in a sexist or otherwise degrading manner is punishable by solitary detention of no less than seven days for first offense, not to mention an Article 15, monetary fine, and extra duty. I should report you."

Tom glowered at her. "Yeah, which you *won't* do because then you'd have to explain what you're doing in a restricted unit without permission." Then he cracked a smile and slapped her—if a bit hard—right on the back. "Jesus, sister. I'm only *joking!* You techgirls really need to lighten up!"

Sharon fumed a bit more, shaking her head at herself for ever even talking to him.

"I can tell you some good shit," he continued, still fiddling with the ring. "Like for ten years they had a mole in Transportation Corp, and he was the Bishop-Chief's right-hand man. This guy knew all the Army's hazmat and weapons routes. That's how the Red Sect pulled all those successful heists."

This was interesting but she expected something more exciting. "What about the organization itself? They seem to be protesting the Christian Federate and any other major global religious-political system. But it's never been revealed what *they* believe in."

"Oh, we know that," Tom said in confidence. "Er, I mean, Federate Intel does. I found out a lot when I TDY'd with them."

He's so annoying! Sharon thought. She had to temper herself. "All right, so what do they believe in?"

"A devil," Tom said flatly.

This stunned her. Many devil-worshiping terrorist cults came into existence after the Christian Federate took over the northern hemisphere. "Devil-worshipers.

So they're allied with one of the satanic factions? The Luciferics, the Ardath-Lils?"

"They aren't allied with anyone. They exist and function within themselves."

"The Luciferics worship Satan through Baalzephon and Panzuzu. The Forge worship Nergal. The Black Adventists worship Aldinoch. What 'devil' does the Red Sect worship?"

"*This* devil," Tom said.

He'd finally found the correct chip-pin; he unlocked the bag and unzipped it, first revealing only the dead terrorist's face.

Sharon blanched, stepping back at the sight of the cadaver. *Oh, God.* The fleshless face grinned through bared teeth. Eyeballs remained bright in their sockets; the effect created an illusion of a raving stare.

"This devil right here," Tom went on. Now he pushed back the body-bag's polykevlar cover entirely, disclosing the utterly nude corpse.

Crusted blood ringed the tiny punctures from the flechette shots. The skin on the arms and legs appeared even whiter than the skull-face.

But the impact of the vision came not from the cadaver's extremities, nor even from the hideous stripped-to-the-bone face.

The birthmark.

The Mark of the Red Sect, she thought.

From nipples to groin, the chilling pattern stretched in a perfect blood-red. Like an inverted triangle, only coarse-edged.

"Stare at it," Tom said, "and you'll see the details."

She did so, and soon enough, like an optical trick, the subtle inconsistencies began to form in her vision.

Nuances of darker scarlet suggested an antediluvian face, vacant ovals for eyes, and an opened maw like a bottomless chasm.

A face from Hell, Sharon thought in a gasp.

Upturned hooks around the nipples sufficed for horns.

"See. I told ya it was creepy." Tom closed and re-locked the bag. "Sometimes I get nightmares from that face."

Sharon had her eyes closed, but a ghost of the image lingered. She grit her teeth to shake off a chill. "When I was in my 400-level of tech school, I took several teratologic and ancient myth classes as well as an entire training cycle of demonology. I never saw any emblem, symbol or drawing like that."

"Same reason you never knew that the Red Sect are demon-worshipers," Tom reminded. "All that information is sitting under a big-time security classification. Nobody has access to it except for Federate Intel, Defense Corp, and the Pope and a few of his bishops in the Vatican Security Counsel."

"But you were *with* Federate Intel for a while," Sharon reminded him. "*You* know a lot of the information. What else do you know?"

Tom's sly grin returned. "I wouldn't be telling you *any* of this if I didn't think you were cool. After all, you *could* blab. Then I'd be in the Lunar Detent Center till the next millennium."

"For goodness sake, I won't *blab!*"

Was it her imagination, or did his eyes roam up over her bosom?

"Remember the crystal-morph scare about five years ago?" Tom began.

"Latest gengineered designer drug," Sharon recalled.

"Organic nano-particles would enter the bloodstream and create their own brain-receptors in the temporal lobe. Instant clinical addiction after one use. The Anti-Narcotics Corp destroyed all the labs in a sting operation. Problem solved. But that wasn't Red Sect, it was a Korean Cartel."

"It was Red Sect," Tom corrected. "Sure, the news-holos said it was the Koreans, but it was really Red Sect. And it wasn't Anti-Narcotics Corp, either."

"Federate Intel?"

"Yep. They busted all the regional labs all over the Federate in less than eight hours. But the distribution point was in Old Besthesda, the ghettoblocks. When F.C.I. Special Ops raided the place, there was only one Red Sect member there, and he'd rigged the whole place with C-11 charges. Just before he snapped the trigger, he yelled out 'Death to the Christian Federate and all enemies of Kilukrus.'"

"Kilukrus?" Sharon questioned. "I don't recall that name from any of my classes. It sounds Gaullic, or like something from the Brythons of pre-Roman England."

"You're getting ahead of yourself. See, there's more to the story. . . ." Tom's words halted at a sudden high-pitched beep that seemed to be coming from his belt.

"What the fuck?" From his belt he plucked a small black device with a small vidscanner on it.

Then his jaw dropped.

"What's wrong?" Sharon inquired.

But Tom snapped into an instant panic. One big hand grabbed her uniform collar and a split-second later he was practically throwing her toward the open pressure door. "Get out!" he yelled. "Get out of here RIGHT NOW! And seal the door behind you!"

"But—"

"NOW, God damn it! There's a fuckin' BOMB in here!"

For a moment, Sharon's heart seemed to stop. But when she turned for the mortuary's exit, she stopped mid-step.

"Let me help you disarm it!" she insisted.

He roared back, "Would you get the fuck OUT of here! Seal the door behind you, then hit the general quarters alarm in the main access!"

The beeping persisted. Tom was scrambling through the autopsy unit, checking frantically through the instrument drawers, looking for something. "What the fuck kind of a fucking morgue is this anyway!"

"What are you looking for?" she yelled back over his rage.

"A fuckin' scalpel or knife, and I told you to get out of here. You'll get killed."

Sharon had already decided she wouldn't leave. Just as she hadn't been scared earlier today when the figure on the slab had tried to kill her . . . she wasn't scared now. She immediately noted the cadmium surgical laser nozzle hanging from its ceiling mount. She grabbed it, slapped it in his hand.

"Good thinking," he said, then yelled yet again, "Now get out!"

Sharon pressed the power button on the laser, still not quite sure what he was up to. But soon she was wincing.

An unpleasant scent rose up; Tom dragged the laser's invisible cutting beam right across the cadaver's abdomen. Innards quickly spilled out.

"What are you doing?"

"Got a gut feeling—no pun intended." Now his

bare hands were reaching into the corpse's opened abdomen. "It's an old Red Sect trick. They'll swallow an RDX ball with a sleeper trigger. That's why my field detector didn't catch it. The circuits can't be detected until the timer activates—Here it is!"

From the gash of tilled innards, his red-splotched hands extricated a small node no larger than a robin's egg. "Don't just stand there! Open the—"

Sharon was a step ahead, having already pressurized and opened the waste disposal chute.

Tom threw the bomb into the hatch, after which Sharon smacked the DEPRESSURIZE & EJECT button—

"Get down!"

—just as the bomb exploded.

PART TWO

"The secret things belong unto the Lord our God."
—*Deuteronomy* 29:29

(I)

Sharon and Tom, their uniforms damp with the sweat of sheer panic, stood painfully at attention in the Mission Commander's quad. General-Vicar Luke was about as hard as they came, surviving two major wars and dozens of field actions. Right now, sitting behind his desk, he looked like a bust of Genghis Khan. Standing to his side—and not looking terribly happy either—was Security Corp Chief Major-Rector Matthew.

"For the digital record, this emergency security inquest and punitive hearing has officially commenced," he announced. "2004 hours, C.F. Standard Time."

Punitive hearing? Sharon thought, fairly outraged. *I*

guess they've already decided that we're all guilty. Some due process.

Also standing at attention right next to her were the ship's physician, Commander-Deaconness Esther, and her ungainly assistant, Warrant Officer Simon. All four defendants had galvanic-stress-analysis bands around their wrists. Any verbal response that was untrue would instantly be detected by the station's lie-detection computer programs.

"Dr. Esther," the General-Vicar stated. He had an odd cleft chin, like two arthritic knuckles. "Was or was not the decedent in the morgue unit properly autopsied?"

"Yes, sir," the tall, statuesque woman replied with more than a trace of nervousness in her voice. "The decedent was autopsied via a standard tomegraphic-microscopy scan immediately after he was killed."

"You performed the scan yourself?"

"No, sir. Since the incident was classified, I couldn't participate. I lack the sufficient clearance. Furthermore, and because of that, I didn't even know what happened until Major-Rector Matthew briefed me a few moments ago. The person who performed the autopsy was my adjutant, Warrant Officer Simon."

Luke's stern eyes searched his holoscreen for any indication that Esther was lying. He found none. "Warrant Officer Simon. Explain to me how a standard post-mortal scan could fail to detect a bomb hidden in a dead man's belly?"

Simon was short, skinny, awkward looking. Sweat ran down his bald head like lines of glycerin. "I-I don't know, sir."

"You're an expert medical tech with a high security clearance, and you *don't know?*"

"I'm s-sorry, sir, I don't know."

"That's great. Then tell me why wasn't an actual physical autopsy performed? Why wasn't the body y-sectioned and directly examined?"

Now sweat dripped off Simon's brows, plipping to the floor. "Cause of death was clear. It was my professional opinion that a physical autopsy wasn't necessary."

"Uh-hmm. Or perhaps you're a Red Sect infiltrator who helped this terrorist sneak on board, knowing that he possessed a bomb."

Simon looked like he was about to keel over. But then Tom spoke up: "Sir, if I may? I can easily explain why—"

General-Vicar Luke's hard eyes snapped to Tom. "Shut up, private. You're a profane indecorous punk with a demerit list longer than the keel of this ship. You'll get your chance to talk, but until then keep your foul mouth shut."

Matthew leaned down to the mission commander's ear. "Sir, I'm well aware of the private's record, but he is a soldier of some experience. It might be prudent to hear what Private Thomas has to say."

Luke grumbled, then redirected his frown back to Tom. "Talk."

"I've seen this sort of thing before, sir," Tom said, "during some joint operations with Federate Intelligence. It's a favorite ploy of the Red Sect. They'd ingest these RDX charges that they'd deliberately encase in de-radiated tritium covered by an electron-negative polymer. This would allow them to walk right over a bomb-magnometer without triggering an alarm; that's how their suicide operatives have been able to get past our security stations at churches, courthouses, Federate buildings, and the like. A medical tomegraph is based on the same technology as most of our public mag-units. That's why the autopsy scan didn't detect the RDX charge in the dead guy's gut."

The General-Vicar seemed to consider this.

Sharon explained the rest. "The bomb was only detectable for a few moments, sir—when its primer-charge was activated via a discreet timer. That's when Private Thomas' electrostatic alarm went off."

The Missions Commander nodded minutely. "I thought you were a navigational systems operator. What were you doing in a restricted property vault?"

Sharon knew she had to be careful how she answered. She wouldn't want to lie anyway. She chose her words carefully. "I was walking down the central manway, sir, when I noticed Private Thomas standing guard before the unit. I'd never known him personally but I had seen him for the first time earlier in the shift when he responded to the milliwave attack at my office."

"Go on."

"While I was conversing with him, his electrostatic alarm went off. He gave me the option of evacuating the area but I chose to enter the unit with him. I thought I might be able to help him render the bomb safe."

General-Vicar Luke's eyes held on his holoscreen, waiting for the program to register a lie. None came.

"It was Private Thomas' bravery and expertise that allowed him to locate the bomb so quickly, sir," Sharon added.

Then Tom kicked in, "And it was Spec Sharon's foresight to prep the waste disposal system in advance. If she hadn't done that, the bomb would've detonated before we could eject it."

Luke's fingers stroked the cloven chin as he continued to watch the lie-detection program. "How do you like that? Everyone's telling the truth. Esther, Simon. You're both dismissed. Carry on with your duties, and may God be with you."

"And also with you, sir," the two medical techs said in unison. They saluted and left.

"The Christian Federate is proud of you both," Matthew said to Sharon and Tom. "You're brave Christian soldiers."

"Yes," the Mission Commander agreed. "And God said: 'Behold, I come quickly.' I'm promoting each of you one grade in rank."

"Thank you, sir," Tom and Sharon said at once.

Luke tossed a hand. "And a three-day pass for each of you."

"I appreciate your generosity, sir," Sharon said. "But I don't need a pass. I live to serve the Lord."

"Very well." Then Luke looked up at Tom.

"I live to serve the Lord too, sir," Tom said. He shrugged. "But I'll take the pass."

(II)

In the United States' presidential and general elections of 2049, a reform party popularly known as the Christian Coalition had swept the House, the Senate, and the Oval Office. Forty years of war, crime, corruption, and an overall devolution of morality caused a social outcry from the few Americans who still voted (only thirty million by that time). Popular demand changed things very quickly. Just as the Founding Fathers had provided for the Constitution to change as society changed, the new government proposed many changes for its populace, and soon thereafter, the 60th Amendment redefined the fundamental law of the nation's federal system. Where previous centuries had ensured the separation of church from state, the two-thirds majority ratification *joined* church with state. Ten states immediately seceded from the Union—they were allowed to. Members of non-Christian denominations were deported to the country of their choice. Jews, in particular, relocated to Israel, which now encompassed most of the former Middle East after the Cold Fusion War. Reproduction out of wedlock was criminalized. A Christian educational base became compulsory. New technology polygraphs replaced jury trials, ending ninety-six percent of violent crime in a single presidential term via summary execution and a disposal of the 1st-through-7th Amendments. Next came the Eugenics Act, which mandatorized in vitro fertilization. Once children reached puberty, they were sterilized but only after sperm and egg samples were inventoried in the national cryolization depository; hence, when couples properly married and wished to have children, the respective egg and sperm were retrieved and joined in vitro, then the fertilized egg was implanted into the wife's womb. Within several decades, advancements in genetic screening enabled this process to screen out genetic defects in the fertilized egg, as well as hereditary propensities for all manner of disease.

Public health conditions skyrocketed. The economy bloomed exponentially. Poverty disappeared.

So did freedom but no one cared.

Over time, other countries sought to join this new explosively successful governance: Canada, much of South and Central America, much of Europe. A succession of popular elections officially acknowledged this transcontinental political merger as the Christian Federate. One and a half billion Roman Catholics voted the Pope into the office of president, replaced all houses of representatives with the Synod of Bishops, and all likenesses of the senatorial branch became the Sacred College of Cardinals. Vatican City was now not only the seat of religious power over most of the world, it was the seat of political power—that is, until the year 2080, when a well-coordinated Red Sect nuclear attack had reduced this domain to a wasteland, to the tune of half a gigaton's worth of ordnance supplied to the Sect by the nation now known as the Alliance of Southern China. Though the Red Sect members involved were never apprehended, most of the Alliance of Southern China was obliterated a week later, by the Christian Federate's Satellite Defense Initiative.

To the tune of fifty gigatons.

The Synod elected a new Pope, and the Vatican was moved to the former Washington, D.C.

Since then—with the exception of minor terrorist cells—global peace ensued. Accelerated discoveries in inorganic transfection techniques allowed science to create new artificial compounds by manipulating molecular bond structures in metalloids and rare earth elements, materials that conducted no heat, materials that

145

deflected radiation, and materials stronger than titanium but nearly weightless were easily manufactured. Cold-fusion-based generators powered the entire Federate with mere water. Magnetic-field-levitation engines circumvented the laws of gravity. Genetic crop hybridization fed the world. Simple "nuclear-drag" techniques launched humankind into outer space at .444 the speed of light.

All in the name of God.

(III)

Was the sign new? JESUS IS WATCHING YOU. It was right below the ID plaque for the women's dom wing. *How could I not have noticed that?* Sharon thought. *After two days underway?* "Bless me, Jesus, your unworthy servant," she whispered to the benevolent visage. As if to answer, the mid-shift blessing flowed from the intercom:

" 'Let judgment run down as waters, and righteousness as a mighty stream. Blessings are upon the heads of the just.' "

Thank you for your blessing, my Lord, she thought, all the while slightly irritated by the new regs that allowed the Chaplain's Unit to mix up scripture. *Amos?* She guessed, *and Proverbs?* She was getting rusty. It wouldn't hurt her to attend a study group soon.

The lumeplates engaged when she entered her dom. *Do—not—despair,* she forced the thought. Kim's bunk and locker had already been stripped. "She's with God now." She snapped on her holomirror, immersed herself in the next task. She'd been promoted twice today; she wanted to wear her new rank—Spec 6—when she went to the galley. She entered the tiny lav, then quickly stripped off her tech utilities and fed the one-piece valcron garment into the reprocessing chute. The multiple jets of the vapor shower refreshed her, the cool sublimation of verapropyl betaine caressing her body. The grim ponderings of the day seemed to wash away with the spray: the corpse in the morgue.

ABZ Genotype Syndrome. A Red Secter . . .

She shivered at the terrible scarlet image.

The demon's face.

Kilukrus, she thought.

Twice today she'd nearly been killed.

Thanks be to God. My comforter and protector. My friend.

The vapor shower hissed on, licking her skin. The Seaton Tech Academy had trained her well in the mentalistic blocks. Without a flinch, she ignored the tiny sensations when the rover nozzles ran up the slit of her sex. She rejected any sexual thought when her nipples distended. *Just a tactile reaction,* she reminded herself.

The vapor sucked out of the shower cell when she hit the exhaust tab. Next she walked nude across the lav, appraised herself in the holomirror. She'd developed late: small white breasts and a narrow pelvic span. She was lean, long, and her short honeyish hair glowed healthily. Back at the Academy, she often felt insecure when she glimpsed the other girls naked. Their larger breasts and pert nipples seemed robust; their curvaceous body lines seemed more desirable. But as she matured, she discarded these notions as trifling and even sinful. The beauty of the body was as diverse as the beauty of a garden. Each flower different but beautiful nonetheless. *My body is a temple of the Lord, and all that God makes is a thing of beauty.*

Her freshly reprocessed fatigues were hanging for her, her new Spec 6 insignias imbued in black on the sleeves. She was about to put them on when she heard her flagtone go off. *Maybe I SHOULD have taken that three-day pass,* she wondered, but when she walked back into the dom she found her holoscreen unblinking.

Of course, she realized. It wasn't her flagtone at all; it was Kim's.

The death report must not have been processed yet. Sharon switched on her ex-dom-mate's intranet screen, just to make sure it wasn't anything important that needed to be reported to whomever took over command of the Data Regiment.

MOS WORK CALL
DATA REGIMENT/ANALYSIS TECHNICIAN

Priority Code: **NON-URGENT**

Re: MADAM and ESA-2 Photospectroscopy Probe Order
De: Data Reg c/o Security Corp

READ: Elemental Probe detects Target-Object (exterior) as programmed. Target-Object composition results: Molecular scan reveals geometric structure of silicate of sodium & aluminum, a pyroxene compound.

ORDERS: File & Store for Analysis
STOP

Sharon took it unto herself to touch the FILE & STORE icon. *Silicate of sodium and aluminum,* she recited to herself. *A pyroxene compound.* She made neither heads nor tails of the electronic missive. Kim had been the regiment's analysis tech, a rather dull occupational speciality which entailed little more than rerouting analysis transmissions into the Edessa's Macro-Analysis Computer. MADAM was one of the ship's long-range sensors (for Mass-Activated Detection and Alarm Mechanism), much like the old-time radar systems, only this worked in space. The MADAM would alert the ship's guidance systems of unanticipated obstructions, such as asteroids and sundry space debris—its main onboard function—but it was also used to uplink to other sensor mechanisms such as . . .

ESA-2, she recognized. *The latest extra-solar array.*

This was the Federate's largest radio-telescope, several square miles in surface area, which was being used to detect new planets and analyze aspects of their composition. The frustrating thing about Kim's job— as was also the case with Sharon's—was that they would spend their entire shifts filing data reports that they knew nothing about. Of course, she realized that she had no official "need to know" and that was how it should be. It kept the ship's operations secure.

Still, it pricked her curiosities at times.

Just some boring compositional scan, she deduced and closed the flagtone's window. Even though she and Kim had never really been friends, it gave Sharon a good feeling to have carried out Kim's last duty order for her.

She was about to turn off the screen when she noticed a far icon. PERSONAL DATA. Most of the Privacy Acts had been repealed but the Federate did allow each member of the Exploratory Corp to have a separate directory in their computers to store personal information. Sharon didn't even use hers—she scarcely had a need.

But—

She didn't see any harm in looking at Kim's data. Kim was in heaven now.

I should've known, she thought at once.

The first file was nothing but an index of male names and commsigns. There were dozens of them.

Sharon had realized all along that Kim wasn't keeping her celibacy vows; she'd overheard many of her conversations with secret male suitors. And even though this was a clear violation of Federate protocol, Sharon never reported it—nor would she report this list. *Only God can judge,* she reminded herself.

She quickly closed the file. Then—

A second file read MISC.

Sharon opened it, expecting simple personnel info or favorite verses—

What is . . . THIS?

—but found something else altogether.

The screen filled with bright, edgy movement—a cyberfile. The small three-dimensional image seemed to be alive in the air.

A hitch gathered in Sharon's chest, a sensation unlike anything she'd ever experienced. On the screen, two naked men took turns fornicating with a woman who was stretched back across a lev-slat. The woman was naked, flushed. Anxious sighs escaped her lips.

The woman was Kim.

Oh . . . my . . .

Even without ever having seen an example, Sharon knew at once what she was looking at: pornography.

And this she could not overlook. Possession of ungodly and/or lewd imagery violated the Federate's felony statutes. Kim would be posthumously demoted, and her obit records would reflect the felony charge. Sharon hated to do it but this was too much.

But when her finger raised to close the file—she couldn't do it.

Her eyes held to the image.

The men must be civilians or non-fed contractors: they weren't bald. One man—with coal-black hair—pushed Kim's knees all the way back to her bosom, accelerating the pace of his fornication. The second man was—

Sharon recoiled. It was the most offensive thing she'd ever seen. It was ugly, wretched, and evil. With gritted teeth she turned the awful images off, then turned around . . . and screamed.

There was a figure in the room.

(IV)

Jesus extended His hand toward Major-Rector Matthew. Beneath Christ's feet was the flag of the Christian Federate, under which read:

BLESSED ARE THE MEEK,
FOR THE MEEK SHALL INHERIT THE EARTH.

It was just another Morale Department poster, of course, but it made Matthew wonder. Indeed, the Christian Federate had inherited much of the world . . . but *meek?*

How meek were we when we nuked Iran and Iraq? he asked himself. *How meek were we when we mag-fielded the Army of the Ukraine and starved them into surrender, or when we EMP-bombed all the power stations in Yugoserbia during the middle of winter?*

Not very meek.

EDWARD LEE

But the Security Corp commander didn't question his orders. Sometimes the Lord God was a god of anger and vengeance. Matthew supposed it all became justified in the end.

Still, he wondered.

This mission, for instance. Earlier, when he'd led a group of securitechs to check the cargo bays, he'd discovered something rather odd. Yes, they'd found a small storage warren with a shimmed lock, obviously the overlooked cranny in which the Red Sect infiltrator had stowed away—the DNA scans proved it. But that wasn't the *odd* thing.

All the main cargo bays were empty.

A resupply mission? he thought. *With no supply inventory?*

This was just one of many things that rubbed Matthew the wrong way. All of the data-retrieval units were running hot; cyphers by the dozens were being received, but Matthew didn't have the clearance to read them. Add to that, the Decryption Unit was off line entirely; no technical staff ever boarded. And add to that—

A terrorist attack on the Data Regiment, and an explosion in the Property Station.

It just seemed odd.

Though Matthew did have a recourse. He fingered the silver cross about his neck, knowing what was secreted beneath its shining finish. During the second California Campaign, Matthew had commanded an extraction platoon with orders to capture a team of Mt. Sutro Front hackers being harbored in the Exclusion Zone of Old San Francisco. The raid had failed on one hand (Matthew and his platoon had wound up killing all of the front members) but one positive result was their discovery of a box of algorithmic biochips. Matthew had been promoted for the find: the chips were programmed to override all Christian Federate decryption modules, a formidable technological weapon. There'd been six of the chips all told.

Matthew had turned in five.

It was a security crime that could imprison Matthew for life. But he'd kept the chip just the same, a safeguard so to speak.

With that chip, he could probably find out what was really going on.

If this is wrong, then I must face God's wrath, he realized. *But . . . if it's right—*

Two tiny indentations were located at the butt of the cross. Matthew crimped them with his fingernails, began to slide the hidden chip out, but before he could extract it even an eighth of an inch—

"What in God's name—"

From behind, a puncture-proof effluxion sack was whipped over his head, its draw cord yanked closed. Suddenly Major-Rector Matthew couldn't see and couldn't breathe.

But he could still hear.

"Under heaven lay umbra," came a dark voice.

Matthew scrabbled backward in his grav chair, arms flailing. His face beat like a frantic heart from the stricture around his neck. He blindly reached aside for the security alarm but—

CLACK!

He flopped to the floor, convulsing.

A de-jam gun had been pressed to his temple and fired. The tool's 1000-foot-pound bolt instantly cracked Matthew's skull, penetrating inches into the brain. Then—

SNAP!

The bolt retracted.

The puncture-proof sack began to quickly fill with blood. Matthew died, heels thudding the floor. He never even had time to ask God to forgive him for his sins.

The only living mouth in the cove spake: "Hail, Kilukrus."

PART THREE

"The children of the kingdom shall be cast out into outer darkness."

—*Matthew 8:12*

(I)

"Calm down! Jeez!" came a woman's voice.

Sharon quickly covered her breasts and pubis with her un-donned uniform. She was totally shocked to find herself facing a tall, shapely girl with long carbon-black hair.

"Who are you? What are you doing in my dom?"

The girl produced a transfer card. "I'm your new dom-mate," she said. "You heard about the dichrololine leak in accessmain six, didn't you?"

The cover story, Sharon reminded herself. What really happened was classified, to prevent a panic. "Of course. My dom-mate, Kim, was killed."

155

"I was domming with some data tech named Leslie, a real snoot if you ask me."

Sharon's heart sunk another notch. "It's not nice to speak ill of the dead."

"Hey, they're in heaven now but we're stuck on this tub." The woman tossed her duffel on the stripped bunk. A robust body was clear beneath the rarely-seen white service fatigues.

"The hair, the white fatigues," Sharon said. "You're a civilian."

"Yeah but I'm grade-5 so don't get any ideas about bossing me around. What are you?"

"Grade-6."

"Shit. So much for that. My name's Brigid, by the way."

"Sharon," Sharon said. "I like Brigid. Is it for Saint Brigid of Northumbria?"

"Yeah. Got murdered by satanists during a pilgrimage to Rome. Hell of a person to be named after." Brigid eyed the holoscreen, raised a brow. "Where'd you get the cyberfile? I thought they were illegal in the Army."

"It's not mine," Sharon snapped. "It was my dommate's, and, no, I wasn't rooting through her privacy files, I just wanted to—"

"Relax, I'm not going to rat you out." She watched a few moments more of the pornography. "Wow. She's pretty over-the-top. Let's watch the whole thing."

Sharon switched off the screen. "No thanks. It's disgusting."

"Looked pretty hot to me." Brigid peeked into the lav. "Oh, great, another vapor shower. Don't they have any water showers on this ship?"

GET UP TO
4 FREE BOOKS!

You can have the best fiction delivered to your door for less than what you'd pay in a bookstore or online—only $4.25 a book! Sign up for our book clubs today, and we'll send you **FREE* BOOKS** just for trying it out...with **no obligation to buy, ever!**

LEISURE HORROR BOOK CLUB

With more award-winning horror authors than any other publisher, it's easy to see why CNN.com says "Leisure Books has been leading the way in paperback horror novels." Your shipments will include authors such as RICHARD LAYMON, DOUGLAS CLEGG, JACK KETCHUM, MARY ANN MITCHELL, and many more.

LEISURE THRILLER BOOK CLUB

If you love fast-paced page-turners, you won't want to miss any of the books in Leisure's thriller line. Filled with gripping tension and edge-of-your-seat excitement, these titles feature everything from psychological suspense to legal thrillers to police procedurals and more!

As a book club member you also receive the following special benefits:

- **30% OFF all orders through our website & telecenter!**
- **Exclusive access to special discounts!**
- **Convenient home delivery and 10 days to return any books you don't want to keep.**

There is no minimum number of books to buy, and you may cancel membership at any time. See back to sign up!

*Please include $2.00 for shipping and handling.

YES! ☐

Sign me up for the Leisure Horror Book Club and send my TWO FREE BOOKS! If I choose to stay in the club, I will pay only $8.50* each month, a savings of $5.48!

YES! ☐

Sign me up for the Leisure Thriller Book Club and send my TWO FREE BOOKS! If I choose to stay in the club, I will pay only $8.50* each month, a savings of $5.48!

NAME: _____

ADDRESS: _____

_____

TELEPHONE: _____

E-MAIL: _____

☐ **I WANT TO PAY BY CREDIT CARD.**

☐ VISA   ☐ MasterCard.   ☐ DISCOVER

ACCOUNT #: _____

EXPIRATION DATE: _____

SIGNATURE: _____

Send this card along with $2.00 shipping & handling for each club you wish to join, to:

Horror/Thriller Book Clubs
1 Mechanic Street
Norwalk, CT 06850-3431

Or fax (must include credit card information!) to: 610.995.9274. You can also sign up online at www.dorchesterpub.com.

*Plus $2.00 for shipping. Offer open to residents of the U.S. and Canada only. Canadian residents please call 1.800.481.9191 for pricing information.

If under 18, a parent or guardian must sign. Terms, prices and conditions subject to change. Subscription subject to acceptance. Dorchester Publishing reserves the right to reject any order or cancel any subscription.

"Of course not," Sharon rebelled. "It's an inordinate expense. The vapor shower works just fine."

"Yeah, and if you stay in it too long, you'll lose your top layer of skin." She walked around the dom, as if scrutinizing it. "God, no wonder I feel like I weigh a thousand pounds in here. Look how high you've got the grav turned up."

"I like it high," Sharon said. "It keeps me toned."

Brigid didn't even ask; she turned the grav knob down. "There. That's better."

What a fuss-budget, Sharon thought.

Now the woman's breasts seemed even larger, buoyant orbs under the white jumpsuit. She smiled. "See. You don't look so flat now, right?"

"Thanks a lot," Sharon muttered, but a quick look down beneath the wrap of her uniform confirmed the comment. Her breasts *did* look fuller. She sat down and crossed her legs, uncomfortable at being seen naked by someone else. "Lower grav is bad for your bones," she pointed out.

"That's bullshit," Brigid said.

"Do you have to use language like that?"

"Jeez, don't be so uptight. We're both in this together, you know." Now Brigid's eyes went from scrutinizing the room to scrutinizing Sharon's haphazardly covered body. "How'd you make Spec 6 so young? What are you, seventeen?"

"I'm *twenty*," Sharon tersely corrected. "I'm a navprocessor and redundancy systems technician. I finished number one in my class."

"Cool. Where'd you go?"

"Seaton Tech."

"God, no wonder you were watching that cyberfile."

"I wasn't watch—"

"I've heard about that place. All girl from start to finish, right? Epiphanite nuns and all that?"

"Yes," Sharon said.

"I went to Meade Cathedral. It was an all-girl class but the majority of the instructors were men. Most of them were real old, though. Not a hard dick in the whole facility."

Sharon frowned at the rough language. It wasn't as bad as Tom's, though it somehow seemed worse from a woman's lips. But she *had* heard of Meade Cathedral; it was a psy-ops training compound for the Christian Security Agency. "So what's a civilian from CSA doing on this ship?"

"Breaking me in, I suppose," Brigid said, testing the bunk mattress. "Probably just for familiarization training. They want all the RV's to know what it's like on exploratory missions."

"RV's?" Sharon asked.

"Yeah," Brigid said. She lounged back in the bunk, let her feet float in the lowered gravity. "I'm a remote-viewer."

Sharon was fascinated at once. A remote-viewer. Psychics who could supposedly project their visual and aural senses great distances beyond their physical bodies. Like the telethesists and paramentals. She tried to act nonchalant as she redressed.

"So you've . . . seen things?"

"Oh, sure. I can't tell you what, of course, but I can tell you that it works. We're screened from birth—it's all natural. Not like the telethesists."

"I heard that the Federate Intel terminated the telethesy programs."

"Yeah, a lot of them simply couldn't survive the implants and surgical procedures, and a lot of the ones that did either went nuts or died later from micro-hemorrhaging."

Sharon remembered seeing some cyberfiles of a telethesy platoon. Large nodes protruded from the sides of their heads to accommodate the extra brain growth. It was hideous . . . but captivating.

"I knew a couple. They could actually channel themselves hundreds of thousands of miles, but a lot of times they'd forget what they saw, just from the sheer experience. Believe me, I'd rather be a remote-viewer any day. I don't want some Defense Corp butcher cutting into my brain." She rubbed her eyes as if fatigued. "They want us for industrial spying and stuff like that. The Japanese Space Agency's all over the solar system now, probably breaking all kinds of free-trade agreements. It's a living but if you want to know the truth, it's pretty dull."

Sharon couldn't conceive how such a specialty could be *dull.* "*My* job's dull. Yours must be thrilling."

Brigid grinned at the remark. "Only when I abuse it."

"What do you mean?"

"Let's just say there's a lot more hanky-panky on this ship than you'd think."

"You mean . . . you *watch* people. . . ."

Brigid nodded. "And, you know, when a girl gets lonely, there's some great scenery in the men's shower quads."

Sharon cringed to know more, but it seemed sinfully voyeuristic.

"The rest of it's a pain in the ass," Brigid went on. "All that sensory-dep and theta-wave meditation. And the attrition rate's over ninety percent. Not many of us ever make it to permanent duty."

"You must feel very privileged."

Brigid shrugged. "The pay's all right, and I get a lot of time off."

"Are you married?"

"Not allowed to be. It comes with the contract. Single for life."

This acknowledgment seemed sad to Sharon. Brigid had obviously chosen duty over wedlock, committing herself to a life of solitude for God's work. An honorable sacrifice.

Brigid leaned up. "God, and there's another thing I hate about these damn Army flights."

"What's that?"

"I'm starving."

"Well then," Sharon beamed. Even this soon, she knew she liked Brigid. She hoped they would be friends. "Let's go to the chow hall and get some appetite suppressants!"

SUSTAINETH ME WITH RAISINS, O LORD.
REFRESH ME WITH APPLES!
EAT YOUR BREAD WITH ENJOYMENT,
AND DRINK YOUR WINE WITH A MERRY HEART!
GOD, LORD OF HOSTS, WE THANK THEE FOR
THIS BOUNTY!

Brigid was shaking her head. "I guess the Morale Department forgot to change the sign when they switched the ship to non-solids. Raisins and apples, my ass." She held her cup under the electrolyte tap, waiting for it to fill with the crystal-green liquid. "And this Tinkerbell pee sure ain't wine."

Sharon, in spite of the rough language, enjoyed Brigid's spirited vigor. "It's a wonderful nutritional technology. All the calories we need in one glass."

Brigid frowned down. "It looks like fairy urine, and tastes like it too." She moved on in the line. "Oh, terrific. Now the main course." A slot on a narrow machine ejected a small synthpaper cup full of pills. "Ah, my favorite. Veal Oscar with Tasmanian crab, artichoke hearts in truffle oil, and, oh, this little red one must be the garlic potato soufflé."

Sharon gave a light laugh. "I don't mind the nonsolids, and I'm glad they changed to it for all sub-light missions."

"Why?"

"It's more efficient, saves money, lowers the Defense Corp budget." Sharon followed the tall sablehaired woman to a table. "Our tiny sacrifice is good for the Federate."

"You're kidding me, right? You'd rather pop these ridiculous pills than bite into a chili dog with the works because it's *more efficient?*"

"Why, of course. No fecal waste to out-process."

Brigid grimaced. "Oh, that's a delightful thought."

Sharon didn't get the objection. "And consider how much a real galley costs the Federate. All that food, all that storage space, equipment and food-service personnel. It's just a minor inconvenience for the good of God's work."

"Sharon, we bust our asses for God, especially on these explo missions. We breathe recharged air, travel at unnatural speeds, risk our lives every living minute in these tubs—all for God. With all that, do you really think God would mind if we got to eat fried chicken once in a while?"

"Well, I guess not. But the way I look at it, the real food is something to look forward to when we get back to the moon." She picked a red pill out of her cup, swallowed it with her green drink. "And the appetite suppressants work just fine for me."

"Whatever turns you on, Sharon."

Most of the rest of the pills were gengineered vitamins and immune stimulants. Sharon was about to swallow another pill when she noticed Brigid plucking out the long yellow one. She slipped it in her pocket.

"Why did you do that?"

"Are you serious? I don't want that Big Brother crap in *my* bloodstream."

Sharon didn't know what she was talking about. "It's good for you. It's an anti-oxidant."

Brigid sighed. "Wow, you really are naive, aren't you? It's *not* an anti-oxidant, Sharon. Everybody knows that."

Sharon plucked out her own yellow pill, reading the tiny print on it. "See, it says right on the side: 'D-L-alpha tocopheryl and selenium selinate.' They're compounds that block lipid degeneration in your cell walls and—"

"Keep your voice down!" Brigid whispered. "And give me that!" She snapped the yellow capsule from Sharon's fingers and slipped it in her pocket. "You keep taking that crap, you'll be a little girl all your life."

The comment hurt her. Her eyes turned down. "I'm not a 'little girl.'"

"So stop acting like one. Don't you know what that is? It's an oxytocin blocker."

"A *what?*"

Brigid whispered lower. "It kills your sex drive. It blocks all reactive sexual responses."

"I-I don't believe it," Sharon said with not much conviction. She'd been taking that pill three times a day since her deplant and ligation at puberty.

"Well, believe it, honey. You young kids barge out of tech school all high and mighty and God fearing, thinking you know everything. I was the same way. But I also learned to trust my elders. People who've been in the grind longer know more. So do yourself a favor and do what I say."

"What are you, my big sister?"

"I might as well be, 'cos you *need* one. I hate to think of what kind of brainwashing procedures they pulled on you at Seaton."

"They didn't *brainwash* us," Sharon insisted. "They simply taught us scripture between training blocks."

"Yeah? And I'll bet they gave you a little cup of orange juice before each scripture session, right?"

Sharon paused. "Well, yes. It was just a refreshment."

"It was sodium athynol, you dumbass. The Army started using it in all of its youth academies back in '184. It's a hypnotic drug, puts you in a wake-trance and makes you susceptible to hypnotic suggestions. It's behavior-modification, Sharon. Teaches you to be repulsed by sex. God *created* sex, Sharon. He made it pleasurable for a reason. But you're letting a crypto-fascist government burn out your natural desires."

All at once, Sharon felt neck deep in questions and rebuttals. "Even if what you say is true, it's for my own good. Sexual congress out of wedlock is a sin."

Brigid stifled a laugh. "Sexual *congress*—my God. You've got *all* the Christian Fed buzzwords beat into your head. Listen, what it all boils down to is this: if you want to stay a virgin till you get married, that's fine, that's great. But it's only a Godly endeavor if you do so by your own free will. Not sub-hypnotic chemical therapy. Not mind control. That's not the free will that God gave you. It's medical tyranny. *That's* the sin."

Sharon's quandary didn't abate. She felt inclined to argue but she couldn't shake the impression that Brigid was telling the truth. "Well . . . aren't you a virgin?"

Brigid snorted, not quite stifling the laugh this time. "Sharon, my hymen bit the dust back when I was fifteen, and it *wasn't* from falling off a horse."

"Well, you went to Federate school just like me. Didn't they brainwash you, too?"

"Not allowed in Civilian Branch. That's why I feel sorry for all you Army girls. What we had instead were CMS's—Christian Motivational Sessions. They'd sit us all around in a big circle, show us pictures of all the sexual diseases from the old days, and yammer about how sex was a sin. I spent those sessions thinking about being in orgies."

"Brigid!"

"Oh, and it was a hoot once I graduated to Meade Cathedral. It was an old complex, used to be a military base before Federate Intel took it over. They had water showers there, not these vapor things." Brigid interrupted herself to chuckle. "Here's how stupid those old sticks in the mud were. To induce us not to touch ourselves, whenever we'd go to shower block, we'd have to wash the girl next to us! Isn't that hilarious?"

Sharon's brow creased. "I—I don't get it?"

Brigid leaned closer. "You know. They thought it would keep us from learning how to masturbate. So instead of masturbating ourselves, we'd masturbate the girl next to us!"

Sharon's face remained blank. "What's masturbate mean?"

Brigid put her face in her hands. "Jesus. Never mind."

The conversation confused Sharon. But just as she wished for a diversion, she noticed Tom coming off the sustenance line. She waved him over. "Hi, Tom."

"Specialist," he greeted and sat down. He pointed to his sleeve. "Check out my new E-2 stripes. Cool, huh?"

"Yes," Sharon said. "Now you're only four grades in rank below me."

"Go ahead and bust my balloon."

"Tom, this is Brigid, my new dom-mate. She's Civilian Branch."

"Sister," Tom said, eyes darting back and forth over Brigid's bosom. "It's a pleasure to serve God with you."

"Likewise."

"Tom keeps getting demoted because he has a foul mouth," Sharon appended. "But he's a nice guy."

"I'm real flattered."

Sharon's eyes narrowed when she noticed Tom taking the yellow pill from his synthcup and slipping it in his utility pocket.

"See?" Brigid said to her.

"See what?" Tom said.

"Nothing." Sharon grabbed Tom's shoulder enthusiastically. "Brigid's a remote-viewer. Isn't that exciting? She can channel through walls, and see things thousands of miles away."

Tom cut a big sarcastic grin. "Yeah, and I can bend spoons with my cock."

"I told you he had a foul mouth," Sharon apologized.

But Brigid grinned right back at him. "That's real funny, Tarzan. By the way, this morning when I was channeling into the men's shower unit, I noticed that cute little scar on your ass. How'd you get it? Shrapnel?"

Tom paused over his electrolyte drink, took a moment to consider the revelation. "Lousy parlor trick, honey. Any guy in Security Corp could've told you about that."

"Um-hmm. Then how could I possibly know that you jerked off twice yesterday?" Tom spat a mouthful of the solution across the table, his face turning red.

Brigid chuckled in a long stream.

"You're making a believer out of me already," Tom admitted.

But Sharon looked at both of them, confused. "What's jerking off?"

(II)

After "dinner," Sharon reported via intranet order to the med unit. Commander-Deaconness Esther explained upon her entrance: "The MAC processed you for a physical, Sharon."

"But I had one just before we debarked."

"Yes," Warrant Officer Simon said, "but since then you've suffered several traumatic ordeals. First, the attacker in your duty station, then the bomb going off in your proximity. We just need to make sure you're okay after all of that."

"Yes, sir," Sharon said. A man in the cove unsettled her. She understood that he was Dr. Esther's medical adjunct but there was something unsettling about him.

Thin neck, pointed chin. Eyes she might describe proverbially as beady.

"Relax, Sharon!" the Deaconness exclaimed. "You look as nervous as I was earlier today during the inquest." The fiftyish woman lost the stiff veneer of her high rank once she spoke. She'd aged attractively, all fine lines, graceful curves, and a bright, warm smile. "I thought I was going to faint."

"Me too," Simon admitted.

The Deaconness frowned at the remark but kept her attention on Sharon. "We mainly just need to do a quick tox screen, to insure that you didn't absorb any of that ethanolamine-based coolant when you threw it at the infiltrator. And the concussion from the bomb could possibly have caused some microscopic ruptures."

"Now if you'll just step into the tome," Simon said, "we'll have this done in no time."

Sharon nodded uneasily, began to take off her jumpsuit. Simon's eyes seemed like a rake over her skin. "Um, ma'am, if you don't mind—"

"Oh, of course." She shot a hard glance to Simon. "You're dismissed."

Simon left the cove in a swift turn.

"He's such a creep," the Deaconness commented when he was gone. "Reminds me of a lizard. I can't stand those Security Corp plants."

Sharon stepped out of her uniform. "Plant? I thought he was a medical technician."

"By training, he is. But that's just a front. On these sub-light flights, Security Corp always puts someone like him in the general duty population. I even heard a rumor once that he was Federate Intel."

"A spy?"

"In a sense, yes. But he's spying on his own people, which infuriates me. And what can I do about it? Nothing. Just go along with their game."

Sharon saw the woman's point. "I'm ready, ma'am."

"Just step into the tome, dear. Put your feet in the outlines."

Sharon entered the tall cylindrical scanner, shivered slightly when the door sucked shut. She never really liked this—mechanical voyeurism—and the outline in which she placed her feet seemed painfully wide. In a moment, the scanning lumes came on, a fluttering meld of violet and vermillion, which ran top to bottom. The light on her skin felt cold.

"Just a little prick," the doctor's voice flowed softly through the chamber, and then a rod lowered, pressed a tiny cup to the side of her arm. She didn't wince when the microneedle pierced her skin for a blood sample.

"How's your cycle? Is it regular?"

"Yes, ma'am."

"Any pains, aches in the pelvic region?"

"No, ma'am. I've never felt better."

"Good." A distant pause as processors hummed. "Thyroid panel, lipid panel, and CBC and platelet count look just fine," Esther said. "Blood sugar, PSA, and RPR—great." A pause. "You know what comes next. Some women love it, some hate it, I'm afraid."

Sharon pursed her lips, closed her eyes. She could hear the tiny servos as the GYN node rose between her legs. The lubricated node—the size of a baby's fist—nudged into her vagina perhaps an inch, then just seemed to throb there. Next, the fleet of nanoprobes emerged. She felt several tickle up her ure-thra, then scores more caterpillared through the natural perforations of her hymen and up into her cervix and reproductive tract.

"PAP, good; ketones, good; creatinine, good."

Sharon's breath oddly began to grow short.

"Ligations secure—zero deformity. Fallopial channels clear, negative for lesions, blockages, and cystic activity." A distant beep could be heard. "Ah, just a moment. Looks like you've got a neoplastic cyst on one of your Graffian follicles. Not to worry, it's benign. Give me a sec and I'll fix it." Like mechanical ants, the nanogroup swarmed, each with different roles: identification, anesthesial, surgical, and cauterization. In moments, the tiny nanobots performed a textbook operation.

But Sharon trembled. A pocket of the most foreign sensation churned up inside between her legs. A sensation she'd never experienced before.

Something like pleasure.

"There. Finished. Sharon, I'm pleased to inform you that you're in perfect health. Sing praise and thanks to God."

At first, Sharon didn't quite hear the doctor's conclusion.

"Sharon? Did you hear me?"

"Yes, ma'am," she blurted out, and quickly quoted Ecclesiasticus: "There are no riches above a sound body." Her teeth clamped her lower lip as all the nanoprobes withdrew, leaving intense, thrilling trails deep in her most private flesh. Her breasts felt stuffed with tantalizing warmth; her nipples stuck out like bolts.

"Praise be to God. Okay, we're done."

The door sucked back open; Sharon stepped out. The confusion overwhelmed her but she kept silent about it. *What's happening to me?* she pleaded with herself. Back under the med unit's harsh lumes, she noticed that she was flushed from breasts to groin, and her nipples seemed embarrassingly distended.

"You needn't worry, dear," the Deaconness assured her, noting the obvious. "God doesn't hold us responsible for autonomic responses. Some women actually orgasm during the exam."

The bare, forbidden word—*orgasm*—embarrassed Sharon further. Her face pinkened. She was speechless.

"A gynecological nanoexam is *perfunctory,* Sharon. It's a cold, impersonal medical procedure. The free will that God gave you is not involved."

Free will. Sharon immediately recalled the comparable remarks that Brigid had made in the galley. *It's only a sin when you invite it.*

But that conciliation did nothing to cease the dizzied dismay, nor her "autonomic" responses.

When she had her jumpsuit pulled up to her waist, Dr. Esther said, "Here," and handed her a small sterilized pad. "Dab your arm."

Sharon noticed the spot of blood on her arm, from the blood sample taken. She swabbed it, felt a tiny sting from the pad's antiseptic/coagulant compounds.

"But what might be more important in this instance," Esther went on, "are the potential psychological ramifications."

"I don't understand, ma'am."

"You're a brave young woman, but you're only human. The terrible things that you've witnessed today could develop into some considerable after-effects. Seeing your covemates killed, nearly being killed yourself by that bomb. Post-traumatic stress is what I'm talking about."

That was the least of her worries. "I'm fine, ma'am. Really."

"Good girl. But if you notice any problems, psychologically speaking, I want you to come and see me at once. That's an order."

"Yes, ma'am."

The Commander-Deaconness took back the antiseptal pad and dropped it into her waste disposal unit. "Go in peace now."

"To love and serve the Lord," Sharon replied, zipping up the front of her uniform.

She left the med unit, winded, abashed. Her nipples tingled more intensely now, as the valcron of her jumpsuit abraded against them. However naive she might really be—and however impersonal the nature of the exam—Sharon knew that the eruption of sensations she'd experienced in the tome were unquestionably sexual.

And she knew something else.

When Commander-Deaconness Esther had discarded the antiseptal pad, there was another item awaiting disintegration in the waste disposal's tray: a long yellow pill.

Brigid was right. Everyone onboard knows that it's really a sexual suppressant—even Dr. Esther doesn't take it!

That might explain at lot. By not taking it herself today, her sexual responses went unblocked for the first time since puberty. And if she continued not to take the pill—as Brigid insisted . . .

Will I be able to control myself?

A struggle tugged inside of her. She felt inclined to return to her dom, to shower off the lusty perspiration.

But then the sublimation nozzles might only inflame her more. Another thought: Go to Confession, seek council.

But she had no confidence that she could frame the words to properly express her emotions—especially to a man.

Get your mind off it.

This option made the most sense. She took herself quickly back to her dom, sat down and turned on her intranet screen. She remembered the odd file-and-store data she'd read earlier on Kim's intranet—the photospectroscopic probe readout from the Extrasolar Array. She thought a moment to recall the information.

"Something about an elemental molecular scan," she muttered to herself. "A pyroxene compound of . . . aluminum and silicate of sodium?"

She input the information and executed a definition command.

An instantaneous reply read:

—Monoclinic geometric crystallization of $NaAl(SiO333)$ commonly [from historical archives]:

a) crystalline variety of quartz, a vitreous amphibole attached to mineral groups known as pyroxenes.

b) Jasper, a gemstone with ancient roots.

Must be a compound analysis from a planetoid or debris belt, she concluded. The holoimage showed several examples of hand-carved trinkets of an opaque greenish stone.

But . . .

A gemstone? Why would such non-descript information be relegated to the restricted data-channels that Kim had processed?

Hmm.

She switched on Kim's holoscreen, expecting it to have been deactivated by now.

It's still up!

Sharon hoped for more analysis files to have been tagged for redeposition, but there weren't any. Then she tried to retrieve the initial file but got this response:

—data-retrieval request denied.

—requested data has been quarantined.

"That's strange," she told herself. What could be so important about this? *So much for that,* she thought. But as she was about to turn off Kim's unit, the flag-tone sounded. Another file was incoming on the system's download band.

Sharon clicked it on:

MOS WORK CALL
DATA REGIMENT/ANALYSIS TECHNICIAN

Priority Code: **NON-URGENT**

Re: MADAM and ESA-2 Photospectroscopy Probe Order
De: Data Reg c/o Security Corp

READ: Cartographical Probe results: positive for Target-Object (interior) configuration.
—fixed geometric object (in exactitude):
    HEIGHT: 1500 unrefracted miles

LENGTH: 1500 unrefracted miles.
WIDTH: 1500 unrefracted miles.

Observations: Target-Object exists as a fixed perimeter in geometric exactitude.

ORDERS: File & Store for Analysis

STOP

Sharon squinted at the accommodating diagram of whatever this "target-object" was. She couldn't imagine what it could be.

This is useless, she decided. There wasn't enough information, and even if there had been, so what?

She clicked the FILE & STORE icon and closed it out. But at least the distraction, however useless, had taken her mind off her previous problem.

Her body felt normal now, unflushed. This relieved her . . . until she remembered something Brigid had said in the galley, the bizarre word.

Sharon input the word into the language program: masturbation.

masturbation: 1) excitation of the genital organs, often to orgasm, by means other than sexual intercourse. 2) more commonly, the act of sexual self-excitation with one's own hand. Judicially condemned by the Christian Federate's Mental Hygiene Board as a venal sin and statutory third-degree misdemeanor. (Public Law 1163-05/2157)

The words seemed to stare back at her. *Sexual self-excitation.* The sharply clinical term sounded forbidden in her own mind. *With one's own hand.*

Without realizing it then, she'd closed the language program and had already re-delved into Kim's personal directory.

The cyberfiles.

The pornography.

Don't, Sharon ordered herself.

In a fit, she shut down the holoscreen, rushed out of the dom and into the corridor. Yes, she wanted to do it, watch more of it, and—

Masturbate?

She didn't know and she didn't want to know. Two more words sounded in her head.

Free will.

Blessed are they who endureth temptation, for when they are tried, they shall receive the crown of life.

She sailed down the accessmain with no idea where she was going. *Away from there,* she thought. That was all that mattered. She knew she should confess— she'd nearly touched herself.

But hadn't she also willingly turned her back on the desire. Hadn't she resisted the temptation after it had already blossomed in her mind?

"Hey, Sharon?" A hand touched her shoulder.

She spun around. "What!"

It was Tom, just exiting a serviceway. Her outburst clearly startled him. "What's bugging you?"

Sharon pulled her composure back in. "I'm sorry, Tom. I'm just . . . a little frazzled right now."

"Well, it just occurred to me," the tall securitech said. "With all the excitement in the property vault, I never got a chance to tell you the rest of the story."

"The rest of *what* story."

"You know, the stuff about the Red Sect's deity," Tom replied. "The demon. Kilukrus."

(III)

She typed the bizarre name into the mythology data-bank:

K-I-L-U-K-R-U-S

"You're sure this is the name of the demon that the Red Sect worships?" she asked.

"Yup."

They'd gone to the ship's library station, which was unoccupied and quiet. Tom sat back on a grav-chair with his feet propped up on a table.

"Well, like I said before, I've never heard of this particular demon," Sharon pointed out, "and I took a lot of demonology blocks in the academy. And—look, see?"

The holoscreen read: SEARCH OBJECT NOT FOUND

"That's because there *is* no demon named Kilukrus," Tom told her.

"But I thought you said—"

"Just listen to the rest of the story. There's more, and it goes back almost three hundred years. Everyone thinks the Red Sect are like the Druids, that they deliberately left no written records of themselves."

"Yes?"

"That's not entirely true. They *did* create a written record—*one* written record. It's just a little pamphlet, hundreds of years old, called *The Order of Kilukrus*."

"Then there'd be a reference to that in the archival banks," Sharon challenged.

"No, no there wouldn't. Not *these* archival banks. Because it's classified. That's why you can't repeat anything that I'm telling you."

Sharon nodded her consent.

"Keep in mind, nobody knew what this pamphlet was at the time—it was simply considered arcana. There was nothing to link this Kilukrus to the Red Sect, until—"

"Until that Federate raid you'd mentioned in the Old Besthesda ghettoblocks," Sharon recalled.

"Right, the distribution warehouse. But by the time Special Ops got there, the place was rigged with explosives. There was only one Red Sect member there, and right before he blew the place up, he shouted, 'Death to the Christian Federate and all enemies of Kilukrus.' It was the first and only time a Red Sect member ever mentioned the name."

"Now I get it," Sharon understood. "Once the name was mentioned, they entered it into the F.C.I. computers and it was immediately matched to this 300-year-old pamphlet called *The Order of Kilukrus*."

"Exactly."

"So it's fairly useless information," Sharon considered. "The Red Sect worship an invented demon."

"That's what you would think at first glance."

"The answer . . . must be in the pamphlet itself."

"Uh-huh."

She was getting flustered. "So what was in the pamphlet?"

"Gobbledygook. It's about ten pages of intaglio text, just line after line of random letters."

"A cipher?"

Tom nodded. "A Scytale Cipher. Ever heard of it?"

"Of course!" she complained, hoping for something more thrilling. "It's one of the oldest ciphers known, and one of the simplest. The ancient Greeks used it!"

"That's true, and the real laugh is it took Federate Intel months to break it."

"I can't believe that. They have the best decryption programs ever devised."

"Call it human error. A Scytale was the very first program they ran on it, but it still came up the same gobbledygook . . . until several months later when someone decided to run it in reverse. And the result was the simplest cipher of them all."

"The pages of the pamphlet were bound in reverse?"

"Right. Backward."

Sharon sat on the edge of her grav-chair. "So what was in the pamphlet? What did it say?"

"Nothing you haven't heard before. It was just the Red Sect's crackpot motto: 'Under heaven lay umbra—' "

"Hiding the chosen," Sharon finished. "Major-Rector Matthew said that Federate Intel thinks the 'umbra' may be an astronomic allusion, that 'the chosen' are hiding within some sort of planetary or cosmic shadow. But, back to the pamphlet. It was just their credo in it?"

"That's right, over and over. Nothing else."

"And the only reference to Kilukrus was on the pamphlet's cover?"

"Yeah, the title. *The Order of Kilukrus.*"

Another possibility popped up in Sharon's sense of deduction. "Maybe Kilukrus isn't a demon at all. Maybe it's a place, or a person's name—in code."

Tom seemed impressed. "You're right, it's another cipher, but it *is* a demon. The Scytale cipher was easily broken once they took into account that the pages were bound backward. So—"

Sharon mulled it over, came to the most logical conclusion. "The Red Sect exist in secrecy, so it's clear they want to keep the actual name of the devil they worship a secret too. The demon they name can't be found in any demonological text. The pamphlet's printed backward. What happens when we spell the name—Kilukrus—backward?

Sharon re-input the name, KILUKRUS, and inverted it. Now the screen read:

SURKULIK

"Surkulik," Tom finished.

"Now that's one I've heard of," Sharon recalled. But it seemed disappointingly obscure. "The demon of falsehoods, something like that, right?"

"The demon of false *identities*," Tom corrected. "And the demon of inversions, which is why they called him Kilukrus, the inversion of his genuine name."

Sharon re-accessed the mythology banks and ran a search. Instantly, the holoscreen produced:

Surkulik: lesser-known demon from old Judeo-Christian myth, first described in Deniere's *Compendium de Hel*, as simply a 'demon in absëns.' Later in the far more comprehensive *The Demonocracies* by Douleth, Surkulik is defined as a 'devil of the seventh order of the Infernal Empire,' and the 'demon of inversions, puzzles, and false faces.' [No illustration available.] See Appendices.

"That's certainly strange," Sharon remarked. "And not very much information." Next, she tried to access the noted appendices but instead got the message:

:original text deleted:

"That's maddening!" she complained.

Tom agreed with a nod. "The original texts have been removed from the computer."

"Why?"

"Either because it's considered minutiae, or it's classified beyond the compartmentalizations of the data archives."

"I just can't believe this," Sharon smoldered. "Without a scan of the original text, how can we find anything out about this?"

Tom gave her a stolid look. "Maybe somebody on this ship doesn't want us to."

PART FOUR

"These things saith he that holds the seven stars in his right hand. . . ."

—*Revelations 2:1*

(I)

She knew she shouldn't.

But she did.

Brigid had long-since trained herself to remote-view short distances without the need of sensory-dep or acetylcholine jumpers. The ship would be going into retros soon; she had some time to play with. It was always so difficult to resist.

Physically, she lay nude on her bunk in the new dom. Psychically, though, she let her vision fly.

Simply by thinking.

Almost like God, she thought.

Through bulkheads and pressure doors. Along accessmains and serviceways. Up lev-shafts and wiring conduits and vent ducts and even through the ship's hull. Brigid's vision soared.

It was not like telethesy or OBE-ing. She simply *saw*. Her eyes were part of a mentally propelled camera, so to speak, registering images but not feelings. Her feelings, she knew, would circuit back to her physical body through the ethereal tether that connected them. She thought of General-Vicar Luke, and suddenly she was looking at him as he changed into his flight gear, grumbling some unheard complaint. She thought of Sharon and suddenly there she was, poring over holoscreens in the Library Unit with the tall securitech she'd met in the galley. She thought, quite errantly, of power, and next her psychical eyes were watching some engineering techs in the aft prep bays bolting a small nuclear-thrust charge to the ship's as yet un-deployed inertial disk.

She thought of—

Men.

—and saw them in various uniforms moving about the ship, and then—

Naked. Men.

—and was in one of the barracks vapor showers. Unlike the showers for female personnel which were never shared by more than two, at least eight strong muscular men stood within the cleansing fog. They conversed with nonchalance as the sublimation jets washed their bodies. But—

Another blink of a thought—*sex*—took her discorporate eyes into a valve cove, where one man desperately sodomized another.

Another blink showed her a young woman in a green admin uniform. She was on her knees in a service closet, fellating a man.

Brigid stared with her psychic eyes, licking non-existent lips and knowing that her physical body back in her dom would be trembling.

Women, she thought in a hot gush. *Having sex.*

Two women, sweat-slicked and nude floated in a human ball, having turned down the grav in their dom to zero. White thighs vised close-cropped heads, faces pressed to groins, tongues churning in mutual cunnilingus.

Go back, she thought in a squirmy desperation. Yes, she wanted to yank the psychic tether and slip back into her real body of flesh and sensation and let her fingers rub out a volley of clenching pleasures, but—

A final thought first, an uninvited flash in her mind. *Death.*

And then she saw—

(II)

General-Vicar Luke strapped himself in behind his flight techs. He always hated this part.

God, he prayed, *please don't let us get killed.*

It had never happened on a sub-light excursion but the cynic in the ship's commander supposed there was always a first time.

The techs recited their ready list.

"Flight Cove to Nuclear Prep, requesting commo check, over."

"Roger, Flight Cove, commo check affirmative."

"Standby for Inertial Dish displacement."

"Inertial Dish and assembly ready."

"Abort advisory check."

"Abort advisory is satisfactory. Fuselage pressure reading?"

"Green at one hundred kilopascals."

"Green on INHIBIT and ATM PRESS CONTROL."

"Circuit test for radiation- and fire-suppression."

"AV Bays One and Two, circuit-test positive. Cabin and payload cove, circuit-test positive."

Just get on with it! Luke thought.

The pilot turned to look at Luke. "Pilot Station green, sir! Request permission to activate all nuclear-drag assemblies, sir!"

General-Vicar Luke felt nauseous. He simply waved a consenting hand.

"That's *green* for *go!*"

Luke could feel the grating vibrations as the Edessa's counter-inertial shield extended.

"All gravity systems off."

"Roger."

"EM deflection envelope systems on."

"Roger."

The pilot refaced Luke. "Permission to detonate, sir!"

One pulse short of vomiting, Luke nodded.

"Ooo-RAH!" the co-pilot shouted.

"Glory be to *GOD!*" the pilot tech countered. He flipped up the red safety shroud on the console, then flicked the simple toggle.

In the center of the ship's rear inertial disk, the .5-megaton nuclear-implosion device detonated. Approximately one-half of the fissile thrust expended uselessly into space. The other half was caught in the ship's retro disk, bringing the Edessa to something close to a complete stop in its fixed trajectory. The ship tremored, inboard lights fluttering for only a moment.

The entire operation took less than ten seconds.

Which seemed like a full hour of horror to Luke.

"Sir, are you all right?"

I guess that means we're still alive, Luke reasoned. "Yes, yes," he choked.

"Forward lox thrust, green for go. Go for point-two seconds."

"Roger."

Now the laws of normal inertia returned. General-Vicar Luke spectacularly vomited up his last all-liquid meal when the ship jolted forward at a mere 17,000 miles per hour.

"MADAM display re-engaged."

"Tracking. Point zero zero six parallel milliseconds from Utility Station Solon. Pre-prep for automatic dock."

"Roger."

One of the comm techs came immediately to Luke's aid, wiping up the mess in his lap. "There you go, sir. Just an accident. Can happen to anyone."

Luke fumed, humiliated. *Thanks a lot, God.* He turned around to see if Major-Rector Matthew had caught the spectacle. Matthew always joined him in the command cove during launches and retros. *He's probably sitting behind me right now, laughing it up.*

But when Luke fully looked around, he saw that Matthew's flight chair was empty.

(III)

The accessmains hustled with activity, as the ship's intercom blared: "This is the C.F.S. Edessa requesting permission to dock at Threshhold 6."

"This is Custom's Corp, free-drift utility station Solon. Welcome, Edessa, and thanks be to God. Permission to dock granted. Autoguides are activated."

"Roger, Solon."

During all sub-light launches and retros, most of the regular crew strapped themselves to flight chairs in one of the ship's four launch coves. Sharon had sat with Tom for the short turbulent duration but her mind seemed diverted. *All this strange stuff all of a sudden. Attacks on the ship, bombs planted in cadavers, elemental data-relays from the Extrasolar radio telescope, and now this bizarre business with the Red Sect's cryptic deity.*

Surkulik, she thought.

A demon of inversions.

A demon of false faces.

What puzzled her most was the simplicity in deciphering the demon's true name: a crude reversion. It seemed to defy the very nature of the Red Sect itself. For hundreds of years they'd kept every aspect of their terrorist agenda secret. No one knew their base, their leaders, their official formation. Beyond random murder and destruction, no one even knew their objectives. Yet the name of the deity they worshiped was deciphered with ease.

And now this most recent crux.

Text deletions in a simple historical data-bank. Why?

And Tom's observation as to why they couldn't find out more about Surkulik: *Maybe somebody on this ship doesn't want us to.*

Sharon didn't really believe that; it made no sense. She struggled, though, for an explanation.

"Wow, we sure got here quick," Tom said, unbuckling his chair straps.

"What did you expect at just under three billion miles an hour?"

As they debarked into the central main, he glanced behind him. "Where's your new roomie?"

"What?" Sharon came back, distracted.

"The civvie chick with the big—"

Sharon shot him a reproving glance.

"—mouth," Tom finished.

"I don't know," she huffed. Was she jealous? *What a preposterous thought!* "She must've gone to a different launch cove. So you don't really believe that Brigid is a remote-viewer?"

The comment left Tom flustered. "Let's just say that she made some compelling points. I know stuff like that exists . . . it just gives me the creeps. Besides, I don't trust Civilian Branch."

"Why not?"

"They get Federate benefits that regular Army doesn't. They're all on the take. She reminded me of one of Federate Intel's sexual operatives."

Sharon didn't understand him. "A sexual—"

"A sex-op. They'll plant these girls anywhere they want, under a phony occupational cover. They'll seduce guys, see if they reveal classified info."

"Have you . . . ever been seduced?" Sharon asked and immediately regretted it.

Tom's frown was plain. "Never by a sex-op."

What did that mean? But irrelevant curiosities burned in her. Tom was handsome, strong. She wondered about his sexual history but didn't dare ask.

Again, the intercom: "All first- and second-shift personnel may debark at Air-lock 4. Excluding Security Corp personnel."

"Looks like you have to stay," Sharon said.

"To hell with that," he told her. "I have a three-day pass. Let Matthew and the rest of those busted humps walk sentinel duty. Are you going onto Solon?"

"Why not? I've never been."

"I've got a better idea," he said. "Follow me."

Sharon followed him without much thought. But what *was* she thinking?

"You find her attractive, don't you?" she asked, without realizing why.

"Who? Miss Defense Corp? Hell, yeah."

"I mean Brigid."

He shot her a quizzical frown. "What's a little girl like you asking dumb questions like that for?"

An instant flair of anger rose up. She was sick of people mocking her for her age. "I'm not a little girl, you—"

"Asshole?" Tom grinned. "Were you about to call me an asshole? Second time in a day."

"I don't use ungodly language like that."

"Well, you'd be right."

"Why don't you answer the question?"

"You sound jealous," he joked. "Understandable. Chicks stand in line to go out with me, and as good-looking as I am, who can blame them? Especially the real young ones like you, the teenagers."

Sharon ground her teeth. "I'm twenty!"

"Yeah? Then I'll bet your birthday was last week."

"You're just too bashful to admit that you have a crush on Brigid," she countered.

"No, not Brigid. Someone else."

Before she could respond, he took her through another accessmain.

Does he mean me? she wondered.

The placid voice echoed the third-shift blessing: "The people that walked in darkness have seen a great light: they that dwell in the land of the shadow of death, upon them the light will shine."

Tom chuckled as he led Sharon into a decidedly *dark* mechanistics wing. "If they're trying to encourage us, it ain't quite makin' it."

"Where are we going?" Sharon asked. She felt impatient, and still irritable over his innuendos as well as her recent brush with temptation.

"My three-day pass entitles me to certain advantages." Tom proudly held up the narrow plastic chipcard. "That means I can go to the obcove. You're my guest."

"I've never been in one." Sharon tried to sound subdued, when actually the prospect thrilled her. The observation cove was the ship's only dedicated astronomical viewing post. Not a direct window, of course (no technology existed yet to produce transparent panels that were radiation- and heat-resistant enough to hold up against the back-blast of nuclear-drag launch), but the digigraphic beacons on the ship's skin would transfer a high-definition display into the obcove's reception panels. This would be Sharon's first opportunity to see deep-space in real-time.

"Up here," Tom bid.

The anti-grav personnel lift took them up to the Edessa's highest strat. And when Tom opened the access with his chipcard, Sharon grabbed his arm and nearly shrieked.

"Gets ya at first, huh? First time I stepped into one of these, I thought I'd opened an airlock by mistake."

Sharon was stunned. Her mouth hung open.

God in heaven . . .

The long curved cove was lined entirely with photorecept panels; it felt as though she were *standing* in space.

The cove offered a flawless view of the quadrant beyond the solar system, a concentrated image that seemed perfect.

"It's the real McCoy," Tom said. "Not like the passive panels they've got all over the ship. Those are just cyberpegs played over and over."

Pockets of stars glowed crisp white-blue before a limitless range of black. She was looking at the northern celestial quadrant, the Ursa constellations—the Big and Little Dipper—plus Cepheus and Lyra, the Zuby Cluster, and the ARC 67 quasar.

"It's beautiful," Sharon whispered.

"Even the Centirion and the Hubble Six can't show it like this." He pointed up to Ursa Minor, the constellation of seven second-magnitude stars known as the Little Dipper. "Gee, and it's only 300 light years away."

Sharon stared at the star system's brightest offering at the end of the dipper's handle. "Polaris, the North Star."

"Navigators have been using it for 3000 years," Tom observed. "I think it changes every 5000."

"Because of earth's ecliptic precessional movement. It used to be Thuban in the Draco system, and one day it'll be Alpha Cephei."

"I'll take Polaris any day. Job called it the eye of God."

Perhaps it was. Sharon shuddered at the spectacle. Just then, the entire galaxy seemed a hand's reach away.

"I knew you'd dig this," Tom said.

"Thank you." Only then did Sharon realize she'd not let go of Tom's arm. She could feel the muscles beneath his uniform sleeve. All hard curves. With the cosmos distracting her, her focus skirted away . . . and forbidden images overwhelmed her.

Forgive me. . . .

She was kissing him, sucking his tongue. Her hand rubbed his groin, marveling at the mysterious hardness that seemed to grow as she rubbed it. His strong thigh pressed up into her pubis, the sensation of which sent a gust of the most primitive pleasure through her guts. The hard pinpoints of her breasts ached as if bitten; then he was biting them literally after his firm hands had peeled her uniform down to her waist.

She could barely breathe. Her lust was smothering her. His hand slid down inside her uniform, down her front, his fingers buried in her sex, which was now overflowing. Her own hand did the same to him, exploring what she'd never explored before. His testes felt like ripe fruit. Next, higher, to the shaft, the whole hot raw thing in her hand. She was squeezing out beads of enigmatic liquid, slicking it back and forth over the strange pulsing rod of flesh. Then—

She was out of her jumpsuit altogether. Naked and flat on her back like a whore in a Gomorran fertility feast.

Fuck me. . . .

"Hey, hey, wait—"

The sinful muse shattered; reality crashed back.

Sharon was kissing him—for real.

His hands urged her backward. "This isn't right."

Her head swam in circles. "Why isn't it?"

"You have vows."

"I—"

"I'm not going to do this! It's illegal!"

191

"Kissing is?" some part of her objected. "Touching? Fondness is illegal?"

"Yeah. In the Army it is, and you *know* that. Let's get out of here. I never should've brought you here."

She couldn't believe what she was saying. "We won't tell anyone. Let's just—"

"No! You're a virgin! You don't just give that away!"

"But I—I—"

More reality fell on her. *What have I done!* Dread fell down on her like a heavy net. She brought her hands to her face. "Oh my God! I don't know what came over me. I'm so embarrassed!"

"Forget it." He sleeved some sweat off his brow. "Come on, let's check out the Solon Station."

Sharon sheepishly followed him back down to the accessmain. *What is wrong with me?* She'd never behaved like this in her life. What would the priest say at her next Confession? What would the General-Vicar say if they'd been caught? *Behavior like this could ruin my conduct record. . . .*

"I don't know about you," he said, "but I need a beer."

In her shame, she barely heard him. "Beer? That's been illegal for almost fifty years."

"Sure, within all the Christian political borders. The Federate rents half of the Solon Station to the Japanese; it's a space commerce post. The Christian Federate has no jurisdiction there. Booze, brothels, casinos, and—guess what? Solid food."

Sharon was totally unaware of this but, just the same, not very interested. Official jurisdiction or not, such indulgences were sins.

And today she'd already committed her share.

As they followed the accessmains to the debark bulkhead, Tom seemed uneasy. She could hardly blame him. Eventually their passage was stopped cold by a throng of crewmembers waiting at the processing point.

"Jesus. I fuckin' *hate* standing in lines."

Sharon dismissed the vulgarity. She squinted into the throng, standing on tip-toes to see past the crush of shoulders and heads. "I don't see Brigid anywhere. I wonder where she is."

"Hey! Up front!" Tom shouted his complaint. "We're growing old back here!"

A detached voice from behind caught them both by surprise: "Specialist, Private. I'm afraid your debark privileges have been revoked. Both of you— follow me."

Tom was about to fire off another vocal objection . . . until he noticed who'd just spoken.

General-Vicar Luke.

(IV)

Sharon and Tom hustled to keep up with the General-Vicar as he headed back to the command levels.

"Sir, uh, with all due respect, I haven't had any leave in fourteen months," Tom explained.

"And perhaps you'd like to spend the *next* fourteen months in the brig," the commander calmly replied, "which, if you ask me, is where a brazen, impertinent punk like you deserves to be in the first place."

This is it, Sharon felt sure. *There must've been surveillance chips in the ob-cove. They saw me trying to seduce Tom. . . .*

"But, uh, again, sir, with all due respect. You just gave me a three-day pass."

"What you deserve is a three-day ass-kicking for that ungodly mouth of yours. Can it, Private, or I'll bust you so low you'll think the bottom of my boot-heel is the ionosphere."

Sharon was wilting, shame piling upon shame. It took all of her courage to ask: "Sir, are we being . . . reprimanded?"

"Reprimanded? Of course not." Luke passed through a security door with his chip-pin. "You're both on the classified duty manifest."

Tom took more exception. "Sir, we weren't informed about any—"

"Shut your hole, Private, before I kick it closed." The General-Vicar explained directly to Sharon: "You've both been selected for a special mission. Regrettably, I can't disclose many details at this point."

"So this really never has been a routine resupply flight?" Sharon asked.

"That's correct. We're letting most of the crew debark at the Solon Station. They have no idea that we're going to leave them there. They'll all be picked up and taken back to the moon by the next freighter. We launched with a full crew to avert suspicion. This mission was planned in advance."

Sharon's excitement collided head-on with her complete puzzlement. *A classified mission—and I'm on the manifest.* This might very well explain the bizarre analysis transmissions that the ship had been receiving. And, now that she thought of it—

"If I may, sir. In spite of the lengths that have been taken to keep the mission secret, isn't it advisable to suspect the possibility of infiltration?"

"Unfortunately, yes," Luke agreed. "The Red Sect member who tried to kill you, for instance, could've been tipped off, could've been stowed away on the ship by Federate collaborators. We have to consider it possible."

"Who else knows about the mission?" Tom had the audacity to ask.

"Not that it's any of *your* business, Private, the only member of the original crew who knows anything . . . is me. And to return to Sharon's point, the possibility of a security breach is the reason why we're abandoning most of the crew. We're only proceeding with the mission with a dozen techs. Mostly Security Corp and anyone else with a sufficient clearance."

"A dozen?" Tom nearly railed. "Who's going to run the ship?"

"To reduce the chances of human infiltration," Luke explained, "all manual control stations have been locked out. Everything—propulsion, life-support, course-projection—are all discreeted. The ship's Macro-Analysis Computer will take over from here—in auto-mode based on a previously initiated program. Human tampering is not an option." Luke looked directly at Sharon. "Navigation is discreeted too, but you've been retained to survey the navigational status monitors for a potential abort display."

"Understood, sir."

"What about me?" Tom asked. "Why was I retained for this mission?"

Luke's facial expression seemed to be one of total disgruntlement. "Because—unfortunately—you're the only securitech onboard who's qualified to fly the ship's lenticular re-entry vehicle."

Tom stopped in his tracks. "You mean . . . we're going to another planet? You want me to land an LRV on *another planet?*"

General-Vicar Luke didn't stop walking. His only response to the query was a simple, unequivocal "Yes."

PART FIVE

"He stretcheth out the north over the empty place,
and hangeth the earth upon nothing. . . ."
—Job 26:7

(I)

"Group! Ateeeeeeeeen-hut!"

Everyone in the command briefing cove snapped to attention as Luke entered, Sharon and Tom trailing behind. "At ease," he said. "Be seated."

Via its solid lox engines, the ship had already thrusted off from the Solon Station, leaving almost the entire crew behind without explanation. Sharon counted only eleven people in the cove. *He said a dozen, didn't he?* Commander-Deaconness Esther was here, and so was Warrant Officer Simon. Everyone else seemed to be Security Corp personnel, everyone except—

Brigid sat at the conference table's far end.

What's wrong with her?

The raven-haired civilian looked blanched, anemic.

"As you all know by now," Luke said, "we've all been selected to take part in a classified mission. Details will be forthcoming, as the need to know progresses. The mission objectives forbid me from outlining the details at this point."

Most everyone in the cove looked either dismayed or aggravated.

"All I can say right now is that we will soon initiate a sub-light nuclear-drag into the north celestial quadrant. This is not an exercise."

A multitude of questions bloomed on the faces of all present, but no one dared ask anything.

Save for Tom: "Sir, if I may, who authorized the mission orders?"

"The Pope himself, under advisement from the Vatican Security Council." The ship's commander scanned the faces of everyone in the cove. "Sometimes God's work is secret, yet it remains God's work. So it says in *Deuteronomy*, 'The secret things belong unto the Lord our God.'"

"Amen," the room replied.

"From here on, the Edessa will run in auto-mode. Most of you are here strictly to maintain security."

Tom instantly spoke up: "Then how come Major-Rector Matthew isn't here? Why wasn't *he* selected for the mission?"

The question left Luke's eyes downcast, troubled. "Major-Rector Matthew's name was indeed on the personnel manifest, which leads us to our first dilemma. He is unaccounted for and presumed dead."

"What!" Tom belted out. The others seemed shocked, with Brigid as the only exception.

What is going on here! Sharon thought.

Luke glanced at Brigid, gave a grim nod. "For those of you who don't know her, Sister Brigid is from the Federate's Civilian Branch. Sister?"

Brigid stood up, still clearly distraught from some unnamed torment. Her voice sounded dry, hoarse. "I'm a remote-viewer," she said, "from Meade Cathedral's Psychical Services Center. Earlier today, I was practicing what we call a 'run,' and I saw a dead body. Somewhere on the ship."

"You mean in the morgue unit, right?" Tom said.

"No. I sensed it was somewhere amidships, in the command levels. I could tell by the blue service lights at the thresholds."

"Was it Major-Rector Matthew?" Dr. Esther asked in alarm.

"There was a sack of some kind over the corpse's face so I can't say for sure," Brigid continued. "But I did make out major emblems on the uniform. After I saw this, I immediately reported it to the General-Vicar, whereupon he informed me that Major-Rector Matthew had been missing for several hours."

"So," Luke added, "it's fairly safe to assume that this is the Major—deceased, probably murdered."

"Murdered by someone on this ship," someone piped in.

Maybe even by someone in this room, Sharon considered.

Tom was frowning, addressing Brigid. "Wait a minute. You're saying that you saw this dead body *psychically?*"

"Yes. I was not physically present at the time."

"Then how do you know he was actually dead?"

"Believe me. When you have the sensitivities that I have . . . you *know*. The absence of a life-force projects a particular psychic reaction."

"I'm not buying that crap," Tom said, standing up. "We'll just have to search all of the fuckin' command levels. Cove by cove. He could still be alive and we're all sitting around like a bunch of putzes."

"Very well, Private," Luke approved. "Take the rest of the securitechs, designate search parties, and commence. You're in charge."

"Come on, let's roll," Tom said to the rest of the techs. They all quickly filed out of the cove.

Luke appraised those who remained: Esther, Simon, Brigid, and Sharon. "The rest of you, come with me."

"Due to our technical specialties," Luke was saying as he led them down a corridor, "the four of us have the highest level security classifications of anyone else on board. That's why I'd like you all to see this. I'll need your input, and your discretion."

Commander-Deaconness Esther queried, "My clearance is only mid-level, sir. Are you sure you want me to—"

"Yes, I am," Luke cut her off. "Your experience as a Federate physician makes your opinion most crucial. It's a *medical* situation."

Sharon couldn't guess what he meant, but with all that had happened over the last hour, she wasn't surprised. But what *did* surprise her then was their current destination: Sharon recognized it at once.

The Property Vault. The restricted morgue suite.

For the second time in a solar cycle, Sharon was entering this strangest of stations. The first time she'd entered, she'd nearly been killed by a bomb. . . .

The body of the Red Sect terrorist remained bagged on the exam-slat. Luke quickly debriefed Brigid as to what had *really* happened, and why this body was here.

"I don't understand, sir," Simon asserted.

Luke looked at him with calculation. "It's interesting that you'd say that, Simon—since *you're* the one who performed the autopsy scans on the decedent."

Suddenly Simon looked less weasely than usual.

"I can vouch for Mr. Simon's qualifications, sir," Esther said.

"I didn't ask you to, Doctor."

"Is there a problem with the autopsy?" Simon asked.

Luke faced him sternly. "As a matter of fact, there is. All of the autopsical analyses—the tomographs, the blood screens, and the DNA probes—were forged. Someone switched the genuine test results—" Luke turned on the holochart above the corpse—"with these *counterfeit* results."

"With all due respect, sir," Simon finally stood up for himself. "Your insinuation is out of line. And if those aren't the real results, then where are they?"

Luke popped a data-chip into the holoscreen's drive. "Right here."

The chart was completely different from the previous one. "No mention of ABZ Genotype Syndrome," Sharon muttered, staring up.

"Correct," Luke said. "The fake DNA probe didn't match with anyone in the global ID base. This man, in other words, isn't Red Sect at all, he was topically altered to appear so. The Red Sect mark, for instance, is artificial. It's the result of a deliberate skin graft that was genetically pigmentated to look like the real thing. And whoever did this thought they were deleting the genuine results and substituting them with the fakes. Unbeknownst to them, the Exploratory Corp changed their processing discriminators before we launched. The MAC picked up the discrepancy at once."

"If he's not Red Sect," Brigid asked, "then who is he?"

"Timothy Peter," Luke reeled off. "Surname Dunne. He is—or I should say *was*—a field operative for Federate Intelligence."

The rest was easy to see. "Our own Federate Intel service tried to sabotage the mission!" Sharon exclaimed.

Brigid finished, "And make it look like Red Sect."

Luke nodded. "That much is clear. But what's not clear at all is why."

Esther was bristling. "Sir, I feel it my duty to point out that quite a few rumors were circulating about Warrant Officer Simon—"

"That's uncalled for!" Simon shouted.

"—that he's a Federate Intel plant! Simon performed the autopsy, which means he had the best opportunity to substitute a phony diagnostic chart—"

"*You're* the one who processed the chart, Esther!" Simon yelled back. "It wouldn't matter that they were discreeted!"

"—and it also means that he knew about the bomb!"

"Shut up, both of you," Luke ordered. "It's been interesting gauging your reactions to all of this—"

Simon again: "Sir, I assure you, I didn't have anything to do with this. The more logical suspect is Esther."

"I said shut up!" The room hushed; then Luke continued. "I don't suspect either of you—you both passed the polygraph; in fact, everyone now on board passed it before launch. This was all prepared beforehand."

"I still don't believe it," Simon griped. He roughly opened the body bag, revealing the nude corpse from the waist up. Everyone winced at the sight of the face-less skull. The incision that Tom had made—to ex-tract the bomb—remained hanging open, but the large scarlet mark across the chest was essentially intact. Immediately, a chill bolted up Sharon's neck.

The face of the demon, she thought. *Surkulik.*

Simon pointed to the mark, challenging the General-Vicar. "You're telling us that's *fake?* That it's some kind of genetically cultured skin graft? I've seen them before, sir; they *all* look the same."

"But the fact that they all look the same just makes it easier to replicate genetically," Esther asserted.

"If you're trying to make a point," Luke said to her, "then make it."

Esther had a scalpel in her hand. "The technology's existed for years. Blood supply and nerve-conduction can easily be grown into an exterior skin graft. But there's only one way to find out for sure."

"Proceed," Luke granted.

Esther rolled down an ultraviolet scanning screen over the cadaver's chest. "There, see? Those microsu-tures are the dead giveaway." She scowled at Simon. "If the autopsy had been performed *properly,* these tiny blood- and nerve-connections would've been de-tected without any need for a tomograph." Next, she carefully applied her scalpel, beginning to cut.

Sharon and Brigid took a step back, cringing.

"Good God," Brigid muttered.

A trace, wet sound could be heard. Within a

minute, Esther had peeled much of the scarlet skin off the cadaver's chest.

Revealing perfectly normal skin underneath.

"It's almost like the new skin was *painted* on," Sharon observed.

"Not painted," Esther replied. "*Grown.*"

The General-Vicar was pinching his cleft chin. "Well, I suppose this is proof-positive of a Federate Intel sabotage attempt. Forged autopsy and DNA results, an easily detectable bomb that goes *undetected,* and now this. Our friends at Federate Intel have gone to exorbitant measures to stop this mission and blame it on the Red Sect. But I can't think of any logical reason."

"And it also means that they killed Major-Rector Matthew," Sharon suggested, "if, in fact, he's dead."

"He's dead, all right," echoed a voice behind them all.

Tom stood in the unit's entrance. He looked morose.

"We just found his body stuffed up into one of the service conduits," he said.

(II)

When the securitechs brought the body of Major-Rector Matthew into the morgue unit, Sharon felt all the blood drain out of her face. Another exam platform was lowered, and the autopsy began, care of Dr. Esther and Simon, while everyone else looked queasily on. The cranial vault had been ruptured within an effluxion sack.

"Sir?" Sharon asked. "You said that no one else knows about the details of the mission?"

Luke was clearly saddened by this latest atrocity. "Yes. Me, and me alone. Matthew knew nothing about it. He did make some comments, though, which clearly indicated that he was beginning to have some suspicions that this might not actually be a typical resupply flight. As Security Corp commander, he noticed the irregularities in some of the processing points, the random analysis transmissions coming in, things like that."

"Where are those transmissions coming from?" Tom was bold enough to ask.

"You'll find out in due time. Nonetheless, it appears that Matthew was killed due to his suspicions. The murderer didn't want him to get the chance to discover more of the mission's classified objectives."

Simon glanced up from the tomograph assembly. "At this point, sir, don't we all have a right to know those objectives?"

"No, you do not. You have no *rights* at all," Luke reminded, "just the privilege to proceed with God's work under the criteria of New Vatican's orders."

"Yes, sir."

"But isn't it possible that the Major's murderer is still on board?" Sharon continued.

"I don't regard it as likely. You've all been polygraphed to the highest levels of Federate scrutiny, and the statistics demonstrate that our latest lie-detection programs can't be defeated."

Tom sputtered something under his breath.

"You have something to say, Private? Feel free to enlighten us with your obviously exclusive wisdom."

"Nothing to say, sir."

"Good."

But Sharon couldn't let it go. "All right, let's just

say it's not any of us." She pointed to the other dead body in the unit, whose genetically implanted skin graft now hung off his chest like a sheet of wallpaper. "That man stowed away. He successfully infiltrated the ship. If he did it—"

"Someone else could, too," Luke conceded. "Your point is well taken, Specialist."

Brigid spoke up next. "You mean there could be someone else on the ship as we speak. Hiding."

"We have to consider the possibility," the General-Vicar confirmed, "which is why our ever-vigilant Private Thomas is going to lead the search detachment and won't stop until every square inch of this vessel has been physically inspected. You hear me, Private?"

"Yes, sir," Tom replied with a smirk.

"Then don't let the pressure door hit you in the ass on the way out."

Tom exited the suite, taking the rest of the securitechs with him.

Sharon and Brigid left a few moments later, hands to bellies, when Dr. Esther removed the effluxion sack from Major Matthew's head. A dark-red stew spilled out of the bag, slopping the floor.

"God, that was gross," Brigid said after she and Sharon had left.

"The poor man. He was a faithful servant of God."

"Yeah, and now he's a faithful *dead* servant of God, which is what we all could be real soon."

"You heard the General. The boarding polygraphs prove that none of us could be spies or infiltrators, and if there's another stowaway, Tom's team will find him."

"There's no damn *stowaway*," Brigid insisted. "I've RV'd all over this ship. If there was someone hiding out, I'd sense it, and my vision would take me there.

You think I saw Matthew's dead body by accident? No way."

Sharon couldn't very well argue; Brigid's gift was as specialized as it was arcane. "I saw you too," Brigid said in a lower tone. "You and Tom."

"*What?*"

"On the ob-deck." A wink. "Don't worry. Your secret's safe with me."

Sharon's face flushed with embarrassment; she was speechless.

Brigid began to walk away. "You should've done it, Sharon. I've got some *bad* vibes about this special 'mission.' You should've gone all the way when you had the chance."

"How-how can you say that?" Sharon fumbled the words.

"My gut's telling me we're all going to die."

(III)

The opteostatic mentometer housing that sat to the side of Sharon's work mod reminded her oddly of some kind of mechanized head—with horns.

And such a shape—with horns—could only remind her of demons.

The demon's face . . . *Surkulik*. Sharon hoped that it was merely the power of suggestion, but the pigmented red stain on the dead man's chest—genetically grafted or not—*did* look like a face when one stared at it long enough. A hideous face.

The image in the memory seemed to drift toward her, as if to kiss her, as the wide sheet of skin was peeled off the killer's chest. . . .

She blinked the memory away, struggling to concentrate. *Pay attention!* she yelled at herself. *Do your job!* Her job was to survey the navigational status monitors for potential abort displays. Simple. *So do it!*

On the other hand, her difficulty in focusing on her task was understandable due to the most recent events. A restricted mission. A possible stowaway. A murder. It was Federate Intelligence—not Red Sect—who'd tried to sabotage the ship. What could account for this? And then she considered something else.

What could account for Brigid—a civilian remote-viewer—being included on the personnel manifest for a classified military mission?

(IV)

The cove stood muted in tinsled dark. The blinking lights on the relay panels behind him seemed to cut out his silhouette in stark black, haloed by furious kaleidoscopy.

"Yours is a privileged role," the General-Vicar said. "The first to be close enough to *see*."

Brigid didn't understand, but she was used to that. It came with the parameters of her job: to *do*, not *ask*. True, she'd been born with her "gift"; she never really wanted it. "God gave it to you," the Abbot Superior had told her at Meade Cathedral, "and you have an obligation to use it—for Him."

But to be honest, in the most secret moments to herself, Brigid didn't know if she even *believed* in God.

General-Vicar Luke had asked her to meet him in the Lab Station. It was just a typical diagnostic lab save for one additional ante-cove: the sensory-dep cell. *I'll bet I've spent half of my life in these things,* she thought. Such cells were known to attenuate the psychic limits of a trained remote-viewer, amplifying mental reception, vastly extending range. Hours ago, now, the Edessa had jumped to nuclear-drag, accelerating at over 75 billion miles per solar cycle. Brigid wondered what they were soaring to.

Luke sealed the pressure door after she'd entered, and keyed in a delock password. No one was coming in without his expressed permission.

"It's time," he said.

The cell before her, with its hatch hinged open, reminded her of the old-style coffins they'd used to encase the dead, back before the Federate Cremation Act had been passed into public law. The inside shimmered in the dark: its bath of distilled glycerene heated precisely to human body temperature.

"I'm ready," she said and unhesitantly began to strip.

The General-Vicar seemed to flinch. "Oh, I didn't realize. I've precious little experience with remote-viewers."

She shouldered out of the jumpsuit, her large breasts bared. "It works best if you're nude."

A chuckle that didn't quite work. "Don't be distressed. I've been chemically celibate for decades. I'll show you my implant certification if you like."

"That's all right." She didn't care. She liked exposing herself—another sin. A tingle lit in the furrow of her sex when she stepped out of the rest of her uniform. But most of the thrill was lost in front of a man with no sex drive. Younger men, men without libidinal tempering—she loved to nonchalantly reveal her body to them, knowing they'd take the image with them, to some dark unmonitored place.

Sin, more sin.

"Give me a moment to hook up."

She stepped into the cell, lay down in the slippery bath. At once she felt caressed by a hundred hot hands; they smoothed over her skin, over her breasts and back and forth over the insides of her thighs. Awash in the dense liquid, she stuck a pair of sensor-cups to either side of her throat, then a chargecup over her heart.

She was floating now.

Nude, totally vulnerable. Locked away behind an unopenable door.

The most grotesque thoughts assailed her. Who was the General-Vicar really? She didn't know him; she'd never even heard of him.

He could be insane for all I know.

HE could be the spy. HE could be Major Matthew's killer.

Perhaps.

She imagined herself being raped in the cell. . . .

"Are you all right?"

"Yes," she answered, snapping out of the nightmare. But it was just more sin. The awful vision only stoked her desires further. She'd nearly climaxed.

"Close the hatch now," she said. "Then use the intercom."

The cell's hatch geared shut, sealing her in hermetically. Total darkness now. Soundless. She was floating on nothing.

The digistats processed her exact body temperature down to a thousandth of a degree, then adjusted the fluid temp. Pure oxygen hissed in at exactly one hundred kilopascals.

"Can you hear me, sir?"

Trace static crackled over the intercom. "Yes," Luke said.

"I'm going to self-induce a theta-wave trance. But before I do that, I need you to give me a focus-word."

"Understood."

She was already sliding away. "Give me the focus-word now."

There was a long dead pause.

Then General-Vicar Luke said—

(V)

"This is a crock of fuckin' bullshit that can suck my dick," Tom said. He lounged lazily on the grav-chair across from Sharon's mod, arms crossed and boots propped up.

Sharon, as usual, shirked at his language.

"There's no fuckin' *infiltrator* on board. There's no *stowaway spy*."

"How do you know?" Sharon asked.

"We searched every inch of this goddamn space-canoe, with IR, parabolic heartbeat sensors, carbon-dioxide detectors—every fuckin' thing. Christ, we even used a methane probe."

"Methane?"

"It's right out of the tactical search manual. They figure if someone's hiding out on a ship or plat, he's eventually gonna have to take a *shit* somewhere. Well, guess what? We didn't find a single pile of *shit*."

Sharon sighed in useless disgust. "And your point would be?"

"Whoever killed Matthew is someone on the personnel manifest."

"Maybe the killer debarked at the Solon Station."

"What, come all this way just to *leave* before the *real* mission starts? Not likely."

Sharon asked outright. "So who do you think it is? There are only eleven of us."

"Could be anyone. That creepy chick with the big tits, or that airhead bitch doctor. Then we've got Simon, a known flake to begin with, plus there've always been rumors that he infiltrated Security Corp to spy for Federate Intel. Next, we've got that old hard-on Luke, who's not telling us a damn thing about what we're doing out here. And after all that we've got five circle-jerkin' bohunker securitechs, none of whom I know from fuckin' Adam in a hole in the ground."

"So you don't trust anyone?"

"Hell, no."

"What about me?" Sharon toyed. "Couldn't I be the killer?"

"Yeah, and I could be the next Pope." He laughed out loud. "Right, a teenager plugging a Security Corp commander in the head with a de-jam gun and stuffing his body up a service conduit. Happens every day."

Sharon bristled. "I'm *not* a teenager," she re-reminded him. "And what about you? You have the worst reputation and record of anyone onboard. Shouldn't the rest of us be suspecting *you?*"

"Sure, if you've all got dog shit for brains."

Sharon shook her head. "There's absolutely no point in continuing this avenue of discussion. So why don't you just leave? I'm sick of listening to you use impious language, and I've got work to do."

Tom's brow arched. "Yesterday you were trying to suck my tongue out of my mouth in the ob-cove, and now you want me to leave?"

The comment incensed her. First came the flood of embarrassment, then a harder flood of rage. "Just get out!" she yelled.

"Jeez, I was only kidding. You teenagers need to lighten up."

"Get the f—"

"Gotcha," he said, pointing at her. "Almost made you use *impious* language." He stood up, meandered over to her mod. He looked at her holoscreens. "What are you working on, anyway?"

"I'm monitoring the nav systems for abort displays," she huffed back. "Now leave me alone."

"I thought you liked me."

"I don't. You're a horrible person. You say things on purpose just to make me angry or hurt my feelings."

"No I don't. I'm just funnin' around. Can't you take a joke?" He looked at her tertiary holoscreen. "What's this one on for?"

"Just some research." She tried to ignore him. "None of your business."

He snooped forward, put a hand on her shoulder as he squinted at the screen. The screen read:

:LOOP SEARCH/ NAM ALLOCATION:
under heaven lay umbra, hiding the chosen

—AND—

red sect

—AND—

surkulik

"Red Sect stuff, huh? But you already tried that at the Library Unit," he said.

"I'm trying it again." However unconscious the gesture, his hand on her shoulder distracted her. "It's a multiple data-bank search. Any hit in one bank loops the trinaries back into a quarantined directory. It pieces together fractals and holds them in the national access memory."

"Ah, I knew that. Every data-bank on the ship, huh?"

"Yes, unless it's an encrypted bank, but typically the only encrypted banks are reserved for operational specs and intelligence grids. Not historical information."

"But the other day, when you were searching those appendices, didn't it say that the original text had been deleted?"

Sharon struggled to rein her exasperation with him. "Yes, it did! Running this kind of search could locate the surface space when the information was deleted! I might be able to retrieve the deletion!"

He paid no mind to her raised voice. "Right, technical stuff. I do technical stuff too, you know. Dig ditches, paint walls, clean out the insides of deep-space garbage hoppers."

This time she almost smiled.

"Oh, I meant to ask you. Any idea what this is?"

He placed a tiny piece of thermal plastic on her mod. She picked it up, only had to look at it for a moment to realize what it was. "Where did you get this?"

"I found it on Major-Rector Matthew's body," Tom replied. "It was sticking out of the bottom of his dress cross. Looks like some kind of a circuit or computer chip."

"It *is* a computer chip," Sharon acknowledged. "It's a biochip. You better turn it in to the General-Vicar."

"Why? What's the big deal?"

"The big deal is that the only place in the world that legally makes these is the Federate Science and Research Facility. The specs are secret." She held the chip up. "See? If this was legitimate, it would have a Federate seal on it. But this one doesn't, which means it had to have been made by hackers. All Federate intelligence systems use biochips to protect their passwords from being broken. They use self-sustaining biogens to serve as the power source. This one looks pretty old but you should definitely report it."

"I wonder what Matthew was doing with it."

"I'm sure the General-Vicar will ask the same question," Sharon suggested. "But what I'd like to know even more is exactly what *kind* of biochip is this? It could be ancillary—for use in a customized—meaning *unauthorized*—processing system. It could simply be programmed for use in a safeguarded file. Or it could've been built specifically to override Federate cryptographs designed by Federate Intel."

"Is there any way to find out?" Tom asked.

"Sure. I could run it through a diagnostic test, but I'd need authorization from the General-Vicar."

Tom's brow raised. "Yeah. And I'll bet you could also run it through a diagnostic test *without* authorization from the General-Vicar. What's the harm? Luke doesn't even know about it, and with this mission and all, he's got a fuckin' shit-load on his mind anyway."

Sharon grimaced. "Was it really necessary for you to say that?"

"What? Mission?"

"What's your point, Tom?"

"My point is it makes more sense to run the test ourselves. It could be nothing. And if it turns out to really be an illegal cryptograph-breaker . . . *then* we'll tell Luke."

Sharon put the tiny biochip in her pocket. "I'll think about it."

"In fact, I'll bet we could run down to the lab right now and test it," Tom prodded on. "The ship's practically empty. No one would be the wiser."

Sharon scowled back. "Don't try to make it sound so innocent, Tom. You want to find out if this chip could be used to decode the onboard Federate Intel banks."

"Yeah? Well don't try to tell me you haven't considered the same exact motherfuckin' thing."

Another cringe at his language. *But . . . he's right,* she admitted. If the biochip turned out to be what she thought it was, she could theoretically bypass the safeties in the ship's Macro-Analysis Computer.

I could find out what's really *going on.*

It was a tempting prospect. She thought of the Book of James: *Blessed are they that endureth temptation,* but the ordinarily powerful scripture didn't seem all that compelling right now. "I'll think about it," she repeated.

"And it looks like you've got something else to think about too." Tom's attention shot to the other side of her mod. "There's all kind of funky shit blinking on that screen over there."

"What!" *Not an abort!* Sharon fretted. She spun in her seat but was relieved when she noticed that her secondary holoscreen was merely signaling a long-range MADAM relay.

"These come in all the time," she said. "It's just a notice from the Extrasolar Array, sort of like a weather report."

Words ticked across the screen:

C.F.S. EDESSA MEAN TRAJECTORY WILL CO-INCIDE WITH THE FOLLOWING NON-THREAT-ENING ASTRONOMIC PHENOMENA: WAIT

"We're waiting," Tom said.

GRID: APPROX 15 HOURS RIGHT ASCENSION

80 DEGREES NORTH DECLINATION

PHENOMENA: ECLIPTIC VESTRAL

APPARENT SUB-ASTEROIDAL DETECTION: WAIT

"What's that mean?" Tom asked.

"The radiotelescopes on the Extrasolar Array just discovered a small asteroid," Sharon told him. "It's nothing particularly special these days. Light refractions have been known to hide asteroids, planetoids, and even large planets for hundreds or thousands of years before they pop up on the surveys. It's because of ion debris and large noble gas rings in galactic orbits. An eclipse, for instance, will suddenly block differential starlight—then the Extrasolar Array detects the asteroid."

"Oh," Tom remarked, unenthused.

"It should process the exact cause in a few seconds." She kept her eyes on the screen. Then—

NOW OCCURRING IN M34 BLUE-DWARF SYSTEM ECLIPTIC VESTRAL DUE TO OCCULATORIC UMBRA

Sharon and Tom both stared at the last word. Squinting, Tom began, "An occulatoric—"
"Umbra," Sharon finished.

PART SIX

"Here we have no everlasting city,
but we seek one to come."

—*Hebrews 13:14*

(I)

Brigid saw black. Just black, with the faintest razor-line streaks of perfect white that could only be stars. She was "running." Flying, bodiless.

She was free.

Her psychic eyes felt bereft of lids. The breath-like discorporate *thing* that was her face felt exponentially more alive than flesh. Now her *soul* was her body, stripped of flaw and physical stricture.

Carry me away. . . .

Time meant nothing. The notion of distance was pointless. On she soared, but racing toward—*what?*

She pondered what might happen if her physical

body—back in its desensitized cell—simply died. Would she be free like this forever?

She could not imagine anything so perfect.

Next, she began to *see*.

She saw a green border, like a fence. She saw an immense square hundreds of miles high that seemed surrounded by the fence. Closer, the fence began to sparkle, as if impressed with swarms of tiny lights or lit gemstones.

Closer.

Then, closer.

She saw now that the immense square was actually a cube. It shined like nothing she could ever describe. *Golden glass* was the only simile she could think of.

The cube had twelve entrances—twelve gates.

The gates stood open, inviting her.

God be praised! she thought and glided into one of the gates, for know she knew where she truly was, just as General-Vicar had promised when he'd whispered to her over the sensory-dep cell's intercom the single focus-word:

"Heaven."

(II)

Heaven? Sharon thought.

The chapter before her eyes described Heaven.

But the moment of truth—or at least truth as some perceived it to be—was at hand.

At 0700 hours, the General-Vicar had called Sharon, Tom, Dr. Esther, and Simon into the conference cove. A holoscreen angled up at each of them, the screen itself lit with *The Revelation of St. John the Divine*.

The Holy Bible's final missive: The Book of Revelation.

"This is most difficult, but most wondrous," Luke told them. "I am now obliged to reveal our mission's objective in its entirety, and when I'm done, all of you—all of you faithful Christians—will realize the magnitude of this blessing."

"What gives, sir?" Tom asked. "There's a lot of weird shit going on in this ship. We deserve answers."

"You'll get them," Luke promised. "All of you."

"Where are the rest of the securitechs?" came Tom's next brusk query.

"They've been posted on routine patrols about the ship. Their purpose here is topical. They don't need to know what I'm about to tell the four of you and, to be frank, I don't think many of them could handle it."

"Why isn't Brigid here, sir?" Sharon asked.

"She is . . . indisposed at the moment."

What did that mean? The cove seemed to hang in silence, as if anticipating a sudden cacophony.

General-Vicar Luke maintained his staunch military poise and tone of voice, but Sharon, for the first time, detected something beneath the trained veneer. Something exuberant.

"I'll begin by telling you this," he said. "Eighteen months ago, our most recently deployed Extrasolar Array began feeding back a series of partial analytical messages from the north celestial quadrant, something—a possible planet or asteroid—located between earth and the constellation known at Ursa Minor."

"The Little Dipper," someone said.

"Grid triangulations confirmed that—what I'll refer to for a moment as—the target-object was relatively close on the tracking point, only about ninety billion miles. The Federate Exploratory Corp immediately launched sub-light probes, and one of these probes landed on the target-object."

Tom scowled. "Come on, sir. What's this all about? And why are we sitting here with New Testament files open in front of us?"

Luke ignored the question and went on: "An asteroid indeed had been charted, but with features that clearly aren't natural."

Now the cove really quieted down.

Luke projected a large holomural at the front of the cove.

A cube, Sharon thought. *And . . . a fence.*

The diagram on the mural matched the inexplicable analysis file she'd seen on Kim's station-link.

"It looks like a tiny fence—" Dr. Esther began.

"Yes, a fence is one way of describing it," Luke affirmed. "Or more accurately a *wall*. The spectroscopic surveys that were uplinked from our probe to the Extrasolar Array determined that this *wall* is composed of exactly twelve different crystalline compounds, the most significant of which is a vitreous form of quartz known as—"

"Jasper," Sharon said aloud without thinking.

Luke looked at her. "That's right, Specialist. A once-valuable gemstone known as jasper. Other constituents of this wall included sapphire, calcedony, emerald, beryl, amethyst, and others. Look at your holoscreens. Read Chapter 22, verse 19."

Sharon read the words of the Apostle John:

And the foundations of the wall of the city were garnished with all manner of precious stones. The first foundation was jasper; the second, sapphire; the third, a calcedony; the forth, an emerald. . . .

"Go to verse 16."
And the city lieth four-square, and the length is as large as the breadth—

"A . . . cube," Simon muttered.

—and the city measured twelve thousand furlongs. The length and the breadth and the heighth of it are equal.

My God, Sharon thought.
The holomural flashed a new image, something Sharon had already seen but had no way of understanding: another one of Kim's File and Store analyses.

Re: MADAM and ESA-2 Photospectroscopy Probe Order
De: Data Reg c/o Security Corp

READ: Cartographical Probe results: positive for Target-Object (interior) configuration.

—fixed geometric object (in exactitude):
HEIGHT: 1500 unrefracted miles.
LENGTH: 1500 unrefracted miles.
WIDTH: 1500 unrefracted miles.

Observations: Target-Object exists as a fixed perimeter in geometric exactitude.

The gravity of the situation roughened Luke's voice: "In the First Century A.D., John describes the city of

Heaven as being surrounded by a wall of precious gems, the first foundation of which is jasper. Then he describes the physical dimensions of Heaven itself: a cube that is 12,000 furlongs high, wide, and long. A furlong is an eighth of a mile."

Another screen flashed:

12,000 furlongs = 1,500 miles

By now, no one really needed to be told, but Luke clarified it anyway. "The technology that God has given us the intelligence to develop has now revealed to the Holy Christian Federate . . . the actual physical location of Heaven."

Tom's voice sounded parched. "And we're going there. Now."

"Yes," Luke confirmed.

(III)

No one said anything to anyone for hours. Sharon sat in her data cove, pretending to work, pretending to monitor the holoscreens as if it really meant anything at this point. Now, the JESUS IS WATCHING YOU sign seemed inhibiting. Tom remained in the same room, pacing back and forth, muttering under his breath. Brigid lay motionless in her sensory-deprivation cell, her consciousness elsewhere. The other securitechs were none the wiser, simply walking their guardposts and checking their bulkheads. General-Vicar Luke sat quietly in his quarters, reading Chapter 21 of *The Revelation of John the Divine* over and over again. Commander-Deaconness Esther stood alone in the obcove, staring at the stars, silently reveling in their wonder.

And Warrant Officer Simon—

(IV)

Hurry, he told himself. *Can't get caught in here.*

The makeshift thesium[240] sheath fit precisely over the switch-coupler, just as they'd told him it would. The radiation-depleted cap would block any and all tampering sensors that the securitechs might be using in their heightened state of alert; it would sufficiently hide the tiny transceiver that Simon had just spliced into the coupler.

Yes. There.

It was just a simple trigger-override . . . but what he'd connected it to was one of the ship's nuclear driveheads. Simon fingered the toothpick sized firing device that he'd attached to the inside of his uniform sleeve. All he need do now was snap the device in half and break the safety circuit.

The drivehead would detonate instantly.

The ship would be destroyed, and its destruction would be picked up by the radsensors on the Extrasolar Array. The Edessa would never return, leaving the Pope and the Vatican Security Council to determine that God's wrath was the cause, that humankind had stepped too far. It would maintain proof of God's existence, but project a formidable warning sign: DON'T COME BACK.

But Simon had no intention of sacrificing himself for the mission. He would flee the ship in an escape skiff, to be secretly picked up later by a Federate Intel rescue cruiser.

There, he thought. *Done. Time to get out of here.*

But when he turned around to leave, there was a flechette pistol pointing right in his face.

Simon froze.

Holy fuckin' SHIT!

His captor stood in a slanted shadow. All he could see was the gun, its ROUND IN CHAMBER light blinking green.

He tried to speak but fear made him mute. No lie, however intricate nor convincing, would work now. He'd been caught red-handed.

Only one option remained.

I-I-I have to detonate now.

It would only take a second for him to finger the firing device in his uniform and snap it in half. Even if he was shot in the process, chances were he could do it before he died.

His hand tremored at his side, his brain ordering it to move.

Do it! Do it!

But he couldn't.

He simply didn't have the balls to sacrifice himself for his duty.

He gave up. "Who are you?" he asked, defeated.

"Who do you think it is, you stupid asshole!"

Commander-Deaconness Esther stepped out of the shadow, lowered the pistol.

Simon nearly passed out. "You scared the shit out of me! I thought I was caught! What are you doing here?"

"Watching your back," Esther gruffed in reply. "The securitechs are all over the place. You were supposed to wait till shift change."

Only now did Simon's heart resume a normal beat.

"I hacked into the post roster. They won't check here again for another twenty minutes."

Esther seemed alleviated, if only slightly. "You should've stuck to the plan. You were supposed to rig the drivehead while I was decrypting the launch sequence for the escape skiff."

"Calm down, it's set to go off at my command. I just wanted to save some time," Simon assured her. Already, though, the sight of her was making him tremble. His eyes roved the obvious curves of her body through her uniform, the large, high breasts jutting.

Her mouth turned up in a half-smile. "Save time?" She stepped right up to him, planted her hand to his crotch. "Save time for who?"

"Fuh-fuh-fuh—for *you* . . ."

They embraced at once, kissing ravenously.

God, I love you, Simon thought. Her kisses melted him.

Esther gently pushed him away after a last, wet kiss. "Not now. Later."

"Why *not* now?" he pleaded.

She began walking away. "I have to go give that civilian bitch in sensory-dep some serious brain-damage," she said.

Simon's heart was thudding as he looked after her, watched her turn and walk out.

(V)

It was a labyrinth.

Perfection . . .

Brigid was like water; she was like music; she was like perfumed air. She *swept* through Heaven's every recess, marveling at the sacred visions. Stratum upon stratum: ten thousand tiers of pristine light for every holy mile. Truly, this could be the tabernacle for un-numbered immortal souls joined in one faith, one love—a single flawless devotion.

A cube. A four-square. Geometrically inviolate, the-oretically without limit. Invulnerable.

The true Temple of the Lord.

It's all true! It's all true! she rejoiced.

The tabernacle's clear golden glass stretched on—forever. Like a crystal whose facets reflected and re-fracted light without end. Life was the light. Light was the spirit everlasting.

She soared and soared, looked on and on. Then—

Wait a minute, she thought.

If this was the tabernacle for the souls of the virtu-ous, then where were they?

Where were the souls?

Moreover: Where were the Angels?

Where was *God?*

Brigid's psychical senses lit up—in terror.

She was remote-viewing into the physical depths of Heaven, but—

Heaven was empty.

(VI)

The nanobots, even at their smallest, could not be ad-ministered by a dermal air-shot, and she didn't dare risk leaving a microneedle puncture on the skin.

Transvaginally would be so much safer.

This is more like it, Commander-Deaconness Es-ther thought. Simon's Federate Intel channels had provided the best decryption programs; she'd broken the security door's unbreakable password in all of a second.

Now she knelt before the open cell, gazing down at the nude, insentient body, envious of Brigid's long mane of hair and vibrant, young skin. Brigid's breasts shined as if shellacked in the warm pool of glycerene. Esther couldn't help but touch them, squeeze them, as she felt a plush flash in her gut. She soothed a finger between the submerged sex, explored the slick folds, rubbed her thumb over the nutlike clitoris.

The urge to masturbate seized her; she could even see herself stripping, climbing into the cell. But she knew she couldn't; she knew she mustn't waste time.

She could come back, she realized. *Then I'd have to drown her.*

Instead, she quickly slipped the aspirate-line into Brigid's vagina, slipped it up deep. The line was filled with saline, and at its other end was the injector full of preprogrammed nanobots. Esther had programmed them herself: using their microscopic cutters, they would progress up through Brigid's prone body until they reached the brain, whereupon they would decimate the central sulcus, leaving the attractive remote-viewer in an untreatable coma. Eventually, the nanobots would be destroyed themselves by the resultant immune-system response of microphages and T-cells.

Esther's thumb rested on the injector's dispersal button. She continued to stare down at Brigid's motionless, shining body.

Where are you? Esther wondered. *Are you in Heaven?*

She pushed the dispersal button.

Stay there.

(V)

"So. You believe all this?"

It was Tom who broke the long silence in the cove. Sharon, in her own musings, had nearly forgotten that he was even there.

Sharon manned her holoscreens. "I suppose so," she said. "Why shouldn't I?"

"Consider the source."

"The General-Vicar? Why would he lie?"

He cast her a sour look. "I don't know, but I can't think of a single reason why I should believe that we've located the actual physical celestial coordinates for Heaven."

"What's so hard to believe?" she countered. "It makes sense when you think about it. Where else would God be but in space? God gave us brains, God gave us the ability to achieve. We've achieved the technological capability to explore deep space. Why shouldn't we use that—a gift from God—to *go* to God?"

"I'm not buying it," Tom said.

"Look at the Bible then. *Daniel, Ezekiel, Job, Numbers,* and many other books all make references to Heaven's exact description, which all correspond to the *ultimate* description in *Revelation*."

"Big deal. The authors ripped each other off. Saint John had a hallucination. Besides, we don't even know if the Apostle John really *wrote Revelation*. The syntax between John's Gospel and *Revelation* are different."

"He was bilingual," Sharon pointed out.

"Yeah, and he wrote *Revelation* while in exile on one of the Dodecanese islands; he was malnourished and mentally traumatized. Most scholars say *Revelation* was written in 96 A.D.—that would put John at at least 75 years old; back then, that was the same as living to be 110 today. You're telling me that a 110-year-old man could've written something as articulate as *Revelation?*"

Sharon wasn't concerned. "Moses lived to be 120. He was 80 when he parted the Red Sea. God extends the lives of the Prophets. I have no problem with that."

"It could just be *interpretation,* Sharon. Symbolism, metaphor. In 96 A.D. John was an infirm old man, probably senile, probably delusional. He had a weird dream and wrote it down. Right now we're nuke-dragging into uncharted space at several billion miles an hour because more than 2000 years ago a senile old man had a *weird dream.*"

"John also wrote 'Jesus cried with a loud voice, Lazarus, come out. And he that was dead came forth.' You believe that, don't you?"

Tom didn't answer.

"And you saw the spectrometric surveys yourself," Sharon went on. "The cube is *exactly* 1500 standard miles in length, width, and height. Is it a *coincidence* that John's dimensions of 12000 furlongs *exactly* equates to 1500 *exact* miles? 1500 *even?* Not 1501? Not 1499.99? The chances of that are billions to one when you consider the fact that the standard 5,280-foot mile didn't even *exist* until the *year* 1500. That's more than 1400 years *after* John wrote *Revelation.*"

Again, Tom had no rebuke.

Sharon turned on the cove's broad holomural, which threw before them the constellation Ursa Minor. Then she quoted *The Book of Job:* " 'He stretch-eth out the *north* over the empty place, and hangeth the earth upon nothing.' The Old Testament and New abound with references that associate Heaven with a northerly direction in general and the North Star in particular. Where are we now, Tom?"

"The North Celestial Quadrant," he droned back.

"And what's that you're looking at right now at the end of the Little Dipper?"

"Alpha Ursae Minoris," he admitted. "The North Star."

Sharon quickly quoted more of the *Revelation:* "John describes God as 'He that holdeth the seven stars in his right hand.' How many stars do you see in Ursa Minor, Tom? Eight? Six? Fifty?"

"Seven," Tom answered.

Sharon rested her case. She should be praying, not arguing with an agnostic.

"I guess time will tell," he said a few moments later.

Yes.

But they both jumped at the sudden sound of an op-stat alarm. Footfalls quickly trampled outside the cove, down the accessmain. Sharon and Tom peeked out, saw Simon, Esther, and the General-Vicar running toward the elevator.

"What the hell's going on?" Tom said.

"We better go find out—"

(VII)

The sight dragged across Sharon's eyes like a thorned branch.

Oh no! Please, NO!

They'd followed the others up to the Edessa's restricted Lab Station. Brigid lay nude in a long, opened tank of viscid fluid as Simon and Esther rushed to administer aid. Aside, monitors beeped, lights flashed.

General-Vicar Luke's face looked sunken by the

gravity of remorse. "She's back, and . . . I suppose I should've considered this possibility."

"What possibility, sir?" Sharon nearly raged. "What's happening here?"

Brigid looked death-white. She didn't move at all when a submerged rack lifted her out of the fluid. In moments they'd gotten her up onto a lev-gurney and hooked it up to a small ICU in the cove. When the overhead lumes snapped on, Sharon quailed.

There was blood trickling all over the place.

Blood leaked from Brigid's nose, ears, and the corners of her eyes. More blood pooled on the exam platform between her legs. Soon it was dripping to the floor in steady *plips*.

Esther air-shot a coagulant, keeping a fast eye on the metabolic holoscreens that Simon was opening all around. Autoneedles descending, their infrared sensors locating veins and infusing new blood.

Tom squeezed Sharon's hand tightly. "She must've been RV-ing," he whispered. "Something went wrong."

"She's stabilizing," Esther called out. She glanced over her shoulder to Luke. "We've stopped the hemorrhaging but . . ."

"But *what!*" Sharon exclaimed.

Esther sighed. "Life support will probably keep her alive, but I'm afraid the bleeding was considerable. She's suffered multiple microscopic arterial perforations and several cerebral strokes."

Luke began, "Will she—"

"Regain consciousness?" Esther said. "No, I'm afraid not. She's lost all motor function as well as a good portion of active blood supply to the brain."

"She'll remain in a PVS," Simon added, "a Persistent-Vegetative State—until she dies."

Sharon felt crushed.

"She agreed to the survey," Luke said dolefully. "But I authorized it. I felt it was necessary, considering the seriousness of our mission."

Tom spoke up. "She was RV-ing, out . . . there, right?"

"To the target-object, yes," Luke said.

But Sharon thought: *To Heaven. She went to Heaven.* . . . "Sir, what did you mean when you said you should've considered this possibility? What possibility?"

"That even as a psychic vessel, her senses could not have held up to—well, to what we hoped she would see."

"I don't understand."

"Scripture makes no secret of the effect that God's true countenance might have on physical humans. 'Too beauteous to be beheld by man.' 'No man hath seen God at any time.' 'Thou canst not see My face: for shall no man see me and live.' In our physical forms of flesh and blood, we are too inferior to view God. That's why God appeared to Moses as a Burning Bush, to Elijah as wind, to Jacob as sapphire light." Luke seemed convinced. "God is perfection, but in our *im*perfection we cannot see Him until we are taken to him in death."

They all looked down at Brigid.

"Brigid's sacrifice is a noble one," Luke continued. "She has seen the face of God."

After they all left the Lab, Brigid began to twitch. Her eyes remained blank, but eventually her lips began to move and then her voice croaked in the dimmest whisper:

"Not . . . God . . . Not . . . God . . ."

But by then no one remained in the Lab to hear her.

234

PART SEVEN

"We hath made a covenant with death,
and with hell we are in agreement."
—*Isaiah 28:15*

(I)

Seven hours later, the C.F.S. Edessa assumed a para-spacial orbit around the newly discovered sub-asteroidal body. The occulatoric umbra had reached its peak, plunging the ship into absolute darkness. Every holomural onboard showed just that: black. No stars. No light refractions. No ecliptic edges.

Just black.

In the launch dock, the ship's Lenticular Re-Entry Vehicle was being prepared for debarkation.

Sharon sat in the LRV's navigational mod, helping Tom go down the pre-flight checklist. The blinking readout displays threw stippled light across her face.

"This just gets dumber and dumber," Tom complained from the pilot's mod. "I can't believe that Luke's making us do this."

"The mission is authorized by the Pope," Sharon reminded him.

"Yeah? Well then the Pope must've passed his fuckin' brains the last time he took a shit."

"That's blasphemy!"

"Aw, stow it, will ya? Is everyone going nuts around here but me?" Tom's scowl cut into his face. "All right, let's just say for a minute that this whole cluster-fuck shebang *isn't* a crock of crap. Let's just say that it really is Heaven down there."

"It *is* Heaven," Sharon insisted.

"Fine. It's Heaven. Peachy. So what are we doing? We're going to fucking *land* on Heaven?"

"Yes."

Tom glared at her. "What the fuck for?"

Sharon ground her teeth at the expletive. "To give thanks to God!" she yelled back.

"Sharon, it makes no sense. It's a fucking affront to logic. You heard Luke. 'Thou canst not see My face: for shall no man see me and live.' We're going to go and knock on God's front door to say hi? It looks to me like Brigid did that . . . and look what happened to her."

"I agree with the General-Vicar. By coming here, we're proving to God that we've made the best of what He's given us. It's the ultimate gesture of praise. God gave humans their instincts. It's in our instincts to seek God. God won't kill us for using the sum of all our knowledge to seek Him."

"Great. He won't kill us. He'll put us all into a fucking coma instead, like He did to Brigid."

"That was just a psychic accident," Sharon felt sure. "Brigid made a praiseworthy sacrifice. We're just going to take some readings, make some observations—heighten our knowledge of God and His domain."

Tom just shook his head. "Well, then I guess being this close to God is making everyone fucked up in the head. Everyone except me."

"You're so arrogant . . . and so afraid," Sharon told him. 'Put out thine hand to God, and God will take it.'" She let it rest from there. *He just doesn't understand.* They continued matching the pre-launch checklist for a while, then Sharon asked: "So who gets to go?"

"Me, Luke, Simon, and the securitechs," he roughly answered.

Sharon fidgeted in her seat. "I want to go too."

"You're not on the EVA list."

"But couldn't you talk to the General-Vicar?" she hinted.

"No. Correction: *fuck* no."

She rolled her eyes. "Tom, I'm asking a personal favor. I want to go too. You could persuade the General-Vicar into letting me go. I can run scanners and probe relays. It's really important to me."

"Well, let me see, let me think about this. . . ." He frowned at her. "Forget it. It ain't happening."

"Tom! *Please!*"

"Not in a million fuckin' years. If you got killed, I'd be responsible, and in case you haven't noticed, I'm the kind of guy who doesn't want to be responsible for *anything* except his own ass."

The prep buzzer went off. The issue was settled. "Time for us to both get out of here," Tom said. "I have to go suit up and get ready to drive this piece of shit. I'm a fuckin' flunky chauffeur in an EVA suit."

Damn it, Sharon thought, and switched off her system consoles.

Tom climbed out of the pilot mod, prepared to leave the LRV. But he stopped at the air-lock, hesitant, then—

"What are you—"

—kissed Sharon hard on the mouth.

Her initial instinct was to recoil . . . but that only lasted a moment. Next she was kissing him back, desperate in his firm embrace. She wanted to be wrapped up in him. She wanted to be carried away. . . .

A second later, though, the kiss broke. "That's in case I don't come back," he said, and was leaving. "Which I probably won't."

She watched after him, still swarmy from the kiss. *God be with you,* she thought and sighed.

(II)

As Simon made furious love to her in the med unit, Esther's own pleasure hummed. The wireless voltaic-clips applied to her nipples and clitoris provided a roving circuit of gentle electrosonic current, tickling her nerves. In truth, Esther far preferred machinery to flesh when it came to sex.

They were both nude, floating in the mid-air of the cove, thanks to the anti-grav harnesses they wore. Simon loved it that way. As for Esther, she simply pretended to love it too, just as she'd been taught. Instead, she concentrated on the electrosonic pleasure provided by the clips.

Generally these games bored her. Her training as a medical officer afforded her this ideal cover from the Federate Army, but long before that she'd been rigorously trained as a sex-op: she'd seen everything. She'd met men—bishops and generals alike—who longed to be beaten, tied up and gagged, whipped, and much else. Hence, Simon's little anti-gravity quirks seemed trifling to a woman of Esther's experience. It had been the director of Federate Intel himself who'd personally assigned Esther and Simon to go undercover together on this mission.

She knew exactly what their plan was.

Esther revolved in the air, and wrapped her legs around Simon's head. His tongue lapped desperately at the groove of her hairless sex. She returned the gesture via fellatio—another act she'd had considerable training in.

She didn't really like Simon at all; he was an arrogant prick, devious as a weasel. But it had been his idea—back when suspicions of a "stowaway" had been rife—that they accuse each other of spying, and it had worked. The hostile outburst had made them both seem innocent when actually they were *both* spies. Defeating the polygraph programs had been the easiest part; thanks to Simon's FCI decryption code, she'd merely overridden their actual results with generic ones. Simple.

She floated backwards in mid-air, rubbing out the last of her climax as Simon's own orgasm broke in her mouth.

Then they just hovered for a time, in the deep-space "afterglow."

They both eventually stepped out of their harnesses, began to redress. The tight smile on Simon's face told her that he actually believed he'd satisfied her.

The stupid fool honestly believes that I love him.

She smiled herself at *that* thought.

(III)

At 0614 hrs, the occulatoric umbra cast by planets in the distant M34 blue-dwarf system began to break. Sunlight—from another sun—began to level upon the newly discovered and yet unnamed sub-asteroidal body, and as that body's rare optical libration began to turn, it became fully visible. Not spheric at all, but a rough angled rock in space with approximately the same surface area of Saturn's largest moon.

At 0616 hrs, the Edessa's Lenticular Re-Entry Vehicle blew its rail-locks. It fell lazily from the ship's launch-bay, then fired a single one-second burst from its primary thruster.

Heading for Heaven.

Seeing the figures on screen hadn't prepared any of them.

"Jesus Christ," Simon whispered as he stared through the LRV's active-glexan viewports. General-Vicar Luke spared a frown at the use of the Savior's name in vain, though he too was clearly shaken.

Tom couldn't believe what he was seeing. No, seeing the mere numeric measurements in no way readied him for the actual visual confirmation of the "target-object."

"I've never even imagined anything so large," Simon remarked.

"It's as big as a planetoid," Tom compared.

Luke cut them off from his flight seat beside Tom. "It's a miracle. It's proof of the incalculable greatness of God."

Tom, at this point, was not inclined to object.

A cube of golden glass. Fifteen-hundred miles square. On earth, its base would cover most of former North America. Its height would ascend roughly 1400 miles past the terminus of the atmosphere, and its sheer mass would cause a regular axial orbit to deviate.

Here, though, it just *hung,* as if it had *grown* out of the barren sub-asteroid's flat surface.

"Alpha bias set at zero," Tom recited, trying to retain some semblance of protocol. "Data bus and OMS inhibitors enabled on my mark."

At 20,000 miles they could see it all. Tom adjusted the LRV's forward trim, upped the port magnification to 3.0, then 100.0.

"God in Heaven," someone said.

You got that right, Tom thought. *A cube. Golden glass. Nothing more.*

"Turn up the magnification," Luke ordered.

"We're maxed out, sir."

Another order. "Engage all sensor systems. I want everything recorded."

"All holosystems are running. Stereoisometers enabled. Spectral chromatographs enabled. Photo-spec, hexo-recorders, and elemental index systems are on," Tom reeled off.

Luke maintained a scrutinizing gaze at the viewport. "But I don't see any—"

The object's surface seemed totally bereft of features.

"You don't see any *what,* sir?" Tom asked.

"No signs of any point of ingress," Simon remarked. "No entrance, no exit."

"No gates," Luke finished. "But they've got to be there. Each vertical surface should possess three gates." He quoted John the Divine: " 'And the City had twelve gates, and the gates twelve angels.' "

"I don't see no angels," Tom said, "and I don't see no gates."

"Each surface of the cube is over two million square miles," Simon figured. "It might take some looking."

"So unless Saint John was drunk off his ass," Tom queried, "when we find one of these gates, there's gonna be an angel waiting for us? Come on, this is crap. It's a metaphor."

"Shut up, Private!" Luke barked. "Just do your job and shut up."

Tom didn't shut up. "Since nobody else is making suggestions, then I will. Saint John also mentioned the wall, the wall of jasper and eleven other precious gems that surrounds the firmament of Heaven. That would be at the foundation of the cube, right?"

Luke considered this. "Yes. Go to the wall," he ordered.

At 1431 hrs, they were there.

At 1450 hrs, they found a gate.

At 1515 hrs, the EVA team disembarked. The feet of human beings walked upon the blazing gold skin of Heaven.

(IV)

Poor Brigid.

Sharon looked down at the comatose body of her friend. They'd moved her to the better-equipped ICU in the Med Unit. Monitor lights flashed feebly. The steady beeps seemed drastically slower than Sharon's own heart beat.

She touched the white skin of Brigid's hand. It felt deathly cold.

Don't worry, Brigid. 'Fear ye not, be still, and behold the salvation of the Lord.'

Sharon left the cove. Her own monitoring duties were moot now; no abort directive would be forthcoming. In the nearest holomural, space stared back at her. The LRV was long dispatched.

Suddenly she felt desperately alone. She thought of Jonah trapped in the belly of a massive fish as God persuaded him to go to Nineveh.

This, she thought, peering into space, *is our Nineveh. We travail to love and serve the Lord.*

Commander-Deaconness Esther was nowhere to be found. *Shouldn't she be here, trying to revive Brigid? But this was just naive and wishful thinking. Brigid's not coming back. Eventually, she'll die, and go to Heaven.*

Sharon's eyes focused on the holomural.

Out there. So close. Heaven . . .

She tried not to contemplate it. Perhaps she wasn't supposed to. Nevertheless, errant questions pried their way into her mind.

What will it be like?
What will they find?
Will they truly find God?

General-Vicar Luke had implied that the mission was expressly not to *find* God; instead, their EVA excursion would be brief and precise—just a quick topographical survey, some elemental probe readings, little else.

But then she wondered about simple human nature. How could they limit themselves to those parameters once they were there? Would it even be *possible?*

Sharon wandered about the ship. It seemed much larger—and so much more vast—when she considered its emptiness. Eventually she found herself in the vacant Central Communications Unit.

They'd be close enough for standard radio contact.

Would she be violating her orders by establishing radio communication? *I don't see why,* she reasoned. After all, nobody told her *not* to.

It can't hurt to at least listen in.

Sharon knew she had no authorization, but she turned the main commset on anyway, then clicked in the LRV's frequency discriminators.

Immediately, the transmission indicator began to blink.

The ship's transmitter is picking up a direct signal from the LRV, she realized at once. But—

No sound.

She couldn't hear the transmission even though the system was on.

Doesn't make sense. She considered looking for Dr. Esther but what good would that do? Esther was just a physician. She had no technical expertise in communications protocol.

Then Sharon considered something else:

Maybe the transmission is encrypted. And maybe . . .

Sharon remembered what Tom had given her.

The biochip that he found on Major Matthew's body.

She'd put it in her pocket, hadn't she?

Her finger slipped into her pocket. She plucked out the chip.

Should I or shouldn't I?

She decided that she should. *There's no harm in trying,* she asserted to herself, *and I'm probably wrong anyway.*

When she plugged the tiny chip into the peripheral jack, it occurred to her at once that she wasn't wrong.

The transmission came through loud and clear: the LRV's cabin intercom evidently.

Voices exploded:

"—for emergency thrust-off now!"

"What the fuck for?"

"Just do it!"

Sharon recognized the voices. Tom and Warrant Officer Simon. They were yelling.

Tom: "Where's Luke?"

Simon: "Dead!"

Tom: "Where are the securitechs?"

Simon: "Dead! All dead! Those things out there killed them all!"

Sharon froze up.

What's happening down there!

She grabbed the handset, was about to call back to them when—

She squealed.

She was grabbed by the hair from behind, yanked backward. She heard a soft *fffft!*, felt a tiny sting at the side of her neck. Then she collapsed.

Sharon was paralyzed.

"Snoopy bitch. I never did like you."

Commander-Deaconness Esther smiled down at Sharon's fully conscious yet completely immobile form. She held an air-shot injector in her hand. "Don't worry, little virgin. It's just a paralytic agent. You won't die."

Sharon's brain commanded her to get up, to flee.

But nothing happened.

She tried to scream, but couldn't even open her mouth.

"Let's go, little virgin," the voice boomed above. Sharon was lifted up and slammed down hard on a lev-slat. Then she was being carried away.

PART EIGHT

"Lucifer, the morning star, hath infinite faces."
                                        —*Mammon 1:3*

(I)

Nightmare.

Or—was she dead?

Utter blackness prolapsed into a nameless demense. The ushers rose. . . .

She saw a vast scarlet twilight and a black moon and six black stars whose black light bathed an infernal terrascape. Beyond stood a city, a firmament of inversions—a raging mephistopolis whose highest edifice winked at its peak like a beacon of luminous blood. Sharon's vision trailed away on stinking, hot winds, shooting through abyssal canyons and abhorrent boulevards as though it were a scream itself. In one canyon, a horde of the naked and the starved had been packed like cattle within a fence of fiery bones. Golem-like attendants shouldered through their midst, hand-picking—with stout three-fingered hands—this horrid night's select play-things. They were dragged over the fence by fingers hooked into eyes, screaming blood, ejecting innards with their shrieks. Heads were prized apart, raw brains rowed through by the fat taloned fingers. One man was being broiled alive on a spit, another was eviscerated with one fast swipe of a talon. The guts were then summarily forced into the victim's mouth and he was forced to eat. Women fared worse, plundered for sexual possibilities that defied all human imagination. Gravid wombs were pricked by ancient bone-slivers, jettisoning fetuses and placentae onto hot slabs of stone. Afterbirth was lapped up by demon-tongues, like stew; children were slowly garrotted by glistening, blood-swollen umbilicals.

Hail, Belphegor!

Oily smoke bubbled from pores in million-year-old rock.

Hail, Asmodeus!

Screams rose as a song.

Hail, Satan!

Dark chuckles abounded as the endless workings of hell ground on and on.

One woman, whose face had been peeled off her skull as effortlessly as a stocking mask, flailed as she was raped *en masse* by these ushers of the abyss, and when they'd all sated themselves, they drowned the woman in a steaming stack of their own feces.

Horns sprouted from the lead usher's wedgelike head. He picked up the woman's flensed face and stretched it over a stalagmite, displaying it, like a trophy, for all to see. It was Sharon's face.

She jerked awake, a dead scream on her lips.

"That must've been some nightmare."

Eventually Sharon's clouded vision began to focus. Dr. Esther was looking with some interest at a diagnostic holoscreen. In a few blinks, Sharon knew that she'd been relocated to the main Med Unit.

"Your EET was all over the place," Esther pointed out, "your little *locus ceruleus* throbbing away, delta activity spiking off the screen." Esther patted Sharon's thigh. "Poor little virgin had a bad dream."

Sharon tried to speak but only a coarse mutter escaped. She'd been spread out on a lev-gurney, her waist braced down. The brace, though, seemed hardly necessary. When she tried to move her fingers, nothing happened. Her toes—nothing. She couldn't even incline her head.

"You'll be able to talk soon. The Curarix will wear off in an hour or so." Esther held up the minuscule biochip. "Where did you get this? From Matthew, I'll bet. We knew he was suspicious about something. Good thing we killed the old man when we did."

We? Sharon thought. She tried to talk again, failed again. But this time, her lips seemed to actually move a little.

Esther held up the silver de-jam gun, clacked its trigger several times to watch the bolt fire and then retract. "You should've seen the way he was flopping on the floor when I punched this bolt into his brain." Then she set down the gun and returned her attention to her console, into which she plugged the biochip. "You're industrious, I'll give you that." Another holoscreen opened. "I'll bet you'd love to know what went on down there, hmm? On Heaven?"

Sharon stared up through dry eyes.

"It really is Heaven, you know. Federate Intel has known all about it since the initial probes were launched last year." Esther smiled. "But we sent the probes without informing the Vatican. *We* know what's really there, but the *Pope* doesn't."

Sharon's thought processes churned through the diminishing paralysis.

Esther's smile tightened. "God's not there anymore, little virgin, and He hasn't been for a long time."

It can't be true!

Esther's graceful hand smoothed up over Sharon's uniform front, smoothed over the young breasts and squeezed.

The words warbled through the grin. "Heaven has been infested by demons. . . ."

Still a dream, Sharon forced the thought. *Still a nightmare. God lives! God is all-powerful and He will protect the righteous!*

"Saint Matthew said 'How great is that darkness!' and John: 'Men love darkness rather than light, because their deeds are evil.'" The hand rubbed more urgently, sliding lower. "And you know what? They were right. God and Christ and all the Angels got so disgusted with the evil of mankind that They left."

Sharon refused to believe it.

"And someone else moved in."

Sharon fought against the agent in her blood, shouting at herself to move. Feeling was beginning to return—unfortunately through the demented caresses of the doctor. Her utilities, now, had been unseamed down to the braces, Esther's warm hand probing the bare breasts.

"Don't worry, the EVA team weren't *all* killed. Simon's on his way back now, in the LRV. And so is Tom."

Tom!

"And now you're wondering, aren't you? You're wondering if Tom is in on the conspiracy too." She switched on the holoscreen which showed a live-feed from the LRV's cockpit. Tom sat at the control, his face runneled in anger. There was a milliwave pistol at his head—held by Simon.

"Poor Private Thomas—a perfect dupe. Too bad you'll never get your chance to fuck him." Esther's hand cupped Sharon's pubis, rubbing intently down. "You wanted to give your virginity to him, didn't you? That vulgar uneducated flunky. I'll tell you what—*I'll* fuck him, and make you watch. Then I'll cuff him in the tome and transfuse his blood with butylmercuric acid. And I'll make you watch that too."

Sharon's paralysis felt like a ton of dead weight on her chest. Tendons stood out in her neck as she continued to try to move.

"But here's something for you to watch first." Esther walked a few steps deeper in the cove, to the exam table on which Brigid lay even more paralyzed than Sharon. Brigid had been stripped naked. "I injected her with nanobots," Esther informed. "They severed all the synaptic connections in the central sulcus—she can't move, but she *can* feel." She sealed Brigid's mouth with a tight palm, then pinched the nostrils shut. In a few moments Brigid's prone body began to convulse.

Stop it! You'll kill her!

Next, the unit's surgical microlaser was powered up; Esther deftly wielded its hand-held emission tip in her hand and—

pzzzzt! pzzzzt!

—cleanly sliced off Brigid's expansive nipples, leaving cauterized circles in their place. Brigid's back arched up once, then slapped back down to the table.

"Feel good?" Esther asked the comatose form. "Well, I think we can do better than that." She set the laserhead down and picked up a clunky-looking attachment that consisted of a large vulcanized cup connected to a stout tube. "I found this in the Engineering Unit. It's a bilge-pump—they use it to cycle condensation out of the fuel-cell traps." Esther nodded to herself. "But it also works great on humans." Now she pressed the cup firmly over Brigid's mouth and hit a switch.

A tremendous mechanical roar ensued. Brigid's abdomen sucked in.

The roar rose against some preliminary resistence and then broke. The entirety of Brigid's gastrointestinal tract was promptly vacuumed out of her abdominal cavity and redeposited, via the hose, into a large shelved collection bottle on the wall.

For a moment, Brigid's body quivered where it lay, then fell still.

"I like that," Esther said. She hung up the cup and retrieved the laser-head. "But, damn it, call me a completist. . . ."

Sharon screamed within herself as the doctor upped the laser's amperage and intricately severed all of Brigid's toes and fingers, then the hands and feet.

Then the arms and legs in neat six-inch rendings.

The pile of smoking debris grew larger on the floor

as each piece fell. Finally the trunk was sectioned, until all that remained on the table was Brigid's head.

"There." Esther glared down proudly at the pile of pieces. "See if your Jesus Christ can resurrect *that*."

Sharon could only stare in bald horror.

"Hmm. Now. What should we do with *you?*" Esther traipsed back over to the lev-gurney. She lit the laser, waved it before Sharon's eyes. "Cut off that cute little nose and those cute little ears? Section your brain?" Esther shrugged. "Or why not just autopsy you alive?" Next, she displayed a milliwave pistol. "Or maybe I'll bake your heart in your chest with this—until it explodes. Wouldn't that be fascinating?"

Sharon's eyes squeezed shut in prayer. *Please, God. Defend me, deliver me, and protect me. And protect Tom. Please, somehow give Tom the strength to get us out of this. . . .*

A red light blinked overhead. An alarm blared.

"They're back, Sharon. The LRV's pulling back into the launch-dock. And now you're more than likely praying, praying to your God that Tom will somehow save you. But look."

Sharon's eyes flicked up to the holoscreen. Tom was unstrapping himself from the operator's chair, was standing up. But before he could fully rise—

Do it! Please, get it!

—he spun, lunged toward Simon, tried to grab the milliwave pistol.

Too late.

Simon was grinning as he discharged the pistol right between Tom's eyes.

The eyes exploded.

Then the top of Tom's head blew off.

Sharon fainted on the gurney.

It was a snake.

A serpent.

As her consciousness reassembled, Sharon immediately thought of the serpent that coerced Eve. The serpent was Satan.

Memory crashed back.

Tom was dead.

Brigid was dead.

General-Vicar Luke, the securitechs—everyone. They were all dead. Only Sharon remained now, still fettered to the lev-gurney, and Esther and Simon. She watched through the slits of her eyelids. The pieces of Brigid's body had been removed from the exam table, dropped into the cremator, no doubt. Sharon had trouble seeing in detail across the cove, but there was one thing she was sure of: a stout snake lay on the table now, four or five feet long, dead or paralyzed. Esther and Simon hovered over the table, intently examining the snake.

Simon seemed pleased. "Federate Intel wanted a specimen, and they got it. They'll keel over when they see this."

"It's beautiful," Esther whispered. Her eyes beamed as if in reverence.

"I cut it off of Luke after it strangled him."

Snakes, Sharon thought. *Lucifer's first disguise.*

Could she really believe it? That Lucifer and his minions had taken over Heaven as snakes?

Her faith was gone now. She'd be foolish to deny the existence of God when proof of the existence of His nemesis lay right here in the cove.

But God had abandoned Heaven.

God had abandoned her.

There was no point in praying now.

Esther's finger traced down the snake's long green-black body. She was touching an aspect of her *own* god.

"You're both Satanists," Sharon croaked at them. "You're both absolutely evil."

Esther and Simon jerked their gazes around.

"The little virgin finally speaks," Esther announced.

But Simon seemed perturbed. "How come you haven't killed her yet?" he posed to Esther. "We've got to leave soon. You should have killed her hours ago."

"Stop being so cold-hearted," Esther toyed.

"Put her in the disposal chute and flush her into space," Simon ordered. He looked down at the snake. "I'll put this in a cryocase and load it onto the escape skiff."

"Go ahead and kill me," Sharon said through parched lips. "I don't care."

"Look," Simon told the Deaconess. "This isn't the time to be squeamish. If you won't do it, I'll do it." He picked up the laser, was about to turn it on.

"But I was saving her for you, Simon." Esther stroked his back. "What kind of *man* are you? She's a *virgin*."

Simon paused to reflect. "Well. Hmm." He looked at the chronometer.

"And I'd *love* to watch," Esther added in a sultry tone.

"We've still got over twelve hours before we've got to be at the pickup point." The beady eyes ran up Sharon's body. "Come to think of it, it might be fun."

"Oh, good!"

Esther came forward with a pair of snips, began cutting off Sharon's uniform, pulling it out from under her in strips.

Sharon didn't care. She just felt numb.

"So pretty. So sleek." Esther grinned down at Sharon's nudity. She parted Sharon's legs on the gurney, ran her hands up and down inside of her thighs. "So warm and fragile and perfect."

So this was it? This was Sharon's providence after a lifetime of serving God? To be raped and murdered on a deep-space exploratory vessel?

Damn you, God, she thought. *The sins of the world aren't my fault. I loved and served You, and You repay me with this. . . .*

Simon grew flustered, fidgeting in place. He rubbed his own crotch at the sight of her.

"At least tell me why," Sharon's voice grated. "At least give me an explanation. Why this *conspiracy* between the two of you? Why set all those men up for their deaths?"

"Because dead men tell no tales," Simon replied, running a finger around his collar. "No one can know about this—or I should say no one outside of Federate Intel's most exclusive power circles. Especially not the Vatican."

"The man who tried to kill me right after we launched," Sharon began. "You forged his autopsy and genetically altered him to appear as a Red Sect member. Why?"

"Just as a safeguard," Esther answered. "In case things went wrong in some unforeseen way, Red Sect would be blamed. The bomb in his abdominal cavity was supposed to destroy the evidence after the fact, but you and Tom fucked that all up. None of that mattered, though, after we debarked from the Solon Station. He was just a suicide operative, brainwashed and modified. In all, it worked out fine."

"But you two are Federate Intel plants yourself," Sharon pointed out. "Why sabotage the mission at all? The Vatican *authorized* the mission!"

"Yes, the Vatican knows that the Extrasolar Array discovered Heaven, and the Vatican authorized the survey mission. But Federate Intel's preliminary probes told us full well what had happened. And that's something that the Vatican can *never* be told."

"There are four billion Christians on earth. They have a right to know."

Simon laughed. "Think about what you're saying. What? We're supposed to tell the Pope that we found Heaven but that God abandoned it? We're supposed to tell all the Christians of the world that *demons* have taken over Heaven? Don't you understand that we could *never* tell them that?"

"But it's the truth!" Sharon shouted.

"That's irrelevant. The Christian Federate is the most efficient governmental system in the history of mankind. No disease, no poverty. Crime is only one percent of what it was a hundred years ago. Our technical superiority has all but abolished global war. The Eugenics Laws are exponentially perfecting the human species. Everyone's productive, healthy, and happy. And we'd lose all that if the world ever found out what we've discovered here."

"It's crypto-fascism! It's all a lie!"

Simon shrugged. "So what? It works."

Esther continued to fondle Sharon's body. "And it works because the system has produced a population of people like you. Human sin will always rage beneath the surface. Just as it says in your dead New Testament: we're all born in original sin."

"But the Federate, by its very design, can maintain control of the world where no other government could." Simon put his arm around the Commander-Deaconness. "Esther and I have been infiltrating Federate programs for years, on behalf of Federate Intelligence. It's not about power, it's about efficiency. We're the true power behind the Pope, and we always will be. I've armed a nuclear-drivehead to destroy the ship. The Vatican will interpret the Edessa's destruction as the wrath of God. Meanwhile, Esther and I will be secretly picked up by a Federate Intel vessel in an escape skiff. And the world will continue to advance toward perfection."

Sharon felt dead already. It was the truth that had killed her. It was God's abandonment, which paved the way for people like this. . . .

"And speaking of original sin . . ." Simon trembled in precursory excitement. He unseamed the front of his uniform. "It's nothing personal, but . . . I've never had a virgin."

Sharon squirmed against the brace clamped across her waist, but most of her paralysis remained. She could barely move her head from side to side. When she tried to move her hands, only a finger or two twitched. She couldn't even close her legs.

And it was between those legs—that splayed, nude V—that Simon knelt.

"Now I'm gonna bust you open," he whispered. "But don't worry. It'll be good for me."

Sharon closed her eyes, took a deep breath, and just waited for it. It didn't matter now, did it? She'd obeyed God's word and saved her virginity for a good Christian man, a man to be wed to in Jesus' name. Instead she would have it savaged by this loathsome pervert. It was Sharon's fury at God that stultified all of her other emotions.

Simon lowered himself closer. His drool dripped in her face.

Just do it and kill me, you evil son of a bitch.

But then she heard two barely audible sounds—

pzzzt! pzzzzt!

And then he was screaming. It was an ear-splitting, nearly machinelike scream grinding out long and hard.

Sharon heard a *thunk!* and snapped open her eyes. In that instant, Simon was gone. He'd fallen off the gurney before he could penetrate her. Esther was chuckling; an awful scent filled the air.

What happened? Sharon wondered.

Suddenly, though, she became aware of a strange weight down around her thighs.

By now the paralysis had worn off enough for her to incline her head. First she looked up at Esther who stood at the foot of the gurney, smiling, hip-cocked. In her hand she held the laser.

"You didn't really think I was going to let him do it, did you?"

Sharon's eyes darted down. Lying askew between her own legs were *Simon's* legs: severed and instantly cauterized at mid-thigh.

Simon howled like some rough animal in a trap.

"I've always hated that skinny, weasel-faced asshole," Esther commented.

"You fucking BITCH!" he yelled. He was palming his way backward, toward the exit, his stumps smoking before him. "What have you DONE!"

"For one thing, I sure as shit fooled you, as well as the rest of your Intel cronies," Esther coyly replied. "And it wasn't easy."

"WHY?" he shouted. "We had it all planned! It was all working perfectly!"

"Simple minds. You think you've got the Pope in your back pocket? You think you're the secret power behind the Vatican?"

"That's the only way it can be! You KNOW that! We've trained together for YEARS! What in God's name are you doing?"

"Getting rid of a ridiculous little pervert, that's what." Esther aimed the laser at him.

"Who got to you?" Simon managed through the waves of pain. "Who paid you off? Was it the Japanese? The Fourth Commitern or one of the Haddinite militias?"

"Wrong," Esther said. "I belong to a faction that's existed, under many names, for thousands of years. Wasn't it clever how your Intel scientists grew the marked skin-graft over your suicide operative? Well, the process can be achieved *both* ways."

"What the *hell* are you talking about?"

Ever smiling, Esther unseamed her uniform, disrobed from the waist up. The years had treated her well; her breasts remained robust, nearly sagless, her stomach flat. Her skin shone in unblemished white.

Then she peeled the skin off.

She'd nicked her side with a small scalpel, began to peel the skin away from her breasts and abdomen in a single sheet.

"Jesus Christ," Simon whispered.

Now her real skin was revealed, the skin she'd been born with. Encompassing most of her chest and belly was the all-too-familiar scarlet pigmentation: the Mark of the Red Sect.

"I was bred for this," she explained. "I was reared for this day, to infiltrate Federate Central Intelligence and foil their greatest discovery. And we will use that discovery for our own end. *Our* god has defeated yours, and we will prove that to the world."

The single bizarre name beat in Sharon's head: *Surkulik, the demon of inversions and false faces.* She stared at the puzzling shape and swore she could see a face.

"You won't get away with this," Simon assured her from the floor. His stumps looked like circles of char. "I won't let you!" He reached up desperately toward his collar, and slipped something out. It was tiny, like a silver toothpick: the firing device for the nuclear drivehead.

"You don't have the guts, Simon," Esther goaded him. "You're just a sniveling closet-pervert who lives for your own aggrandizement. You're not *man* enough to sacrifice yourself for your ideals."

Even legless, defeated, and thoroughly undermined, Simon managed a smile. "Watch me," he said, and then he snapped the tiny firing device in half.

His entire face drooped when nothing happened.

Esther laughed. "I disarmed the drivehead hours ago, you shit-head. And now I'm going to disarm *you*."

pzzzzt! pzzzzt!

Two quick zips of the laser lopped off Simon's arms at the elbows. He fell back flat against the floor, stumps flailing. More machine-like screams rocketed through the unit.

Esther winked at Sharon. "This laser's getting a bit old, isn't it? What do you say we try . . . *this?*" and she picked up the milliwave pistol.

She applied the milliwave beam to Simon's forehead. The brain began to boil, steam jetting from nostrils, ears, and mouth. More crackling resounded, like something in a deep-fryer.

Simon was long-dead when she finally put the pistol away.

Sharon knew what was next, and it all conformed to everything they knew about the Red Sect. In their random terror was their undisclosed statement. To torture, murder, and destroy, without ever saying why.

"Now you do the same to me," Sharon reasoned.

The doctor sighed in an elated exhaustion. Sweat shined like varnish on the scarlet breasts and belly. In this moment of exuberance, Esther looked as vibrant, invigorated, youthful as Sharon herself.

"No," she said. "It's nothing like that at all. You have your Bible, but we have our own testaments too. They're just as old, just as hallowed. Sharon, I was able to infiltrate Federate Intel due to a divine plan. You're part of the same plan. I'm surprised you haven't realized that yet."

Sharon's voice sounded like creaking wood. "What do you mean?"

"Under heaven lay umbra, hiding the chosen. I was chosen, in *secret*. Surkulik is a great god, a deity of inversions hidden behind falsehoods. Those same inversions and falsehoods have protected me from the scourge of the Vatican and all its technology, just as they have protected you. Your Federate medical background is false. Your birth records are false. Even your genetic register and the certification of your tubal ligation are false."

The tiny snick of the scalpel at Sharon's side told her what she already suspected by now. The lambent white skin of her chest and belly was peeled off, exposing the Red Sect's genetic brand beneath.

An air-shot zapped at her neck.

"Go to sleep, little virgin."

Sharon awoke in snatches. She was inside the escape skiff. Esther had re-armed the nuclear drivehead and destroyed the C.F.S. Edessa. It was not a Federate Intel vessel that had picked them up. It was a Red Sect vessel. In and out of consciousness, Sharon remembered little. Her dreams were horrid and vast.

Eventually they returned to Earth.

When she was allowed to remain in a normal waking state, she found herself secluded within a secret Red Sect facility, deep underground. As she had been during her final hours on the Edessa, Sharon was braced to a gurney here too, but by her ankles and elbows now. She was fed intravenously; she was tended to by quiet nurses whose eyes seemed to sparkle with envy. Every so often Esther would come in to see her.

"The transfections are working marvelously," the woman told her. "Twenty more young faithful girls such as yourself are successfully gestating."

Sharon's state of pregnancy soon became obvious, her belly growing more rotund every day. "Who is the father of my child?" she asked dully.

"Technically, Tom," Esther informed. "After Simon killed him, I extracted some spermatozoa, cryolized it, and brought it back. Your egg was fertilized ectogenically and replanted into your womb. Of course, this was after I spliced some additional gene markers into your egg."

Sharon didn't understand. "Additional . . . markers?"

"Reproductive markers. All cells have them in their DNA coils. I extracted hundreds of them from the specimen Simon retrieved."

Then Sharon remembered. "The snake," she said.

Esther laughed. She moved a small holo-terminal over to Sharon, opened the screen. "You're a smart, inquisitive young woman. Here. Investigate. And you won't even need a biochip for full access. We've long-since broken all of the Federate's earthbound pass-words. I'll give you a hint. Access the vocabulary banks, then remember that Surkulik is a god of puzzles, inversions, and falsehoods. And remember our prayer. It's *your* prayer now, Sharon."

Esther walked away, leaving Sharon to occupy herself with her former skills. She immediately accessed SURKULIK and ran a like-find request.

The screen read:

one (1) entry found:

target word SURKULIK is like:

adj. [from Latin: surcul<<sus or surculus]:

SURCULOSE: producing or possessed of suckers as in woody surus branches or tentacles.

Then: *Tentacles,* the thought tapped in Sharon's mind. *The snake . . .*

It wasn't a snake. It was a tentacle.

Next, she recited Esther's hint: *And remember our prayer. God of falsehoods. God of puzzles and inversions.* The name itself—Kilukrus—was an inversion of Surkulik, whose puzzle was originally hinted at via the simplest puzzle of all: the Red Sect's bible, *The Order of Kilukrus*, was bound in reverse. Hence, Surkulik was Kilukrus in reverse.

Next she input the Sect's intercession:

Under heaven lay umbra, hiding the chosen

She decided on the next simplest cipher in history—an acrostic—and highlighted the first letter of each word:

<u>U</u>nder <u>h</u>eaven <u>l</u>ay <u>u</u>mbra, <u>h</u>iding <u>t</u>he <u>c</u>hosen

This spelled:

uhluhtc

Meaningless, she thought.
Then she ran it in reverse:

cthulhu

Frustrated, Sharon turned off the holoscreen. She idly rubbed her belly. The word meant nothing to her.

SHEEP MEADOW STORY

Jack Ketchum
Writing as Jerzy Livingston

> "Let's go have hamburgers on a beach,
> surrounded by mermaids flapping their wings."
> —John Hinckley, in a letter to Jodie Foster

THURSDAY

> "A merry heart doeth good like a medicine:
> but a broken spirit drieth the bones."
> —*Proverbs 4:4*

Stroup took the cell phone off his belt. He hated the goddamn things but sometimes they came in handy. He dialed. She answered.

"Lesvos Taverna. May I help you?"

"You want to help me?"

"Sir?"

"I'm gonna get you, Carla."

"What?"

"I'm gonna get you."

"Who is this?"

"I'm gonna get you NOW!"

He hung up. He swung the pump shotgun out from under his raincoat and stepped across Columbus. Traffic swerved and skidded. Not even the cabbies cursed him. Not with the shotgun there.

He stepped through the open glass door and looked around. The hostess screamed so he shot her in the face. The bartender screamed so he shot her in the tits. Some Indian or Pakistani busboy didn't scream, just stood there holding a full tray of empties. Stroup shot him anyway.

Patrons dived for cover beneath their tables. He'd disturbed their lunch. Waiters and cooks and kitchen staff hit the floor. Women screamed. Men shouted. He figured she'd be hiding in the office. Like some STAFF ONLY sign was going stop him. He checked the toilets anyway, pushed open the stalls. Nobody on the shitters.

He walked through the empty back room to the door and tried the doorknob. It was locked. Like some locked door was going to stop him. He blasted the shit out of it and pushed it open. Carla was cowering behind the desk. She looked nice there. He almost felt like fucking her.

"Stroup! Oh jesus, Stroup, it's YOU! Why are you DOING this?"

"Not me, baby. People don't kill people. Guns do."

"Are you CRAZY?"

She was close to hysterical. It was something new at least.

"You've fucked with me for the last time, Carla."

"PLEASE, Stroup!"

"You called me an incompetent nobody, Carla."

"I didn't mean it, Stroup. PLEASE!"

"You own this dyke souvlaki joint, right? You're such a hot shit? Well, own this."

He pumped the shotgun. She tried to rise so he shot her in the legs. They were good legs. Once. She went down screaming even louder and in a different way than he was used to and even though he more or less liked the sound of it he put the barrel into her open mouth and fired again.

She painted the walls and floor and furniture.

Stroup turned and walked away.

Some guy at the bar was sipping a martini.

"You're Stroup?" he said.

"What's it to you?"

"My name is Maxwell Perkins."

The guy was old and dressed in a nice clean suit.

"I'm a big fan, Mr. Stroup. I've read everything you've ever written, in fact. I think you're a genius. And I'd like to offer you a three-book deal. Would a million per-book advance be acceptable?"

"Make it two million and you got a deal."

Stroup ejected a shell. Maxwell Perkins smiled and extended his hand.

"Done," he said.

He woke up smiling.

It didn't last.

He looked at the clock. The clock was set for 9:00 but it was only 8:45. Good dream but it had him up fifteen minutes early.

In the bathroom he splashed water on his face and lit a cigarette and exhaled and went to nuke the coffee. The coffee was three days old and tasted like a rat had died in it. It was hot though.

He sat on the edge of the bed drinking his coffee and considered a shower and shave or at least brushing his teeth and a change of shorts and then considered what he had on his plate today and growled and decided all of that could wait. He had work to do. He needed the money. Yesterday he'd rejected two short stories, a coffee-table photo book—naked pictures of some guy's geriatric wife—a self-published Mormon geneology and Lillie Mae Hipps' poetry collection A BOWL FULL OF LOVE. Lillie Mae's stuff was all handwritten and the title poem had a funny misspelling—a *bowel* full of love—but that wasn't why he rejected the thing. He rejected it because it was shit.

They were all shit.

Fifteen years now he'd been working as a reader for the Cosmodemonic Literary Agency and not once had he come across anything that *wasn't* shit. Maybe the other readers got the good stuff. He didn't know. Out of the hundred-fifty-dollar, two-hundred-dollar, or three-hundred-dollar fee the Agency charged these wannabees he got to keep ten percent. For that he had to write a two-to-four page letter explaining why they wouldn't be taking on THE HAUNTED ABORTION CLINIC or the autobiography of some illiterate junkie or CARLOS, THE FARTING CAT for literary representation.

He had to encourage them to try again and write some more miserable swill and send more money.

At least with computers and the net he could e-mail copy for the boss' approval or disapproval and got to work at home. He could roll out of bed and just knock it out. He'd started in a room with a dozen kids fresh out of college all pounding on their IBMs and the sound in there was like eight hundred tap dancers all working on different routines all at the same time. You could smell the fear-sweat to *produce* and do it *fast* like rotten eggs.

He'd been the oldest guy working there. He guessed he probably still was.

The phone rang. His answering machine picked it up.

"*It's your quarter,*" his voice said. "*Leave a fucking message.*"

Whoever was calling didn't. Either he'd scared them off again or it was some goddamn solicitation. At nine in the morning. The machine was on twenty-four hours a day. He hated fucking solicitations.

He took the coffee over to his desk. Saw the inevitable pile of manuscripts. He picked them up once a week. That was all he ever saw of the shop.

On top was something called APPLE KNOCKERS' DELIGHT. The cover-letter said it was a novel. The hero was a guy named Jimmy Ballocks who was a hundred-ten years old and screwing a twenty-year-old schoolteacher. He credited his staying-power to organic gardening. Apples in particular.

Two-hundred-fifty pages.

Jesus.

By four-fifteen he was ready to wrap it.

He'd taken a break to shave, shower and shit and another for his mid-day beer. He wasn't the drinker he used to be but that beer was always tasty.

The phone had rung four more times, all hang-ups. Maybe he should include some heavy weapons-fire on the message. That might do it.

The final manuscript of the day was another book of poems by Martin Wellman. Old Marty had already been to Stroup's personal well five times before but kept plugging away at getting himself some representation. Stroup's personal favorite had been the poem "Toilet" from the last batch. He'd kept a copy.

It's always there when I'm in need
You'll find that the Toilet is a true friend indeed
It never complaints or nags about what you put in it

It just sits there to accept and spin it
Too much to drink and your stomach will reverber-
ate
But you got the Toilet there to eat what you ate
And now you've got to pee
The Toilet says, "squirt it in me . . ."
It went on like that.

Talking toilets. He'd encouraged Wellman on that one. Only complained about the obvious meter difficulties. What the hell. If ravens could talk why not a crapper?

Maybe the guy had read his Edgar Allan Poe.

While he was dressing he turned on CNN. The Republicans were behind in the polls. In Georgia a guy and his wife were arrested for dragging the family dog half to death behind the rear bumper of their car. The dog wouldn't come when they called him. In Florida another kid had walked into another high-school with another Glock and shot up the halls. A teacher and a sixteen-year-old girl were dead. Six others wounded. No wonder he'd had that dream last night. It was in the fucking *air*.

He finished tying his shoes and got up thinking he ought to change the sheets next week and walked out of the apartment and down one floor to the street.

He was meeting Marie at her place at six. Same as every Thursday. An hour and a half to drink.

Some asshole drug-money gold-chained darkie had the windows of his brand-new BMW open as he crossed Broadway on the northbound side and the speakers were blasting rap. *Thunkthunkthunkthunk*. Unintelligible street-spook lyrics. He thought he heard his name mentioned but that couldn't be. Martin King died for this. Made him wish for a grenade. Just pull the pin and toss it into the passenger seat. Exit *thunk*, exit BMW, exit asshole darkie.

He counted seven respectable white citizens on their cell-phones on the single block between 68th and 69th. One of them a chunky young female jogger, her tits bound tight by a running bra, her tits mashed down into her chest. He wondered how she heard whoever she was talking to with that fucking walkman on her head.

Between Broadway and Columbus he counted seven strollers, two of them double-wide. He had to walk right into the street to get around the three black nannies walking side by side. What he really wanted to do was plough through them like a bowling ball through the four, eight, and seven pins. Little white baby-bodies flying. The mothers all looked like they used tanning salons and Starbuck's decaffeinated coffee. They summered in the Hamptons and not one of them had lost her figure in the slightest during childbirth. Immaculate procreations maybe.

He stepped into the End of the World Cafe and sat down at the bar at the corner where he could watch the window if he wanted. Liana knew what to pour him. He lit a cigarette and sipped his Dewars rocks and stared at the rows of bottles. The bottles at least were friendly.

The bar was dead. Just one old rumdumb down at the end with his eyes on Liana. Stroup couldn't blame him. Liana was from Jamaica and taller than god and had smooth cream-and-coffee skin. But the bar was going to hell in a handbasket despite her. At this rate it'd be lucky to last the summer. Their Happy Hour consisted of half-price beer and well-drinks and

Stroup drank Dewars. Their Happy Hour meant nothing to him.

He reflected that Carla's calamari joint was only a block north. Taverna Lesvos was doing fine.

Carla had gone dyke on him in '96.

He never went there.

He stubbed out his cigarette and lit another. With what these babies cost these days he was going to have to cut down.

Sure.

The door opened and two women walked in. Girlfriends. Laughing. The thin one in the short skirt had good legs and no bra. Not bad. Her girlfriend was the usual. Overweight, with everything on her a size too small except maybe the shoes. They always traveled that way. *Fat and skinny had a race* and no real race at all.

They sat down at the bar in front of the window so that he had to look at them if he wanted to look out the window and ordered frozen margueritas. A couple of minutes later the blender was roaring, giving him a headache and Stroup was growling deep into his chest. Had to stop that so he did. Liana brought him another Dewars. That was better.

He inhaled and blew out smoke.

"Excuse me?" said the one with the legs.

"What can I do for you?" Stroup said.

"Do you think you could put that out, maybe? Or at least blow your smoke in another direction? I'm sorry. I'm allergic."

They were all allergic these days. All Manhattan had developed sudden allergies.

Diana brought them their drinks. They smiled. At least the blender had stopped screaming at him.

"I'm looking out the window," he said.

"I'm sorry?"

"The smoke is blowing toward you because I'm looking out the window. You're sitting in front of the window and I'm looking out it. You see? See that one with the good tits there? I'm looking at her. That's why the smoke is going in your direction."

"*Tits?*"

"Tits, yes. She's gone now. You just missed her. Too bad."

She looked like she'd found a turd floating in her tequila. She turned and whispered something angry to her friend. Her friend was scowling, nodding. The roll of fat on her neck ebbed and flowed and ebbed and flowed. Stroup sighed.

"Listen, ladies. This is a *bar*. People still smoke at bars in this city. It's a fact of life. Now, you've got this whole fucking *empty* bar here and you're sitting right in front of me. See all that space down there? Or else you got the tables. Why not try a table? It's cozy. There's no smoke. There's probably nobody around uses the word "tits" in mixed company. Though yours are nice by the way. I notice you're not wearing a bra. Good choice."

"Stroup," said Liana.

"Aw, hell, Liana. You want me to leave, I'll leave."

"I didn't say you should leave. Just be nice."

"I am being nice. I told her she has good tits. She does."

"Stroup."

"All right."

He finished his cigarette and did not immediately light a third one. Then he did. He blew some smoke. The woman with the legs sighed and shook her head and the two of them took their drinks to a table far away from him.

Ralph walked in and took their place. He ordered a beer. Now he had to look at Ralph to look out the window. The women were better. Ralph was always going on about some rotten movie he'd just seen or his rotten new haircut which was rotten because he'd paid some kid in barber school five bucks for it or else he was telling bad jokes. He looked a little like George Burns and maybe that was why. The difference was that Burns was funny. Ralph was about as funny as stillborn puppies. He was sixty-five and called himself a senior citizen. Stroup was only twelve years younger and would call himself a senior citizen when the Reform Party took the White House or Liana decided to fuck him, whichever came first.

"You hear the one about the doctor, asks this old lady patient of his how long she's been bedridden? 'Not for about twenty years,' she says, 'not since my husband was alive.' "

"No, Ralph. I hadn't."

"You hear the one about the doctor puts his stethoscope to some old lady's chest and says 'big breaths' and the lady says yes, they used to be?"

"You got something against old ladies today, Ralph? Or is it just me you hate?"

"You hear the one about the doctor asks his patient how he's doing with his medications? Guy says fine, except for the Patch. Doctor says what's the problem with the Patch? Guy says you told me to put a new one on every twelve hours and I'm running out of places to put them."

"Fuck you, Ralph. You're the goddamn village idiot."

Ralph laughed.

Stroup finished his Dewars and ordered a third one and drank half of it.

"So when are you going to fuck me, Liana?" he said.

"When hell freezes over, Stroup."

"Or the Reform Party takes the White House?"

"That's right."

"That's what I thought."

Two drinks and five doctor jokes later he was headed up Amsterdam toward Marie's. He made a stop at Pathmark for smokes. The Indian woman with the gold tooth waited on him which was good because the Indian woman knew he smoked Winston red softpack and the others didn't know Winston red softpack from Virginia Slims green in a box. They were smokers themselves some of them but the cigarette rack seemed to baffle them.

The Indian woman always smiled and handed him the change right. The others didn't. The others were stupid as dirt. They handed you change from a twenty with the ten on top face-up and the singles on the bottom so you had to reverse the order to put them away in your wallet. He wondered where that started but almost everybody did it now.

As he was walking out the door he thought he heard his name mentioned but that couldn't be.

Marie lived in a brownstone up on 78th Street. Only two floors up so even Stroup could make the stairs. Marie was a Personal Trainer and semi-professional bodybuilder and worked at a Fitness Center which used to be called a gym. Her pecs were better than Stroup's had ever been. She said that Stroup was the first man she'd gone out with who wasn't in shape. He said don't worry about it, he'd get in shape someday. Just not now.

She was a native Norwegian without an ounce of fat on her unless you counted the small smooth tits and her body was lithe as a snake. Not too massive like some of them. Some of them looked like they'd shoved footballs down into their thighs. He liked to watch her work out naked standing at the full-length mirror, the muscles making sudden unexpected appearances, the sweat running down those long sleek legs, the tiny verticle slit of shaved pale blonde pubic hair glistening.

He rang the bell and waited.

He imagined her working out right now.

His hard-on browsed his pants-leg looking for escape.

He rang again.

"Who is it?"

He talked into the speaker. "Rudy Guiliani. You're under arrest. It's Stroup. Who else?"

She buzzed him in. He climbed the stairs.

He tried not to show her he was winded.

"I called you," she said. "I kept getting the machine."

"That was you? I thought it was some bastard trying to sell me something."

"I kept getting the machine."

He walked over and kissed her and she didn't smell like herring for a change. She had her countrymen's weakness for pickled herring which was sometimes an almost fatal weakness to Stroup's way of thought. They'd be fucking and the stink would pour off her like a Stavanger sewer.

She was wearing grey sweatpants and a tight blue tank top. She looked good.

"Why didn't you leave a message?"

"I do not like to use the machine."

"You've used it before."

"Yes, but I do not like to."

"What're these?"

He pointed to the two dozen long-stem roses on the coffee table.

"Roses."

"I know that."

"That's why I do not like to use the machine."

"Because of the roses?"

She sighed. Stroup let go of her.

"I do not want to tell you on the machine. It's not right. I am getting married, Stroup. I am sorry."

"You're kidding."

"No, it is truth. I am sorry."

"To who?"

"Raymond. These are Raymond's flowers."

"Who's Raymond?"

"A client. A black man. You know I always like black men. He is in very good shape. Very strong. He proposed to me today. I told him okay."

"Is he rich?"

"A little."

"How can you be a little rich?"

"Please, Stroup. Do not make this difficult. I am very fond of you, you know. But you know, we have never been, what would you say, exclusive."

He guessed that was true enough. He was seeing Brauna tomorrow night as usual.

Still he felt oddly lonely standing there. Maybe it was the abruptness of it. You leave your apartment expecting dinner and a good hard fuck and what you get is walking papers. Or maybe he'd just miss her. The past three months they'd had a lot of laughs—she was pretty funny for a bodybuilder. She thought *he* was funny. She told him he was great in bed. He knew for a fact that she was.

She gave him a hug. A peck on the cheek.

"I am sorry, Stroup. It's been nice."

"It has. I'll miss you, Marie."

It was true. He would.

He turned and walked away and down the stairs and out the door.

He wouldn't miss the herring.

The air-conditioning at the Food Emporium was doing its impression of late December. He walked up the fresh meats aisle just to see if they had the plate of broiled Italian sausages out and they did. He impaled three on a toothpick and walked over to frozen foods. He got a Swanson Hungry Man dinner out of the freezer and dropped the toothpick on the floor.

The girl at the check-out counter looked at the Hungry Man dinner and then looked at him. Then she scanned the box. You bought a single Hungry Man dinner, they knew you were all alone.

She handed him his change. Ten on top face-up, singles below, receipt on top of that, and on top of that, the coins. He tilted the bills so that the coins slid off into his hand and pocketed them and reversed the order of the bills and shoved them in his wallet. He threw the receipt on the counter.

He realized he was growling.

The Hungry Man dinner was dark-meat chicken, corn, whipped potatoes and apple-cranberry-crumb dessert. The closest thing you could get to KFC in this goddamn yuppie hood. While it was cooking he poured himself a drink and then another. He checked his e-mail. Two distant relatives had sent mass communications of a religious nature. He deleted without opening. Ralph had sent him more doctor-jokes. He deleted without opening. He had an e-mail from Brauna confirming tomorrow night.

That was something.

He ate watching CNN. The Democrats were behind in the polls. The kid with the Glock in Florida said he was only fighting back, that there was an organized plot at school to impregnate his twelve-year-old girlfriend with the child of Behemoth Yuggdoroth Nit.

A Cornell research group had just published a paper finding that inept, basically useless people tended to be confident—even *dead certain*—that they were smart, witty, and always in the right. The truly talented, on the other hand, tended to underestimate themselves. Figured that if they could do it, anybody could do it. The scary thing, the report said, was that you could always talk to the talented and convince them they were better than they thought. But the inept were intractable.

When he got up to dump his chicken bones he thought he heard his name mentioned but that couldn't be.

He poured himself an after-dinner drink and decided to work on the story. He turned off CNN and fired up the Gateway. The story was about a nosebleed he'd had in Florida. The nosebleed had been intractable too. He'd needed surgery.

The story was a comedy.

A half hour into it the telephone rang. *"It's your quarter. Leave a fucking message,"* his voice said.

"Stroup?" said Carla. "Pick up, Stroup."

Jesus. No way.

"I know you're there, Stroup. Ann saw you walk into the building. Don't make me come over there, Stroup."

Ann was his upstairs neighbor. A mousy little friend of Carla's and a goddamn snoop who seemed to have no life of her own whatsoever. He'd caught her once going through the landlady's garbage.

Maybe it came as a result of being named after an indefinite article. He didn't know.

He picked up the phone.

"What," he said.

"You *know* what," Carla said.

"No I don't. Hurry it up. I'm working."

"On what."

"A story."

"A story. You call that working."

"Yes I do."

"Working is what a person does for a living. Has any story ever made you any money, Stroup?"

"This one will."

"You know why I'm calling."

"The other money."

"What?"

"The *other* money. The money I owe you. Not the money I'm going to make on the story."

"Six months back rent, Stroup. Your half. That's two thousand, seven hundred and six dollars and ninety cents. You've owed it to me now for nine months, Stroup."

"I know."

"What do I look like, a credit card?"

"You should never have left home without it."

"Goddamn you! I need that money. I need it now."

"Why now?"

"What?"

"Why not yesterday? Or last Thursday? Why now?"

"That's none of your business, Stroup."

"You want my money it is."

"It's *my* money. I *carried* you for six months, re-member? So you could pay off your goddamn medical bills after that stupid nosebleed."

"What stupid nosebleed?"

"Don't be funny, Stroup."

He sighed. So did she. Here they were, sighing to-gether. Must be love.

"Randi and I want to go on a vacation," she said, "if you must know. We *need* a vacation. The restau-rant is driving us crazy."

"I hear great things about your calamari."

"To hell with the calamari. What about my money? You signed a note, Stroup."

He had. He was drunk. Drunks are stupid.

He should know.

"You'll get it."

"When."

"Soon. Tomorrow. Next week. The week after next."

"WHICH, goddammit!"

"TOMORROW OR THE WEEK AFTER NEXT. Whichever I *say* it's going to be, you get it? I put twenty long years into you so don't you piss on me for a couple thousand bucks and don't you yell at me or I'll come over and *fry* your ass, you understand me? Now go tickle Randi's titties or whatever the hell it is you two do together and don't you call again. Good-night. Goodbye. Fuck off."

He hung up the phone.

It didn't ring again. He half expected it to but it didn't. He wondered if she really needed him to pay her. The business was supposedly doing well but what did he know.

He went back to the story but couldn't get it down. He had another drink.

He had no chance of getting her that money at all.

He was barely breaking even here. He'd have to quit drinking. And smoking.

No chance.

Turner was running MARNIE. He thought Hitchcock was a crock. THE BIRDS was okay and REAR WINDOW and the first half of PSYCHO but he was also the guy who introduced QUE SERA, SERA into the canon.

IFC was running NOSFERATU, THE VAMPIRE so he lay back on the bed and watched that instead, Isabelle Adjani doing all her silentmovie poses, all beautiful wide dark eyes and melodrama. The movie was just slow enough to bludgeon him to sleep.

FRIDAY

"Let not your heart be troubled,
neither let it be afraid."

—*John 14:27*

By quarter after four he was ready to e-mail his daily re-
jection letters over to Cosmodemonic for approval. Olgie
Lamar from Arkansas had finally sent in the last five-
dollar payment on the one-hundred-fifty bucks for her
book about her husband who'd been killed by a drunk
on a snowplow. It had taken her eleven months to get
up the money. Some months she hadn't sent anything
at all, she said, because the goats hadn't given enough
milk.

The book was illiterate from the get-go. So was the
letter about the goats. So were all her letters.

Stroup encouraged her to try again.

He had a novel outline from Walla Walla State
Prison from Joseph Johnson.

*A small boy at the age of five, who had experience
sex with his sixteen year old babysitter.*

A woman get raped and have her hair pulled clean out her head.

The main character get in touch with a seven-year-old pimp who get them some girls. Later find out the girls are male foggies.

One of the main character get tricked into having sex with a corpse.

Another getting the Blue Ball Claps and his penis grow to length of four feet by two. They cure him by smashing it with a sledge hammer.

The four main character meet this gorilla guy who they shoot, cut, hit, and run over with their car but he just keep getting up.

One of the characters catch lice from a prostitute.

Another character get kidnapped and his ass raped and get an overdose of heroin. That near the end, the most touching part of the whole book.

The novel was called COOL AS SHIT and the author's cover-letter informed him that if he ever wanted to read "a good sexy book, which wasn't dirty at all but funny," then COOL AS SHIT was for him. "It's magnificent book," Johnson said, "all it needs is publisher. Who is daring enough to make a millions of dollars."

Stroup told him to try again.

He had a short story collection written from the points of view of a varied group of insects. ANIMAL FARM with an ovipositor.

He had something called DIARY OF AN ANAL-RETENTIVE HOUSEWIFE.

Stroup told them to try again.

On the divide in the middle of Broadway half a dozen kids about five or six years old ran around him giggling playing tag or some damn thing like he wasn't even there. Maybe he wasn't. Their twenty-something mother or babysitter or whatever the hell she was looked on and smiled. Except for the fact that he was standing there he could have hoped for an out-of-control beer truck to jump the divider.

The reek of stale popcorn and warm fake butter wafted out to him from the Sony Multiplex on 68th. He vowed he'd never eat that shit again. The vow sounded very familiar.

On Columbus a pair of teenage girls, ballet students, duck-walked right into him and damn near knocked him into traffic.

Lincoln Center was trying to kill him here.

The End of the World was empty again. Stroup took his usual seat. Liana poured him the usual drink. He was meeting Brauna at eight. They were going to a party. Plenty of time.

The bar had their radio on and the song was bothering him. Something about *video killed the radio star*. Who gave a shit about video or radio for that matter. *Video killed the radio star* over and over.

What bullshit.

"Liana, could you maybe switch stations, please?"

She shook her head. "Sorry, Stroup. Manager says this station only. Light Rock. Easy listening."

"Easy listening? You call this easy?"

"It attracts the customers."

"You don't have any customers, Liana. Just me."

"We will, though."

"When? How old am I gonna be then?"

"How old are you now, Stroup?"

"Fifty-three. And don't change the subject. What about the CD player?"

"Out of order."

"Tape deck?"

"Busted."

"Jesus, Liana. You're presiding over a goddamn wake here."

The song ended. HARVEST MOON came on. He more or less liked that one.

"I hear you got dumped last night," Liana said.

"Jesus, Liana."

"Marie was in with her boyfriend."

"Fiancee."

"Fiancee. Sorry to hear it, Stroup."

"I'm sorry you heard it at all. Can't anybody keep their mouth shut in this town?"

"It would have been obvious anyway. He's black. You're not."

"Good-looking?"

"Very good looking."

"Shit. You want to pour me another?"

"Sure."

Ralph came in and started bitching about his haircut.

"I don't want to hear about it, Ralph."

He was right, though. Whoever cut it had let the hair grow over one ear and clipped it short over the other. Ralph was lopsided now.

"You ever eat at Vinnie's?"

"Where's Vinnie's?"

"Third and Fifty-ninth."

"That's the East Side, Ralph. I don't go there."

"The food was lousy. Don't go there."

"I won't, Ralph."

There was a woman of about thirty on the sidewalk outside talking to a pair of guys who looked ten years younger than she was and the guys with their baseball caps on backwards were standing in his way with their backs to him so he had to shift to try to see around them which he did because the woman was a looker. Long wavy auburn hair which she was primping with both hands and smiling brightly at them. V-neck cleavage of the best possible kind and no bra, tight ass in the tight jeans, tight shirt over the tits. The woman glanced in his direction a couple of times and seemed aware of him watching. If she was aware of him watching then why didn't she tell these two bozos with her to move their skinny asses? You just couldn't figure a woman.

Take Liana now. Ex-model. What the hell was she doing slinging drinks and bowls of goldfish to guys like him and Ralph? It was like hanging the Mona Lisa off an oil derrick.

He watched the woman walk away, the hair swaying, the tight ass swaying. The guys were watching her too, turning to each other, saying something. He knew what they were saying. You could see it in their eyes. *My cock right now is the lonesomest sonovabitch in the world* is what they were saying.

He could sympathize.

A guy walked by with a wide bright swirl-patterned tie, yellow and green and orange.

He hated wide bright swirl-patterned ties. He hated ties in general. He'd see one and want to turn it into a noose right then and there.

Ralph said, "You hear the one about the . . . ?"

Oh, jesus.

On the way up Columbus to Brauna's a delivery boy on a bike going against traffic almost hit him, a kid on a skateboard going against traffic almost hit him, and a rollerblader going against traffic almost hit him.

That was only three near-misses in a six-block walk. Stroup figured he was lucky.

Brauna designed hats for fancy boutiques and department stores and lived in a doorman highrise. They knew him there. Nobody even questioned him now. He was King of the Walk one or two nights a week. He nodded to the doorman and the guy behind the desk. They smiled. They could afford to smile. They had a union. They made more than Stroup did just by standing there. At Christmas time they got enough tips to fly the wife and kids to Tahiti.

He took the elevator up to four and Brauna opened the door. She was wearing a smile and nothing else so Stroup went right at her.

He grabbed her wrists with one hand and pulled them over her head and pushed her up against the wall. She liked to have her nipples pinched, they were already stiff waiting for that so Stroup took one between his thumb and forefinger and pinched and twisted hard and she gasped against his mouth and then moaned when he put his tongue inside her and rolled her ass against the wall on one side and her cunt against his cock on the other. He pinched the nipple until his fingers ached and then let go. He'd get to the other one in a second.

He let go of her and unbuckled his belt, unzipped his fly and slid his pants and shorts down over his hairy ass and assumed the position. She was already wet so getting in was nothing. Getting in was easy. She moaned and bucked. Stroup realized he was growling. He had to cut that out so he did. He pumped her hard and then took both nipples between thumb and forefinger and pulled them until his fingers and her nipples were nestled in his armpits. She started to scream. He couldn't remember if she'd shut the door. He looked. She had. She came and he came and Stroup zipped up again.

"Hi, baby," he said.

"Hi, baby. You want a drink?"

He lit up a cigarette. "Sure."

She went into the kitchen and poured them each a scotch rocks. They sat down on the couch from Bloomingdale's.

"Thanks, baby."

"My pleasure. That was good, Stroup."

"I know."

"God, my nipples hurt!"

"They damn well ought to."

"I love it when you do that. I can feel it run straight down into my cunt. Like it's electric, know what I mean?"

"We'll have to wire you up sometime."

She laughed. "Wire me up. I'm already wired up."

"That you are. Suppose it wasn't me?"

"Huh?"

"You came to the door starkers. Suppose it wasn't me?"

"I cheated. I used the peephole. I had a robe handy in the closet just in case."

"Nice surprise."

"Mmmm." She finished her drink and stood up and clinked the ice. "I'm having another. You?"

"I already had a few. In a couple minutes maybe."

"Okay."

He watched her fine dimpled ass vanish into the kitchen. She was shorter than Marie, a brunette, not quite the racing model Marie was but beyond the funny little mole on her chin that sprouted the occasional wiry black hair you couldn't fault her.

She came back with a fresh one.

"There," she said. "I'll finish this one and start to get ready."

"What's the party all about, anyway?"

He didn't go to parties much. Too many people there.

"My friend Zia's got a new apartment. She wants to show it off I guess."

"Zia? Your broker?"

"Uh-huh."

"Jesus, Brauna."

"You've never met her, Stroup. She's very nice. You'll like her."

"Where is it? Soho?"

"The East Side. Just off Madison."

"*Jesus*, Brauna."

"Oh, stop bitching." She slapped his arm. "You make it sound like Wisconsin."

"It is Wisconsin. Dead River, Wisconsin."

"What are you so grouchy about anyway?"

"Carla's hitting me up for cash again. I may have to kill her."

"Forget Carla. We'll have fun. I've never taken you to a party. You want something? I've got 'ludes and some pretty good dope. I was going to buy coke but Zia says not to bother, there'll be plenty at the party."

"Another drink is all. I'll get it. You go and get ready."

The East Side, for chrissake.

Maybe they could grab a bite at Vinnie's.

* * *

He'd read somewhere that dirt was nothing more than something out of place. A cigarette in a pack wasn't dirt but a butt on the living room floor was. Fur on a cat wasn't dirt but a tuft of it lying in a corner was. Sand in your shoes. Soap scum in the bathtub. Dust was mostly composed of flakes of shed human skin. Misplaced.

Dirt.

By that reckoning Stroup figured he was dirt.

Zia's apartment was huge and minimalist-modern and she'd crammed it with people to whom ordinarily Stroup wouldn't have given the time of day. Nor they him had he not come in with Brauna. Lawyers. Brokers. Surgeons. Bankers. Agents. They moved through the rooms like a lolling school of sharks and you knew that if somebody so much as pricked a finger there was going to be blood in the water. He had never seen so many suspenders in one place in his life. It looked like the casting call for AMERICAN PSYCHO in there.

He kept drifting back and forth to the wet bar hearing things he didn't like to hear. *Sensational* and *far and away* and *at this point in time* and *awesome* and *by the very same token* and *be that as it may* and worst of all as far as Stroup was concerned, *the exact same thing*. The only thing that was *exactly the same* about these people was that they were all smug whores with too much money.

He kept hearing about their fucking *plans*, their *aims*, their *long-term goals*.

The only goal Stroup had as far as he knew was to outlive Al Sharpton.

Brauna kept disappearing on him. And every time she did she'd come back a little more crazed and manic-sounding. Coming out of this bedroom or that bathroom. *Bolivian Marching Powder* was what it was. Stroup abstained. He didn't like to mix his poisons. Brauna on the other hand was a walking blender full of quaaludes, scotch, wine and coke and god knows what else.

Brauna was having a hell of a time. With what she was barely wearing and those stiff nipples at attention she was very popular with the boys.

Finally he cornered her.

"Sniff," he said.

"What?"

"You're getting sloppy with the white stuff. Left nostril. Sniff."

She did.

"None of my business but do you think you should be doing a whole lot more of that? You're spilling your scotch."

She was.

She exploded at him anyhow.

"You're fucking RIGHT it's none of your business! JESUS, Stroup! FUCK YOU! Who do you think you ARE? To be telling ME what to do? You goddamn LOSER! You write fucking AD COPY for a living!"

"It's not exactly ad copy, Brauna. More like burglary."

"YOU MADE ME PAY FOR THE FUCKING CAB, STROUP!"

He hadn't. She'd volunteered the cash. He just hadn't refused it, that was all. He made it a point never to refuse money. She could buy and sell him.

People were looking. Fuck them. Still it was time to get out of there.

He took her arm.

"Listen, Brauna. . . ."

She pulled away. For the second time that night her ass made contact with a wall. It was a tight ass and a soft wall. You could hear the thump over the Whitney Houston.

"Don't you tell me to LISTEN! I'm not your fucking WIFE! I'm not your ANYTHING! YOU'LL SCREW ANYTHING THAT WALKS, Stroup, you asshole! And you want me to LISTEN?"

"That's not true. I won't screw anything that walks. I am, however, polyamorous."

That seemed to confuse her. She made a comeback.

"Get the fuck OUT of here, Stroup! I NEVER WANT TO SEE YOU AGAIN! You understand?"

She headed for the bathroom.

He turned and all he saw were suspenders. He didn't try to stop her.

In the cab across town which this time he did have to pay for he thought he saw Carla at the corner of Central Park West and 66th but it turned out to be the movie star Lori Singer. Singer was a blonde and Carla was a redhead so he wondered how he'd got that wrong.

He thought he heard his name mentioned over the cab's dispatch radio but that couldn't be.

He had the blues again he guessed. He told the cabbie to let him off at 66th and Columbus just so he could walk the rest of the way home. It was warm and breezy. The air would do him good.

At the corner of 68th and Broadway a couple of kids in their twenties wearing jeans and tee-shirts and both of them slightly overweight were necking in front of the bank. They looked happy. Contented.

Probably they were in love. Love was a Wonderful Thing. Three tall jocks in the latest Gap sweatshirts walked by. Once they'd passed the kids by a few yards and just as Stroup hit the curb opposite one of them turned around.

"Take it INSIDE!" the guy yelled.

The kids stopped necking and looked.

"You WISH you had something to take inside, you asshole," Stroup said, "except for your miserable excuse for a cock. You useless piece of HORSESHIT!"

The lovers were looking at him now. A crazy man in their midst.

"Carry on, guys," he said.

SATURDAY

"Set me as a seal upon thine heart, as a seal upon thine arm: for love is strong as death; jealousy is cruel as the grave."

—*Song of Solomon, 8:6*

Midway through ADVENTURES OF A CAT-TLE-BURGLER the doorbell rang.

Stroup peered through the peephole. Some young guy with a backpack.

"Yeah?"

"Mr. Stroup?"

"Uh-huh?"

"Messenger service."

He opened the door. The guy handed him an envelope, a receipt and a ballpoint pen. Stroup signed his name.

"Have a nice day," the guy told him. *Have a nice day* was an imperative. He didn't like imperatives. Pushy.

He closed the door and opened the envelope.

A summons. Carla was taking him to small-claims

court. He was told to appear in person on such and such a day at such and such a time. *The goddamn stairmaster-using, aerobic-training cunt-lapping shaved-twat nympho bitch.* She was taking his ass to court.

He tore it in two and then thought better of it and scotch-taped it back together again. The last thing he needed was trouble with the law. He tossed it on his desk.

Midway through MY HOLE AND I the phone rang. He heard his boss' voice on the other end. His boss was calling on a Saturday. That was unusual. His boss was telling him to pick up. So he did.

"Max?"

"Stroup? Glad I caught you."

Like he had a life, maybe. Like he was going somewhere.

"You're calling on a Saturday, Max. That's unusual."

"I know. Listen, Stroup. There's no way to say this but straight out. You've been downsized."

"What?"

He was small enough already.

"Downsized, Stroup. The agency's tightening its belt. You and three others."

"Which three?"

"That doesn't matter. I'm sorry, Stroup. You always did good work. You got it in on time. I appreciate that."

"So why are you firing me?"

"I'm not firing you. You've been downsized. We can get kids who'll do the work for less."

"Less than ten percent? Are they crazy?"

"Ambitious, Stroup. They want to work for a prestige agency."

"That's what we are, a prestige agency?"

"No need to be bitter, Stroup."

"After fifteen years you're dumping me and I'm not supposed to get bitter."

"It's my day off, Stroup. Give me a break."

"I'm sorry to spoil your day, Max."

"Could you mail us back your manuscripts? Naturally we'll pay you for whatever work you've completed."

"Naturally."

He hung up.

ADVENTURES OF A CAT-TLE BURGLER was worth twenty dollars to him. MY HOLE AND I was worth thirty. THIS GUN SWEATS WHEN IT GETS HOT was worth another twenty. He had a handful of short stories worth fifteen each.

He threw them in the garbage.

His phone rang. Max again.

"You wouldn't throw those scripts away, would you, Stroup?"

Stroup hung up on him.

He looked out the window. It was a nice sunny day.

He made himself a tuna sandwich and turned on CNN. He felt distracted. He could hardly pay attention. He kept glancing at the dresser drawer.

The Republicans were behind in the polls.

The kid with the Glock in Florida had confessed tearfully that it was he and not his schoolmates who'd impregnated his twelve-year-old girlfriend with the child of Behemoth Yuggdoroth Nit. He'd shot up the school so that somebody would stop him from doing it again. Stroup thought that was considerate of him.

In Connecticut some guy was suing the police department. He'd taken the cop test and they turned him down because his score was too high. The Deputy Police

Chief said that anybody that smart would probably get bored with the job.

When he got up to bring his plate into the kitchen and passed his desk with the summons on it he thought he heard his name mentioned in connection with the cop story but that couldn't be.

He sat down again. He lit a cigarette and watched more CNN. He glanced at the dresser drawer. The Democrats were behind in the polls. Some diabetic in L.A. went into the hospital to have his ulcerous foot removed and they took off the wrong one. The diabetic was switching hospitals.

In Pakistan a court ordered a teenage girl who'd eloped with her older bus-driver boyfriend to be given a hundred lashes prior to being stoned to death. Her father evidently agreed. He'd reported the elopement.

The goddamn news was getting to him. He started surfing channels with his good old universal remote, the lazy man's friend. He got a college football game and a tennis game and a goddamn New York Yankees game. He got Super Sabado. He got an antique show and a cooking show and MURDER, SHE WROTE and some wildlife thing about snails and tree frogs and Weather On The Ones and NAVY SEALS and MATLOCK and MOMMIE DEAREST.

Fuck it. Back to CNN. He thought for a moment that he'd clicked on in the middle of Willow Bay saying something about his sex life but that couldn't be.

He considered calling up a buddy. But then he couldn't recall having any buddies. Must be one or two around somewhere.

Or maybe not.

He went over to his desk and re-read the summons. That was his name, all right. S-T-R-O-U-P.

He looked up Carla's number at the restaurant. Some woman answered.

"Taverna Lesvos. May I help you?"

He realized he was growling. He had to quit that so he did.

They had the ball game on. He could hear it in the background. Classy joint. For this you paid six bucks a drink.

"Carla there?"

"I'm afraid not. Is there anything I can help you with?"

"Randi around?"

"I'm afraid not."

"What are you afraid of?"

"Excuse me?"

"Never mind. Any idea when she'll be back?"

"Carla?"

"Yes."

"May I ask who's calling?"

"Her ex."

"Oh. I really don't know. Probably not until this evening. They took a picnic lunch over to the Sheep Meadow. It's such a lovely day."

"The Sheep Meadow?"

"Uh-huh."

"I thought they were supposed to be working their asses off over there. I thought you were always swamped up the wazoo."

"Excuse me, sir?"

"Me? Hell, yes. I don't give a damn what the hell you did."

He hung up on her. He walked over and re-read the summons. They even had the amount he owed there. Two thousand, seven hundred and six dollars and ninety cents. She was hitting him for the ninety cents.

He glanced at the dresser drawer. He opened it and took out the .38 revolver from under his socks and underwear. He'd arranged to have the revolver straw-purchased for him in Georgia some years ago when he still thought New York was a dangerous place and not just a damned annoying one.

He checked the chamber and put it in his pocket.

He took the remote off the bed and put it in his other pocket and then went out the door.

The bar at Taverna Lesvos was packed. Up front near the TV they were standing two-deep. Everybody riveted on the Yankee game.

It was amazing. New York had *invented* baseball. Who the hell *were* these kids? Hadn't anybody ever told these assholes that the entire point of a baseball cap was to keep the goddamn sun out of your eyes? Maybe wearing them backwards was some sort of anti-redneck maneuver. Or maybe a form of rebellion. Like refusing to eat your spinach.

He stood at the far end of the bar as far from the game as possible and ordered a scotch. The bartender was a blonde who had to be all of seventeen. He waited until the bases were loaded and the Yankee pitcher was winding up and then took out the remote and turned on the Food Channel. Stawberry souffle, it looked tasty.

The boys at the bar moaned and shouted and pointed at the TV like Donald Sutherland pointing at Brooke Adams in INVASION OF THE BODY SNATCHERS. The bartender didn't seem to know what in hell was going on. The bartender looked flustered. By the time she got hold of her remote and switched they were pitching Bud Lite.

More moaning and groaning.

Then after a while the place settled down again.

Meanwhile Stroup pocketed the remote and waited until somebody hit one deep into left field and the Yankee fielder was running hard to get under, hustling real good. He turned on the Home Shopping Network. They were selling jewelery there. Nice stuff. Young executives-and-CEOs-to-be yelled and stomped their feet and raised their fists into the air like Nazi Youth watching a parade of Jews go by.

The bartender was doing something with ice and a shaker but she was a little bit faster this time and got to the remote just in time for everybody to watch the players retire from the field.

Guys groaned and bitched and finally quieted down.

He ordered another drink. Smoked a cigarette.

He waited until the Yankee first baseman was rounding third and heading for home on a terrific grounder to right field and turned on the Weather Channel. It was pouring in Duluth. Sunny in California. California needed rain.

There was serious rage in the room now. Well-bred wasps turned into Chicago gangsters before his very eyes. They were screaming at the bartender to *fix the fucking TV, dammit! what the fuck is going on?* They spilled beers and slapped the bar with their baseball caps which at least was a decent usage for the damn things and leapt and roared

He felt like a bullwhip in a herd of cattle. It felt good.

When he switched to The Learning Channel on what looked to be a Yankee homer the place went the rest of the way to hell and somebody shouted *SCREW this SHIT! I bet they got the goddamn game on over at the End of the World!* And *Yeah!* somebody else said, *LET'S GET THE FUCK OUT OF HERE!* and they did.

It got nice and quiet in there.

He sat a while with the remote in his pocket thinking how much Liana hated baseball and how these guys were going to be disappointed there too and finished his scotch and paid and tipped generously and left the bar.

He crossed Central Park West at 67th and walked through the parking lot at Tavern on the Green. Tourists walked in and out past the liveried doorman. Half-lame carriage horses stood blinkered and waiting and hoping not to die in traffic.

He dodged sweaty long-distance runners and bicycles on Park Drive and walked past the spanish hot dog vendor and through the cyclone-wire gate to the narrow dirt path leading down and gazed out over the wide green grass below. He checked the nearby trees.

No Carla. Just a pair of blonde three-year-old kids and their Indian nannies. Strollers by Armani.

Carla was lazy as a grub when she wasn't working or eating pussy. She also had delicate skin. It was bright out. She'd go for the trees.

He dropped the remote into a garbage can.

He wasn't going to need it anymore.

He headed east along the northern border. Smelled fresh-cut grass. The grass smelled good. But how these sun-crazy mad-dog bastards could stand the damned humidity he didn't know. The guys all had their shirts off and the women all wore halters or bikinis. Too bad it wasn't the other way around but still there were a lot of tits out there. Nice to see.

He saw headphones and strollers and blankets and frisbees and kites. He thought one of the kites had his name on it but that couldn't be. He saw black kids and white kids playing together. They were running around a tree and laughing.

The area across from Mineral Springs' red brick refreshment stand looked like a pretty good bet to him. There was a low outcropping of rock surrounded by a dozen or so tall trees and it was just a short walk from there through the gate to get a frozen yogurt or a smoothie or a bagel or a pretzel or bottled water or a lemonade or a hot dog or whatever. He saw people sitting or lying in the shade in front of every tree he passed, dozens of happy sleepy people. He saw a woman blowing bubbles for a tiny wide-eyed baby in a carriage.

One popped on his nose. Direct hit.

Soap-spit. He hadn't seen it coming.

Then he spotted Carla. That flaming red head of hair. She and Randi were on a blanket and propped against an oak tree just a few yards away. Carla was feeding Randi potato chips. They were laughing. He realized he was growling. There was no point in stopping now so he didn't. He put his hand in his pocket and walked over.

They still hadn't noticed him but that was about to change radically when his eye went to a blonde thirty-something guy in a varsity letter-jacket, green, number thirty-four according to the jacket and the guy was standing leaning against a tree maybe forty feet away and Stroup was thinking *what the fuck is this asshole doing in a letter-jacket in this heat?* when the guy pushed away from the tree and opened his jacket and pulled out something short and black that looked like a combination pistol/machine-gun and started spraying the field and trees from left to right.

Stroup hit dirt. He saw the bubble-lady go down with red exploding from her shoulder and a kid with headphones double over like somebody'd kicked him in the stomach. He saw a boy maybe seven years old take one high in the forehead and then his father lurch toward him before his hip burst open just above his wallet.

People were screaming. Scrambling for cover.

The guy's automatic was swinging toward Carla. She and Randi hadn't even gone down. They were holding one another, wide-open targets, easy scores.

This guy was gonna do it for him, he thought.

This guy was gonna shoot them.

The fuck he was.

He pulled out the .38. He flicked off the safety and aimed and squeezed.

The guy yelped and stumbled back surprised and looked down at his belly. His belly was a mess. Stroup had made it that way. The guy screamed. Stroup squeezed off another one and the guy's balls were missing suddenly. Stroup was shooting in a nice vertical pattern he thought down the guy's body. Had to finish up higher, though. The guy was still howling when his jaw flew off against the tree.

Stroup pocketed the gun and stood. Carla was looking at him. He walked over.

"I saved your life, Carla," he said. "Didn't I?"

Carla was white. So was Randi.

"Y-yes," she said. "Yes you did, Stroup."

"You want to forget the goddamn rent now?"

"Uh. O-okay."

"You sure? You don't sound sure."

"I'm sure."

"Thanks, bitch," he said.

He turned and walked away.

It was a little after six and he was watching New York One when his boss called.

He was watching coverage of the shooting for the fifth time. He was drinking scotch.

It looked like the black kid and his father were going to live and the bubble-lady too but the guy with the headphones was a goner. So was the shooter. The shooter had been identified as one Will Obey, originally from Center Loin Cut, Texas. He'd told friends the day before that he was pregnant with the child of Behemoth Yuggdoroth Nit. His friends hadn't believed him.

So far nobody had mentioned Stroup's name but that couldn't be.

He turned down the volume. Had to do it manually. He was going to have to buy a new remote, goddammit.

"Stroup?"

"You're calling me on a Saturday, Max. You're calling for the second time. That's unusual."

"I know."

"You can't fire me, Max. You already did that."

"Downsized, Stroup. Downsized."

"I don't care what the fuck you call it."

"Listen, are you watching the news, Stroup?"

"Matter of fact I am."

"Carla called me."

"Who?"

"Carla. Your ex. I know it was you, Stroup. She told me everything. You're a goddamn hero, Stroup. You saved people's lives out there."

"I don't know what the hell you're talking about."

"I think we can get a book deal."

"A what?"

"A book deal. It was Carla's idea, but I think she's dead right."

"At least she's dead something."

"What?"

"Never mind."

"Look, we do it anonymously. You write the thing under a pseudonym. Nobody's ever going to find out it was you."

"They found out about Ed McBain, Max. They found out about Richard Bachman. And what's his name? Ketchup or something."

"We'll be careful. Those guys weren't careful. Those guys were clumsy. I know plenty of writers who've never been found out. You want to know who J.D. Salinger really is? You're not a bad writer, Stroup. This book could be the beginning of something really big for you."

"And Carla gets a piece of it, right? That's the deal?"

"Well, yes."

"She mention a figure?"

"Well, yes."

"It wouldn't be something around two thousand, seven hundred dollars, would it?"

"Thirty-five hundred. But look, advances for this kind of thing have gone crazy these days. We do it strictly true-crime. If it were fiction we'd be lucky to make a dime. But we do this thing right, we could make a million. Would a million dollars be acceptable?"

"Make it two million and you got a deal."

"I think I can safely say, *done*."

After a while he went to bed. He didn't know what he dreamed.

He woke up smiling.

It didn't last.

—*For Carolyn, with a serious nod to The Buk*

OFFSPRING

JACK KETCHUM

The local sheriff of Dead River, Maine, thought he had killed them off ten years ago—a primitive, cave-dwelling tribe of cannibalistic savages. But somehow the clan survived. To breed. To hunt. To kill and eat. And now the peaceful residents of this isolated town are fighting for their lives....

ISBN 10: 0-8439-5864-2
ISBN 13: 978-0-8439-5864-5

To order a book or to request a catalog call:
1-800-481-9191
This book is also available at your local bookstore, or you can check out our Web site **www.dorchesterpub.com** where you can look up your favorite authors, read excerpts, or glance at our discussion forum to see what people have to say about your favorite books.

RICHARD LAYMON

SAVAGE

Whitechapel, November 1888: Jack the Ripper is hard at work. He's safe behind locked doors in a one-room hovel with his unfortunate victim, Mary Kelly. With no need to hurry for once, he takes his time gleefully eviscerating the young woman. He doesn't know that a fifteen-year-old boy is cowering under Mary's bed....

Trevor Bentley's life would never be the same after that night. What he saw and heard would have driven many men mad. But for Trevor it was the beginning of a quest, an obsession to stop the most notorious murderer in history. The killer's trail of blood will lead Trevor from the fog-shrouded alleys of London to the streets of New York and beyond. But Trevor will not stop until he comes face to face with the ultimate horror.

ISBN 10: 0-8439-5751-4
ISBN 13: 978-0-8439-5751-8

To order a book or to request a catalog call:
1-800-481-9191
This book is also available at your local bookstore, or you can check out our Web site **www.dorchesterpub.com** where you can look up your favorite authors, read excerpts, or glance at our discussion forum to see what people have to say about your favorite books.

EDWARD LEE

SLITHER

The trichinosis worm is one of nature's most revolting parasites. Luckily, these worms are rarely more than a few millimeters in length. But guess what? Now there's a subspecies that's thirty feet long...

When Nora and her research team arrived on the deserted tropical island, she was expecting a routine zoological expedition. But first they found the dead bodies. Now members of her own team are disappearing, and when they return, they've...changed. And is there any sane explanation for the lurid, perverse dreams she's been having? Indeed, there are other people on the island. But the real danger is something far worse.

ISBN 13: 978-0-8439-5414-2

- -

To order a book or to request a catalog call:
1-800-481-9191
This book is also available at your local bookstore, or you can check out our Web site **www.dorchesterpub.com** where you can look up your favorite authors, read excerpts, or glance at our discussion forum to see what people have to say about your favorite books.

DEMON EYES

L. H. MAYNARD
&
M. P. N. SIMS

Emma had just started her new job as personal assistant to Alex Keltner, the charismatic and powerful head of Keltner Industries. So when he asked her to attend a party he was throwing that weekend at his secluded estate, she knew better than to refuse. It would be her first party amid the extremely wealthy and powerful elite….

It will be a party she'll never forget…if she survives. At first it will be simply odd. Mysterious warnings. Strange, seductive guests. An atmosphere of lust and sexuality. Video cameras in the rooms. But as the weekend progresses, Emma will slowly learn the true nature of the guests and her mysterious host—and the real, grotesque purpose of the party.

ISBN 13: 978-0-8439-5972-7

To order a book or to request a catalog call:
1-800-481-9191
This book is also available at your local bookstore, or you can check out our Web site **www.dorchesterpub.com** where you can look up your favorite authors, read excerpts, or glance at our discussion forum to see what people have to say about your favorite books.

THE DELUGE

MARK MORRIS

It came from nowhere. The only warning was the endless rumbling of a growing earthquake. Then the water came—crashing, rushing water, covering everything. Destroying everything. When it stopped, all that was left was the gentle lapping of waves against the few remaining buildings rising above the surface of the sea.

Will the isolated survivors be able to rebuild their lives, their civilization, when nearly all they knew has been wiped out? It seems hopeless. But what lurks beneath the swirling water, waiting to emerge, is far worse. When the floodwaters finally recede, the true horror will be revealed.

ISBN 13: 978-0-8439-5893-5

To order a book or to request a catalog call:
1-800-481-9191
This book is also available at your local bookstore, or you can check out our Web site **www.dorchesterpub.com** where you can look up your favorite authors, read excerpts, or glance at our discussion forum to see what people have to say about your favorite books.

ATTENTION
BOOK LOVERS!

Can't get enough
of your favorite **HORROR**?

Call **1-800-481-9191** to:

— order books —
— receive a **FREE** catalog —
— join our book clubs to **SAVE 30%**! —

Open Mon.-Fri. 10 AM-9 PM EST

Visit
www.dorchesterpub.com
for special offers and inside
information on the authors you love.

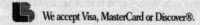

We accept Visa, MasterCard or Discover®.